ROUGH CUT

Also by Bruce Cook:

Fiction

Sex Life
Mexican Standoff

Nonfiction

The Beat Generation
Listen to the Blues
Dalton Trumbo
Brecht in Exile

ROUGH CUT

Bruce Cook

St. Martin's Press   New York

Library of Congress Cataloging-in-Publication Data

Cook, Bruce.
    Rough cut.
      p. cm.
    "A Thomas Dunne book."
    ISBN 0-312-05149-2
    I. Title.
PS3553.055314R6 1990   813'.54—dc20   90-36111

First Edition: November 1990

10 9 8 7 6 5 4 3 2 1

For Bob, Katy, and Cecilia

ROUGH CUT

Most of my work I get from lawyers. I guess you could say that over the years I've built up "relationships" with a few of them in Century City, Beverly Hills and downtown. Sometimes the jobs come under the heading of research—legwork, checking things out. More often, a regular client comes to them with a confidential problem, looking for a legal remedy that may be possible with my help and may not be possible without it. When they need me, they need me. I provide a service.

Once in a while, though, the lawyers throw my way the things they consider too hot to handle. These are situations that are at the very least potentially matters for the police. So then they get in touch with Antonio Cervantes. Me, Chico.

That's how it turned out the afternoon that I drove out to Santa Monica to meet with a man I'd never seen or heard of before. His name was Geisel—Hans-Dieter Geisel. All I knew about him was that Ted Gittelson, a full partner in the firm of Meyer, Greenfeld and Gottschalk, said I should see this guy. The funny thing was I'd never done business with Gittelson before. He was an entertainment lawyer, a negotiator, a reader of contracts, no doubt good at his trade but not the kind who often has need for a PI like me. He said he got my name from Packy DiMarco, who is downtown in the courts. Packy and I go back a long way to when I was on the LAPD, and he was a feisty little criminal lawyer who won more cases than he lost. They finally got him out of their hair by making him a judge. So this was a referral from a referral.

Ordinarily, if it was okay with Packy, it was okay with me. But there was something about this job that bothered me, and so I decided to call him and ask him about it. I got right through to him.

"Yeah, Tony. What can I do for you?"

"You already did it, Judge," I said. "Thanks for putting in the word for me."

"Oh, that. Sure. Anytime." There was an impatient silence at his end.

Finally I asked, "You know this guy Geisel?"

"Who?"

"Hans-Dieter Geisel. He's the guy who's got the job."

Packy laughed. He had sort of a snicker. "Oh, Christ, a kraut. What'd I let you in for? No, I don't know any Hans-Dieter Geisel. But I know Ted Gittelson—known him since law school. He's okay. If he set you up with Geisel, then you don't need to worry about the guy."

"Gittelson asked me if I had a gun. He said to bring it."

"He did?" Another pause. "Well, have you got one? You're licensed, aren't you?"

"Sure."

"Then bring it."

"Okay. But you don't have any idea what this is about?"

"Not the slightest."

"Well, thanks, Judge, you've been a lot of help." He couldn't miss the edge I put on that.

He answered me the same way. "Anytime." Then he added, "You know, Tony, you can always turn it down."

2

"I know," I said. "Thanks. I mean it."

"Have a nice day, Tony."

That ended it. He was right, of course—I could always turn it down. But I was pretty sure I wouldn't.

Things had changed a lot since my trip down to Mexico. I was with Alicia now, and she was about eight-months-plus pregnant with her kid, not mine. I looked across the room at her. She was settled in a chair, watching a soap opera on television, "learning" English. Even like that, swollen with child to about twice her size, Alicia Ramirez y Sandoval looked good to me—luscious, ripe and ready. Although she hadn't made any formal claim, she counted on me for everything—and to tell the truth, I liked it that way. After Mexico, I was a little money ahead, but with the hospital expenses coming and then the kid to take care of, we were going to need a lot more. No, short of murder by contract, I wasn't likely to turn down Hans-Dieter Geisel.

I was lucky enough to find a parking spot on Ocean right across from the Café Casino, where I'd been told Geisel would be waiting. There was nothing really classy about the place except the clientele and maybe the location, which more or less went together. You go inside, and it's nothing more than a glorified cafeteria. The food is about as good as cafeteria food gets, and they've got good wine and imported beer. But still, you have to stand in line with your tray, push through, and pay the cashier. After looking around a little and seeing nobody who seemed to be looking for me in return, that's just what I did—stood in line, got a Dos Equis, and went out to find a table on the terrace to sit and drink it.

It's the terrace that makes the place what it is. Even I have spent some time in Europe, and I know what they say is true: There's no place in the world so much like the Riviera as that stretch of the California coast that runs from San Diego to Santa Barbara. And right there in the middle of it all, like a would-be Nice or a little San Remo, is the city of Santa Monica. Right in the middle of that, across the street from the ocean, is the terrace of the Café Casino. There, on any day of the week, the tables are crowded with men and women who sit in the warm sun, gazing out at the ocean. They sip coffee and wine, and speak to one another in every known European language. Even English English.

Who were these people? Not tourists. As I moved among them, looking for a table, I noticed they seemed to be as much at home here as I was. Maybe more. They waved, called back and forth to one another. This was their town, too. They were members in good standing of Los Angeles's unassimilated European population—the foreign press, movie people, and maybe a few with independent means who had come to live on the American Riviera because it was cheaper than the one back home.

I found a table off to one side, sat down, and poured my beer. Just as I was taking my first sip, a young man appeared and hovered above me for a long moment before he spoke.

"Mr. Cervantes?"

I nodded, said nothing.

"Hans-Dieter Geisel."

I offered my hand, and he shook it vigorously, at the same time making a quick little bow from the waist. He was German, all right. With just a nod from me, he sat down in the chair opposite mine.

"How did you know me?" I asked.

"You were pointed out," he said.

Looking beyond him, I searched the tables for a familiar face. I couldn't find one—not one. Nobody was even looking my way. Then I turned back to Geisel. He wasn't quite what I had expected—younger, still in his twenties, tall and handsome in a blond California sort of way. He was dressed California, too, in jeans and blazer. And I hadn't detected much of an accent.

"Okay," I said, "I'm here. You found me. What is it you want to talk about?"

4

He pulled his chair closer and dropped his voice to not much more than a whisper. "I am the personal assistant to Mr. Heinrich Toller. You know the name?"

"Sure. Movies."

He nodded. "Exactly. Movies. Let me be frank. Mr. Toller has at present some difficulties. Some of these are financial. Not all. You may have seen something in the newspapers?"

I had. They called Heinrich Toller the High-flying Dutchman. He had made his start in the movie business as a very young producer in Berlin before Hitler took over. Just one movie there, but that one got him in trouble with the Nazis—won him a place on some list. So after the Reichstag burned he got out as quickly as he could.

In the next few years, he managed to stay just one jump ahead of them, even got a movie made in England—but in the process he passed some bad paper and did some time for it there. Even so, he somehow got into the States, and he sat out the war in Hollywood, one of the gang of refugee artists and intellectuals they write books about today.

After the war things really picked up for him. He'd managed to get one movie made over here without going to jail for it. And that was enough to get him assigned by the American Military Government to put the German movie industry back on its feet. He wasn't a Jew. He wasn't a Communist. So he was elected. Hans Toller may not have rebuilt the German film industry all by himself, but he did manage to get a couple of pretty good pictures made while Berlin was still in rubble and then switched his base of operations to Munich and got that big film studio built there. Then, in the sixties, he went international and, during the next couple of decades, produced four of the best movies anybody had ever done. They made him famous—but so did his life-style. He ran his business from a yacht in the Mediterranean, like some Greek shipping magnate. But after the great movies, there were some bombs and some others that did no more than break even.

Finally, he surprised everyone by coming back to Los Angeles. He bought, or probably leased, a building in West Hollywood and put up a big neon sign that shouted TOLLER FILMS. The *Tribune* called him a mini mogul. The thing was, though, when he hit Hollywood his luck got even worse. He had one flop at the box office after another. Private investors and the loan departments of a number of banks got on his case. There were rumors he was on the brink of Chapter Eleven. But somehow or other he kept right on making pictures. Nobody knew where the money came from.

Young Hans-Dieter Geisel didn't need to be told any of this. He knew it all and a lot more. So I just shrugged and said, "I read the article about him in the *Tribune Sunday Magazine*."

"Our difficulties were exaggerated," he said coolly. "What the press builds up it likes to tear down."

"Yeah. I guess that's right. Sometimes."

"It's true!" he declared, in a way that sort of defied contradiction. He was pretty sure of himself for a guy in his twenties. "I give you just one example of unfair treatment. Very little was said in that article about Ursula Toller, and nothing at all about her production of *Faust*."

"Oh, yeah. That's his daughter, right?"

"Of course! His daughter! She has her father's eye for detail. He has entrusted her with his most important project. It will win all the Oscars and be an international smash hit!"

Smash hit? You could tell this guy had been reading *Variety*. I leaned back and looked at him. *"Faust?"*

"Sure! Right! *Faust!* Only it's completely updated, you see. It's a marvelous concept"—he named the English playwright who had written the script and explained that this time around the good doctor had been transformed into a nuclear physicist (why not?) and Mephistopheles into—"But this can wait." He interrupted himself with a wave of his hand.

"When does it start?" I asked, just trying to be polite. He looked at me in surprise. "Don't you read the trades? No, I suppose you don't." He sighed at my ignorance. "Shooting has just been completed in Munich. The raw footage is being brought here by the director for editing." Then: "This is where you come in." Full stop. Like I should have understood.

"I do? Where? I don't get it."

"Let me make clear for you what kind of film this will become. It stars Richard Terkel and Catherine Costello and Dietrich Neuheiser, and it is directed by Derek Denison, and . . ."

"Look, let me make it easy for you," I said. "You're counting on this one to save the company. I understand that. But I repeat, where do I come in?"

He shrank a bit, cleared his throat and began again less aggressively. "Yes, well, there is something to what you say. We have high hopes for this picture, and it could improve our financial situation. But it requires the supervision, the *touch* of Ursula Toller."

"So?"

"Somebody is trying to kidnap her. Perhaps kill her, I don't know."

I looked at this big, handsome kid trying so hard to look and act American. He gulped, and I thought for a moment he was going to shed a tear or two right there in front of everyone on the terrace of the Café Casino. But no. He regained control and began this story:

One night, a week ago, Fräulein Toller was returning, in one of the family cars (a Mercedes, of course) from the last day of shooting in Munich. It was late, after eleven; there had been a wrap party. In the car with her were two employees of the Toller organization.

"Wait a minute," I interrupted. "Which two employees?"

He seemed mildly annoyed. "There was the chauffeur,

7

Otto, and another man whose name I don't know. He was, I believe, English."

"What was his job?"

"Bodyguard."

"Oh."

"They were driving the Zurich autobahn. Do you know Munich?" Then, before I could answer, he frowned at me and said, "No, I suppose you don't."

"I've been there." It was true. I had. Two days on a weekend pass.

He seemed genuinely surprised. "Perhaps you remember, then. the Autobahn leads up out of the city into the mountains. It's there Herr Toller maintains his Munich residence. Not too far from the Gruneberg exit. It is fairly deserted there—especially at that time of night."

"Sure," I said. I had no idea what he was talking about.

"So!" He resumed. Although they varied the route from time to time, this was the way she traveled home most often. On the night in question, they had turned off the autobahn and were moving along the road "at a good, steady rate" (which in Germany probably meant about 100 kph). There was a car behind them—but far back and not moving up. Things were going well enough until a truck running without lights pulled across the road without warning and came to a sudden stop directly in front of them. The Toller chauffeur, Otto, had no chance to steer around the truck, but he did manage to slow the Mercedes down so that the collision, when it came, was not so severe. The nameless bodyguard wrestled with the door and finally got it open. He jumped out. But just as he did, the car that had been trailing them at a distance pulled up and shots were fired. The guard was armed and returned the fire. As all this was happening, the chauffeur was working to free the Mercedes from its entanglement with the truck. He finally managed to do that and swung around it, escaping with his mistress, Fräulein Ursula.

At this point Hans-Dieter fell silent—like it was the end of the story.

"What happened to the bodyguard?" I asked.

He looked at me in an odd way, as if I had brought up something that was embarrassing but fairly unimportant. "That was unfortunate," said Hans-Dieter. "He disappeared. Otto went back the next morning to the place where it happened, and the police had found no body. There was, however, a trail of blood on the road, as if someone was dragged."

"So they just took the body along with them." The obvious conclusion.

He shrugged lamely. "He might only have been wounded."

"Get real," I said. "The bottom line is he was left behind by the chauffeur and what's-her-name, Ursula."

"Well, yes, but he had been well paid. It was his job."

I studied him for a moment. There wasn't much to say to that, was there? Well, maybe something: "You want me to take his place, is that it?"

"You must understand . . ." He looked away, a little fluster of embarrassment disturbing his nice features for just a second. He knew he hadn't been saying quite the right things. "Yes, we thought . . . someone who knows Los Angeles. You were recommended."

"Nice."

"Uh . . . you brought a gun?"

I flapped my jacket at him so he could get a glimpse of it. "Tell me something," I said. "In fact, tell me a couple of things. What did the police in Munich say about this? Who did they think ran the operation?"

"Well . . . it was not really reported."

"Huh?"

He cleared his throat. "No. As I said, Otto went back there the next morning, and the police were there. It had been reported that shots were fired. Otto asked them questions, and they asked him questions. He said he, too, had heard the shots and was curious. Then they sent him away." Again he ended as if that explained everything.

"But *why* wasn't it reported? That was *dumb*."

9

"That's something that doesn't have to concern you. Not now, anyway."

"You expect me to go into this completely blind?"

I was putting him into a corner, making him uncomfortable. Good. He looked around, glanced off at the ocean and finally back at me. At last he said, "Well, you must understand that for a while it has been necessary for Heinrich Toller to seek financing from private sources. You might say unorthodox sources."

Jesus, Mary and Joseph, I thought—unorthodox sources. That could mean anything—oil money, but more likely drug money, the Mafia, the Medellín cartel, maybe even those guys in Thailand. I asked myself if I really wanted to get involved in this. I looked Hans-Dieter Geisel in the eye. "*Illegal* sources?" I asked.

"Unorthodox sources."

"I think I understand. Try this: It was not reported because the Tollers were afraid that this was personal, that whoever tried to do it was after more than ransom—that they were interested in collecting on debts past due."

He had actually started to sweat. "Perhaps something like that."

"And that's why you're afraid they might try it again over here. Because these are the kind of guys who don't give up so easy. They like to show how long their arms are."

"Well . . ."

"Never mind. Look, this is going to cost you."

"Oh, of course. You'll be very well paid."

"So was the other guy. And what did it get him? No, you're really going to have to pay through the nose on this one. I think two thousand a day would be just about right."

"*Zwei tausend?*" he barked out in German. "*Das ist doch Wahnsinn!*" He pounded once on the table, and conversation stopped around us. That's when negotiations began.

The drive to the airport was quiet enough. I mean, it was supposed to be quiet, wasn't it? You get into a white Mercedes limo, and you move into traffic, and you're not supposed to hear anything—not the rumble of the tires on the pavement, for sure not the engine, just maybe the quiet hiss of the air conditioner, and in this case quality control at Stuttgart had even taken care of that.

Hans-Dieter Geisel sat beside me. The moment the doors had shut with that soft but emphatic *chunk,* he had picked up a thick sheaf of eight by ten, covered and bound like a script. That's what I thought it was until I looked over and saw that the pages were mostly figures. Maybe a budget. Who knows? Who cares? He studied it in silence as we drove down Wilshire.

At the wheel was none other than Otto, the fearless chauffeur who had saved the Fräulein that fateful night a week ago on the mountain road above Munich. He drove okay, but I thought he sure didn't know LA.

"Hey." I nudged Geisel. "We just passed Lincoln. That's

the way to LAX. Lincoln into Sepulveda, and you're right there."

He didn't even bother to look up. "No."

"It's faster. Less traffic."

"We're not going to LAX. We're going to Long Beach."

"Long Beach? Why?"

"Because that's where the company plane is coming in."

With that, I settled down as best I could for the long haul. I stared out the window, and before long we were on the 405, moving sluggishly with the afternoon traffic.

Hans-Dieter Geisel was pissed off at me. I was costing him more than he wanted to pay. I had settled for $975 a day. I don't know why that figure exactly, except we both landed on it at the same time. I had promised myself I wouldn't budge below a thousand, but then he told me my services wouldn't be required once Ursula was safely home each night.

"The Toller house is like a fortress," he had said.

"Terrific. But seeing the daughter around Munich got one guy killed already."

"We don't know that. He may even have been in on it."

With that blood on the highway? "Look," I said, "there's also the matter of payment. I'm not demanding a thousand in unmarked bills at the end of each day. But from what I read in the newspapers, you guys could go bust any day, and I might wind up standing in line to get paid ten cents on the dollar. If that. I'm taking a chance on you."

That really got to him. His jaw went tight. But he managed, barely, to keep his cool. I shrugged, and he gritted his teeth, and we both said, "Nine seventy-five."

Then, as we walked down the stairs from the Café Casino to Ocean Boulevard where Otto was standing before the waiting limo, I glanced across the street and remembered. "Hey," I said, "give me a minute to get my car off the street."

"We haven't got time. We must pick up Fräulein Toller at the airport."

"But I'll get a ticket. Maybe they'll tow it away."

"With what you're being paid, you can afford it."

The deal was, I was supposed to be with her or on call twenty-four hours a day for a month. If my services were required after that, we would renegotiate. Why a month? What would happen or not happen by then? Geisel wouldn't say. Well, okay. On the upside, I might walk away with close to thirty thousand. On the downside, I might get dead.

I brooded all the way out to Long Beach about what I was going to do with Alicia. She wasn't just pregnant, she was going into her ninth month. We needed the money—that much was sure—but if I wasn't going to be around, then she ought to have someone with her around the clock. I'd have to look into that. Somebody who could speak Spanish; somebody who could get her to appointments at the obstetrician; somebody who could drive her to the hospital if I wasn't around when her labor started. That was going to cost me. That thirty thousand was starting to shrink fast. Jesus, I thought, how did I ever get into this? But I knew. I knew.

I guess the one in Long Beach is what they call a satellite airport. Most of the flights in and out are regional. A few go cross-country. And there's a lot of what comes under the heading of general aviation, nonscheduled flights—mostly private aircraft heading out and coming in from every direction.

There seemed to be a lot of that general aviation overhead as we left the 405 at the Lakewood exit. Geisel was looking critically at his watch, as if there were a problem.

"Are we late?" I asked him. The traffic had not been unusually bad—just routinely bad.

"No, I'm just trying to estimate how long it will take us to get back into the city."

"Longer than it did getting out here."

He made a face. "Well, I expected *that*. There's a six o'clock meeting—in fact two of them. Ursula meets with

13

the editing team, and I will see certain financial people. Do you think . . ."

"About an hour this time of day."

He nodded, satisfied.

The next time I looked we were gliding down Lakewood, then slowing, stopping, and taking a left into the general aviation gate. We pulled up in front of a large but not very impressive structure, the Aerotran building. I glanced over at Geisel and saw that he had tossed his book of figures aside. This was the place.

Before I could turn the handle, Otto had the door open, and I got out. Not a word from him yet. Black suited, black tied, he even wore a black visored cap the way chauffeurs in the movies do. Well, what the hell, he was a movie chauffeur, wasn't he?

Geisel jumped out, then Otto bustled on ahead and opened the glass doors into the building. There Otto left us. Ahead lay another door marked Capitol Aviation Services. Geisel walked up to it and stopped. After a moment I realized that he was waiting for me to open it for him. We stood there and waited . . . and waited. Finally, without so much as a glance at me, he threw it open with all the strength he had. Nothing spectacular happened. There was a pneumatic brake on it.

It's good to get things settled right at the start. I'd open doors for the Fräulein; I'd go on ahead and case every new location; I'd stick to her like Elmer's glue. She was my responsibility. I didn't owe Hans-Dieter a thing except ordinary courtesy. Opening doors for him wasn't part of the deal.

We were just inside the office, getting a smile from the receptionist, when a man came forward and stuck out his hand to Geisel.

"Good to see you, Hans-Dieter. You're right on time."

"The plane has landed?"

"No, the tower says she'll be setting down in three minutes. Should be out back in five." He looked over at me as

14

they shook hands, but Geisel made no introductions. Even so, the guy gave me a polite nod. I nodded back. He was smooth but crisp in his style. I'd give him about eight or ten years in the military—an officer and a gentleman.

He led the way through the office, down a corridor and to a rear door. He held it open for both of us. Suddenly Geisel stopped dead. Had he seen something? My hand went to the handle of the Smith & Wesson .38 Police Special under my jacket, and I stepped quickly around him, trying to see what he had seen. There was nothing there—just a couple of airplanes. Nobody.

Then I heard him say to the other man, "I must make a telephone call."

"Well . . . sure. Come on, I'll find you a phone."

"No—no, I'll find one for myself." And he disappeared back down the corridor.

"Use the one in my office," the military man called after him. Then he shrugged and stepped outside with me.

We stood awkwardly for a moment, glancing back and forth at each other. Then he gave me a crooked smile and said, "Germans."

"Yeah."

"Nice folks."

"Seem to be."

"But very demanding—especially in the food line."

I grinned at that. Heinrich Toller had a reputation as an eater of distinction. He was probably a pain in the ass to anyone trying to cater his flights. "Yeah," I said, "I'll bet."

"You're not."

"How's that?"

"German."

"No," I said, "I'm of the Mexican persuasion."

"Thought so. My name's Tom Turner."

He held out his hand, and I shook it. "Antonio Cervantes."

"I saw how you moved right into it there at the door," Turner said. "You're a professional."

"Well, I've been at it a while."

"It shows. LAPD?"

"Yeah. Ten years."

"Vietnam?"

"No, Germany—sixty-nine and seventy."

"The MPs?"

"Yeah."

"Well, it'll be interesting to see how you get along with these folks."

That was about all Turner and I had to say to each other, because moments later Geisel came hurrying through the door. I let him talk to Turner about whatever he needed to talk about and walked out to give this particular situation a closer inspection. Well, somebody could pop out of one of those planes, I supposed, and you could put a sniper up there on top of the Aerotran building, but no situation's perfect. This one looked pretty ordinary to me.

Right on time the plane appeared. You could see it coming from a long way off, a Lear 35, taxiing over from the other side of the field. There was something almost stealthy about it, relatively quiet for a jet, as it moved closer and closer. Two aircraft maintenance men had appeared, one of them waving the Lear jet forward.

I turned back to Turner. "Your guys?"

He nodded.

The plane came to a halt about twenty yards away and then shut down. A few moments later the passenger door opened and stairs flopped out. Hans-Dieter ran over and stood expectantly at the foot of them.

Ursula Toller appeared in the door, looking right and left. She was dressed in pipe-stem jeans and a mink jacket. She wore sunglasses and in her right hand she carried something like a leather tote bag.

Geisel dropped his head in a precise little bow and called out his welcome—at least that's what I think he was saying, but it was all in German, so I couldn't be sure. I'm pretty sure I did hear a *willkommen* in there someplace, though.

16

She came down the steps, still looking right and left, taking it all in. Then she paused on the last one and said something to him, and he said something back. Then, in response, she swung the bag she was carrying in a perfect roundhouse and let him have it right on top of the head.

I learned later that Geisel had brought her bad news. The footage on *Faust*—all that had been shot and printed back in Munich—had been held up in customs in New York. Why? He had no idea. A technicality. The New York office was looking into it. The director would have it here with him tomorrow.

That was it. That was enough. The bearer of bad tidings had to be punished. She lowered the boom on Hans-Dieter.

Although certainly not tall, she pretended to be. She swaggered forward, taking long strides as she headed in my general direction. Geisel trailed behind. She stopped about three feet away and looked me up and down.

"You are the bodyguard?" She pronounced it *boh-dee-gart,* and spoke in a low tenor, a man's voice. Very sexy—if polymorphous perverse turns you on.

"That's me," I said.

"Shouldn't you be bigger?"

Then I looked her up and down the way she had me and tried to make eye contact with her through those sunglasses. "No," I said at last, "this is the size I'm supposed to be."

With that, I turned and headed back to the building. At the door I made sure they were behind me, then indicated they were to wait there. I checked out the corridor and then gave a once-over to the office before going back and waving them through the door. All this was as much for Turner's benefit as theirs. If he thought I was a pro, I decided I'd better act like one.

Outside, the limo was waiting at the curb. Otto clambered out the moment he caught sight of me, and by the time Geisel and Ursula emerged, he was there, holding the

17

door, smiling broadly as he bowed to the Fräulein. She acknowledged it, and that was that. Geisel told me to ride up front with Otto.

It was not a fun trip. Traffic was even tighter than on the trip out. And instead of going with the flow, Otto kept changing lanes looking for some momentary advantage. This wasn't always so easy with the limo, but it didn't seem to faze old Otto. When a hole the length of the car (or sometimes less) would open up in a lane that happened to be moving faster than ours at that moment, he went for it—and to hell with whoever was behind us. The hour it took to get back on the freeway was punctuated at about three-minute intervals with honks and toots from angry drivers and occasionally with the ripping screech of brakes. And although he never spoke a word to me, he kept up a steady stream of curses under his breath—a lot of *verdammt* and *Arschloch* and *Scheisse* repeated over and over again. Once or twice he let go in full shout.

In back, they added to the din. No, that's not quite right. The glass between us, which should have shut off all sounds from their end of the car muffled to whispers the screams, howls and growls of their conversation. Again, not quite correct. It was a monologue and not a dialogue. Poor Hans-Dieter was reduced to monotone responses; all the rest was Ursula. She was obviously displeased. She let him know that—at great length.

And that was how we made it to the Venice Boulevard exit. Otto turned off there—at last!—and headed east, making for our destination in West Hollywood by some back route he had learned.

I was breathing easier by the time we turned left on La Cienega. Some blocks ahead lay the Toller building. I remember the first time I saw it. It was night. I drove by, and there was the name splashed all over it in neon. I wasn't so much impressed as amused. I knew enough about how Hollywood works to know that this was *not* the way to get the right kind of attention. But it was Heinrich Toller's way—

18

and that was how he had always done things. His way. And just a little while after that first drive by, the Toller organization began the long slide, which the grand and glorious production of *Faust* was supposed to reverse.

There it was, impossible to miss. Not quite dusk, but it was already lit up. Otto surprised me by driving right by it. Then I saw that there was no left turn allowed at the building. He proceeded to the next corner, turned left and started back around the block. It was funny about the west side of Los Angeles. You got off any main stem, and you'd find yourself in some cozy residential neighborhood. There might be little California bungalows or luxury condos, but still, it was all sort of suburban.

So we circled this ordinary suburban block. Nice houses, nice lawns, nice flowers, too. I must have been admiring the view out the side window because I was completely unprepared for the crash when it came. I caught a blur of something out of the corner of my eye—and then, *blam*, not so much the noise as the impact. It threw me hard to the left. If I hadn't been strapped in, I would have landed in Otto's lap.

Only where was Otto? He was already tumbling out of the car, grabbing under the seat.

I unhooked and dove out of the door on my side and landed on my hands and knees. From there I saw what had happened. We had been hit just beyond the front wheel on my side by a car that had come rocketing out of an alley. It was about four feet away, crunched up against the limo. I remember the thought flashed: This is it! Just like it was in Munich.

I looked back. The .38 was in my hand. But there was no following car in sight. Nothing. I jumped up and saw who was in the car that hit us—a flash of pink and purple. And then I sort of relaxed, turned, and then I really froze. I saw that Otto and Geisel were on the other side of the limo. Hans-Dieter had a nasty little automatic that turned out to be a Beretta and Otto had an Uzi. They seemed a split second away from letting go at the two in the car.

"Don't shoot!" I screamed at them. I must have yelled it about three times.

Then I turned back to the kids in the car—punkers. The pink-haired guy was taking the purple-haired girl out for a joyride in his dilapidated Chevy Bel Air. Their eyes were wide open with fear. Maybe mine were, too, because I was right in the line of fire.

"It's all right," I yelled at them, hoping I was right. "Don't get excited. Nobody's going to get hurt."

Tucking my .38 into its holster, I turned around to Otto and Hans-Dieter and saw they were still posed like they were before. I raised both hands, palms toward them, and forced a smile.

"Put those fucking things away," I said. "You want a massacre?"

Reluctantly, they lowered their guns.

I let out a long sigh. I could tell this was one job that wasn't going to be any fun at all.

3

I came in late enough that night that I half expected Alicia to be asleep. But no. The TV set was on. I heard it through the door. The key was in the lock, but before I could turn it, the door flew open, and there she was—head back, bellowing at the top of her husky voice, "'Eeeeere's Chico!"

Sure enough, Johnny Carson was there on the screen.

Alicia gave me a big kiss and the kind of upper-body hug a pregnant woman must give with her distended belly in the way. Nice. A real homecoming. Then she marched me over and pushed me down in a chair.

"Sitt daun," she commanded in phonetic Berlitz English. Switching off the TV, she plopped into the chair across from mine. "Juat du iu du tude?"

"*Did* you do," I corrected her. "What *did* you do to-day."

She frowned.

"You know," I prompted, *"hacía."*

"Ay, Chico! I will never learn this English tongue!" she wailed in Spanish. "For me it's too much."

"No, Chiquita. You are very intelligent. Remember? You said so yourself."

She nodded. "Oke. Juat did iu du tude?"

"Perfect."

She smiled, then gestured quickly for me to continue.

Because I had a long story to tell, I started out in Spanish. *"Pues, he encontrado este hombre aleman. Era casi un joven. Entonces—"*

"Chico," she interrupted. *"En Ingles, por favor.* Ai jaev tu laern."

So I started over in English, resigned to a slow recitation, with the possibility of interruptions along the way. But she was right. She had to learn.

I told her about Geisel and Toller and the movies, and she brightened up at that. I knew she was thinking she might get discovered—her big chance. When I described the kidnapping attempt in Munich, I left out the part about the bodyguard. But when I mentioned how much they were paying me her eyes went wide. Just like a kid's.

"Itt's e uoens in e laiftaim oportunite."

I blinked. That came out so fast that I wondered where she had picked it up. Once in a lifetime opportunity? Of course—from some dumb television commercial. I just agreed that it was a pretty good deal and didn't say anything about the downside.

The rest was uncensored—the pickup at the Long Beach Airport; the near disaster on the sidestreet behind the Toller building; the long wait for Ursula as she railed hoarsely at the editing crew about the need for speed, then showed them lists and lists of numbered sequences, and ended by giving a pep talk to those bored professionals that would have been more appropriate between halves in a locker room; and then finally with Ursula to the Toller mansion, above Beverly Hills off Benedict Canyon.

Would they give me a lift back to my car in Santa Monica? Forget it. They called me a cab. When I got to Ocean at last, the Alfa was still there. It had been ticketed, of course, but thank God it hadn't been towed. So here I was at home.

I explained to Alicia that I'd be gone most of the time from now on. She understood. I told her I'd be getting someone to stay with her all the time I was away. She didn't think it was necessary. Well, necessary or not, that's how it would be. She shrugged and said no more about it.

It was getting late. I was tired and had to be up at seven in order to pick up Ursula at eight-thirty. So we went to bed. But after a little touching we made love. It was Alicia's call. It had to be this late in her pregnancy. She'd know when it was time to quit. We managed to work around her belly. We always did.

Afterward, as we lay together in the dark, staring at each other without quite seeing, she touched me and said softly in Spanish, "This woman you guard, is she pretty?"

Should I lie? "Oh, she's all right—if you like blondes."

"You do. Your wife, she was a blonde."

"Yeah, well . . . she's not as pretty as you."

"She's not fat like I am, though."

"You're not fat. You're pregnant."

"That's right. One more month." With that, she grabbed my head and kissed me hard on the mouth. I tasted tears on her cheek as she pulled away. Then she turned away and made ready to sleep.

We said nothing for a couple of minutes, then she rose up suddenly and said, "Oh, Chico, I forgot to tell you something."

"What's that, Chiquita?"

"A man called about nine o'clock."

"You talked to him?"

"Yes."

"You should leave the machine on."

"I know, but I want to try my English sometimes."

Uh-oh. I wondered how much had been lost in translation. "And so?"

"It went well. I got his name. Walker or Walton or some

23

gringo name like that. I wrote it down—and his telephone number. He was very polite, and he could speak some Spanish, too. Only it was this funny Castilian Spanish with all the thetas. He said he wanted to talk to you about a job."

"Well, I have a job now."

"This was different. It was for all the time. Anyway, the number is by the telephone."

"Okay," I said, "I'll look at it in the morning."

"Good night, Chico."

"Good night, Chiquita."

Just before I left to pick up Ursula Toller, I got on the telephone and called my cousin Pancho in Silverlake. He's my mother's sister's son, or one of them, and I see him maybe once or twice a year, call him maybe two or three times just to talk. In other words, we're not that close, but we're family, and with people like us that still counts for something.

Pancho owns a small jewelry operation in the exchange downtown. He's legal, more or less. He doesn't fence, wouldn't think of it, but he has sources down in Mexico for gold and silver, and most of his best pieces are contraband. But how could you prove it? Besides, as Pancho said once—it was at his daughter's wedding, and he was feeling expansive—it's a tough business, very competitive. Everybody needs an edge.

Anyway, I knew that at eight o'clock in the morning chances were good he'd still be around. He picked up on the second ring.

"Hello?" In English.

"Pancho, this is Antonio—your cousin, Antonio."

He changed to Spanish: "Ah, Chico, how goes it, man? Business good?"

Me, in Spanish: "Business is very good." I decided to get right to the point. "That's just the problem. You see, this lady is staying with me . . . and . . . she's pregnant—"

24

"Chico, you bad boy!" I heard him chuckling, practically twirling his mustache.

"Well, okay." There wasn't time to explain, and I didn't think I ever wanted to. "The problem is, I've got a job that's going to keep me tied up every day until late at night. I need somebody to stay with her. I need somebody who can drive her to the doctor for her appointments, somebody who has a car."

"I understand."

"I can pay pretty well. Seventy-five dollars a day . . . maybe more . . . whatever it takes."

"Oh, no problem then," said Pancho. "This lady, she's Anglo?"

"No. Mexican. Very."

He laughed a big ho-ho-ho laugh. "And you were always one for the blondes!" Then, in a stage whisper: "Our girls do it better, huh? They like it more?"

Whatever turns you on, Pancho. "It's a very nice arrangement," I said a bit stiffly.

Another big laugh. "Good, Chico. I'll have a woman there by noon."

I thanked him and was just hanging up when Pancho spoke up again, suddenly serious. "Oh, Chico?"

"Yes, Pancho?"

"There's no danger? You know what I mean—the business you're in . . ."

I thought about that a moment. Then I said at last, "No, I can't see that as a possibility." It was true, I couldn't.

"Good. I had to ask."

"I understand. Say hello to Lupe for me."

That was that. Next to the telephone I had noticed the name and number Alicia had left there—Wallace, and a number with a West Los Angeles exchange. I tucked it into my pocket and promised myself I'd call first chance I got.

My watch said I'd be late. I ran into the kitchen, gave Alicia a kiss and a squeeze and told her a woman would be there that morning. "Make sure she speaks Spanish before you let her in," I called from the door. And then I left, slamming the door behind me.

Hans-Dieter Geisel wasn't kidding about the Toller place. It really was a fortress. I had gotten a sense of that but no more the night before. It was located high up one of the side roads off Benedict Canyon just about where that shortcut to the valley begins its long, winding ascent to Mulholland. When we had rolled up to the gate, Otto had flashed his lights in code—two short and two long—and only then had the electronically controlled gates rolled open. Otto escorted Ursula into the house. I was made to wait for a cab in a kind of bunker that had begun life as a gate house. There was an armed security guard there who was watching a Clint Eastwood movie on a miniature Sony set next to the gate-camera monitor. He said his name was Newell. That was about all he said. He glanced from time to time at a board full of lights, some green and some yellow. High tech bored me. I didn't ask questions. A long way off I could hear some dogs barking. There was probably another guard out there somewhere making the rounds with them. When at last the cab came I was glad to get away.

That was last night. When I came to a stop before the gate at about 8:35 A.M. I tooted out the same signal that Otto had given with his lights—two short and two long. Nothing happened. I waited. Looking around, I saw the place was even bigger than it had seemed before. I couldn't really see the house very clearly because of the gate and the protective shrubbery, but the high fence surrounding the place seemed to stretch on forever—well, anyway, down and around the bend in the road. That kind of acreage cost in the millions up there.

Still no action at the gate. I switched off the engine, got out of the car, and began waving at the video camera that scanned slowly back and forth across the driveway. "Hey!"

I yelled at it. "I'm here—Antonio Cervantes. I'm supposed to pick up Miss Toller." The camera continued to track slowly. Not knowing what else to do, I put two fingers in my mouth and whistled shrilly, loud and long, the way I learned to do as a kid in Boyle Heights.

At last the gates began to slide slowly open. I jumped into my car and drove through. I was headed up the drive to the house when a security guard, a different guy, jumped out of the gate house and waved me down. Like a good boy, I stopped.

"Get out of the car," he ordered. "I have to pat you down."

"Pat me down? I'll save you the trouble. I'm carrying a .38 Police Special. It's loaded. It's supposed to be loaded because I'm baby-sitting your boss's daughter."

"Yeah? Well, you were on the schedule for an eight-thirty arrival."

"So I was five minutes late."

He checked his watch. "Ten minutes," he said.

I didn't like this guy. He was big and officious, a bad combination. "You kept me out there for five."

"Let's see your ID."

Really, it was a reasonable request, but by this time I was so annoyed that my first impulse was to pop the Alfa into gear and leave him standing there. I fought it—and won. With a sigh, I hauled my wallet out of my hip pocket and fished out my PI license.

He took it, looked it over, and handed it back. "Park over there," he said. "I'll call the house and find out what they want me to do with you."

Do with me? That tore it. I burned rubber as I left him behind. Glancing back in the rearview, I could see that he was gesturing for me to come back and that his mouth was working. He must have been yelling pretty loud, but all I could hear was that V-6 winding up to about 5,000 rpm.

I parked to one side of the big circular drive, got out, and looked around for the guard. He was jogging for the house but was still about a block away. I went to the door and banged on it loudly with the big hand-shaped knocker that had been provided. It swung open promptly and a maid let me in. The last glimpse I had of my pursuer showed me he had already turned around and was stalking back to the gate house. Then the maid shut the door, made sure who I was, and told me to wait in the library. She seemed to be German, too. Somehow that didn't surprise me.

The library was just that—a library, not some oversized anteroom with a few neat shelves of books for show. I'll never forget my shock when I once was in a Bel Air mansion. I found myself alone in an area designated as the library and discovered that all the books were phonies—bindings plastered into the wall. Well, you could tell the books here were real. They were all over the place—leaning this way and that in shelves that went well up above my head, in piles on a long, littered desk, a few on the floor, and one facedown and open on a chair, as if it had been left there the night before. I picked it up and looked at it—Montaigne in French—and set it back down on the chair. Then I began looking around at the rest—odds and ends in no particular order, paperbacks and hardbacks, new and old, in German, French and English. I opened one and then another. ("Looking for anything in particular?" "No, just browsing.") Finally, I found something that interested me. Figuring I'd be waiting for a while, I settled down in a chair and began to read.

When the old man stuck his head in the open door, I glanced up and started to rise. He gestured for me to stay where I was as he walked over to retrieve his book from the chair. He had a slight hitch in his step, something with his right knee. At least I thought that was where the problem was. Over light blue pajamas he was wearing a long, dark silk robe that covered his legs pretty well, so I couldn't exactly tell right then. His hair was still messed from sleeping, and he hadn't shaved yet.

Book in hand, he started back out of the room, then stopped, turned, and looked at me oddly, "You're reading," he said. It sounded almost like an accusation.

"Well, yeah," I said. "Is it okay?"

"Of course it's 'okay.' Why shouldn't it be 'okay'? What do you think these books are here for? To read!"

He walked over and stood squarely before me. He certainly wasn't a tall man or even an especially wide one, but he seemed somehow to occupy a considerable space. "So?" he asked. "What do you read?"

I handed the book over to him. He held it out and put his head back to read the spine. Then, lower lip thrust out, he nodded approvingly. "De Quincey," he noted. Then he opened it up to my place, looked down at the page, and burst out laughing. "Perfect!" he roared. "You're the detective, aren't you?"

I nodded.

"So. What would interest a detective more than 'Murder as One of the Fine Arts'?" He handed it back and immediately looked apologetic. "A bad joke, eh? Obvious?" He shrugged. "Well, forgive me. I don't have so many good jokes these days." He turned away then, and with Montaigne tucked under his arm, thrust his hands deep into the pockets of his robe and shambled out of the room with that game-legged gait of his.

I watched him go and had just opened up the book again when he reappeared at the door. "Take De Quincey with you," he said. "You'll have a lot of waiting to do today." Then he was gone again.

So that, I said to myself, was Heinrich Toller. Well, all I could think at that moment was that his daughter was one hell of a lot better looking than he was. But I liked him more.

She showed up about half an hour later, a little before nine-thirty. There were quick steps on the stairs. Then, breaking into view, she beckoned me from the hall. "Come," she ordered, "we're late." Then she disappeared.

I jumped up and tried to overtake her, and failing that, followed her out the door—held open for us by the maid, of course. There was a surprise out in front. No Otto. No sedan. (The white limo was battered but driveable.) Instead, there was a red Porsche Carrera in the driveway. Hers, as it turned out.

"Let's go in my car," I said.

"You mean that one?"—pointing disdainfully at the Alfa.

"Yeah. Why not?"

"It's dirty, and it needs repair. You should take better care of it." The left front fender was still coated in gray primer.

She walked quickly to the Porsche.

"Then let me drive," I called after her.

"No. We're in a hurry." There was no arguing with her. She was already behind the wheel, and a moment later the powerful little engine roared to life. Defeated, I got into the seat beside her.

I barely had a chance to get the door shut, much less buckle up, before the car surged forward, gears whining, tachometer jumping, as we hung tight on the wide curve of the circular drive. Ursula came out of it in full throttle, headed for the main gate. I was afraid for a split second that the security guard might be looking the other way. But no. He was as efficient as he was officious. The gate parted (a little too slowly for comfort) wide enough for the Porsche to sail through, with about a foot to spare on either side.

That was just about the way the rest of the trip went. I wouldn't pretend it was one close call after another, but there were a few. She pretended there was plenty of room for passing in that long, winding stretch where Benedict Canyon is at its narrowest. Once, we got caught as the middle car on a blind two-lane curve. She managed to steer through it, but I saw her muttering to herself. Was she praying or cursing?

It wasn't fun, but it was fast. And it was noisy, too. Even on the sidestreets past Sunset she kept the engine revving high in the lower gears as we blasted through Beverly Hills. If I had asked her to slow down, she wouldn't have heard me. If she had heard me, I was pretty sure she wouldn't have done it.

When at last she pulled into her star-marked space in the parking garage under the Toller building, hit the brakes hard, and switched off the engine, I exhaled so loudly in the silence that it must have sounded like a sigh of relief. Maybe it was.

She turned to me then, pulling off her sunglasses. "There," she said. "Could you have done it faster?"

"I could have done it better," I said. "Look, if you wind up in the hospital or get killed in an accident, you'll be just as useless to this movie of yours as you would be kidnapped or murdered. Is that what you want?"

"What I want is respect." It seemed to me an odd thing for her to say.

The old man was right. I had a lot of waiting to do that day. But as I sat, there was a lot of activity going on around me. The director—Derek Denison, red-faced, English, loud and commanding—had arrived overnight with all the footage on *Faust*. He had intended to cut the film in London and, in spite of his jet-lagged state, he wanted to make damned sure everybody knew he didn't like this change in plans in the least.

"But Ursoola," Denison drawled, "tell me once again. Who is this fella you've engaged to cut my film?"

"Frank Schoenkamp. He won an Oscar."

"Yes—ten years ago for . . . what was it?"

"*Deep Thunder.*"

"Yes. Silly picture, wasn't it? And *why* couldn't we just bring Timmy over from London to do the job here?"

"Derek, you know that as well as I do. He's a very active

member of the Communist Party of Great Britain. Persona non grata here."

"Ah, yes. Damned silly Yanks. It does put us in rather an awkward position, doesn't it? Well, if you're sure this fella—what's his name? ah yes, Schoenkamp—if he'll follow my orders and not get creative, then perhaps it may just be possible. But good God, Ursoola—a rough cut in a month?"

I wasn't exactly present in the office during all this, but I was sitting just outside the door and heard it practically word for word two or three times as I tried to concentrate on De Quincey.

When Denison asked to use her phone privately, she came out of the office tight-lipped, rolling her eyes angrily. He kicked the door to her office shut behind her.

It was that kind of day—two huge egos tapping gloves, getting it together for the long bout that lay ahead.

Later they went off to the postproduction studio out on Bundy, Hans-Dieter and Derek in one car and Ursula and I in her Carrera. She drove more sensibly this time, yet again without saying a word. Even so, she smoked two and a half cigarettes on the short trip there, and that said a lot.

There was a pay phone across the corridor from the meeting room where they gathered with the editing team. Once I was sure they would be inside for a while, I went over to it and dialed home.

A strange voice answered—a woman. When I told her who I was, she said Pancho had sent her over. Her name was Pilar, and she was a neighbor of his. She sounded like an older woman and seemed pretty reliable. I asked to speak to Alicia.

"Oh," said the woman, "she's sleeping now. This is her nap time."

There was a minor commotion then. I could hear Alicia's voice but couldn't quite make out what was being said.

Pilar, flustered: "Just a moment. Here she is."

"And please shut the door," Alicia called out in Spanish—then to me: "Chico, this woman, she's terrible—a tyrant. She treats me like a child."

"It sounds to me like you can handle her," I said.

"But you should tell her, Chico. Tell her I'm the boss."

"I'll get around to that," I assured her. "But tell me, were there any calls on the machine? Any calls at all?"

"No, nothing." But there was a pause, and she added, "Oh yes, just one thing."

"What's that, Chiquita?"

"That man called again."

"What man?"

"The one who called last night—Walker . . . or something."

"Wallace," I suggested.

"That's it," she agreed. "Why don't you call him? He's nice."

I grunted. "Okay. I will."

"And tell this woman Pilar a thing or two when you get home," she said. "You'll do that, won't you?"

"Sure," I promised.

As soon as I got off the telephone with Alicia I called the number Wallace had left.

"Intertel!" The voice of their operator. There really was an exclamation mark the way she said it.

"Um," I bumbled, "is there a Mr. Wallace there? I'd like to speak to him."

"I'll connect you."

Another female voice: "Mr. Wallace's office."

"Could I speak to him? this is Ch—" I caught myself. "This is Antonio Cervantes."

A moment of silence. Then, coolly: "Could you tell me what this is about?"

"No, I couldn't," I said, then making it plain for her: "Mr. Wallace has called me, twice, and I am now returning those calls, as I was asked to do."

"Uh, well, could you hold on just a moment?"

Another pause. Finally, a male voice, booming, con-

33

fident: "Mr. Cervantes? Bill Wallace here. Thanks for getting back to me."

"Well . . . okay."

"Look, I'll come right to the point. I think we've got a job you might be interested in."

"I see. The thing is, I'm working a job right now."

"I . . . don't . . . think . . . you . . . quite understand. Intertel happens to be the largest business-intelligence operation in the world. We're not talking about subcontracting. We're talking about permanent employment."

"How did you hear about me?"

"Why not come up and talk things over? We'll cover all that then."

"It's not so easy. This job I've got takes up a lot of time."

"Couldn't you get away for a little while?"

"Well, maybe."

"Look, I burn the midnight oil here just about every night. Why don't you give me a call when you're free tonight? I'll probably be here, and you can come up. We can talk more informally that way."

I hesitated. Why not? I told him I'd give it a try. Wallace gave me a night number and the address of the place in West Los Angeles.

I'd just listen to what he had to say.

4

I t certainly wasn't late when Ursula and I rolled through
the gate at the Toller place—just a little after seven. She
had cooled down considerably by then. On the way back I
even caught her humming little snatches of something at
the red lights.

All in all, I guessed that it had been a pretty good day for
her. The director had arrived with the footage. She had
handled him pretty well. The editing of the film would begin the next day.

Her day had ended back at the Toller building in an
hour-long conference with Hans-Dieter. I sat where I sat
before, just outside the door, De Quincey and I. Although
I was curious and attentive enough for a while, I didn't
catch much of the conversation because it was all in German. At one time I might have gotten more. I picked up a
kind of half-assed, work-a-day knowledge of the language
back in Frankfurt with the MPs. But that was a long time
ago. All I could get from that day's conversation was the
drift. They were talking about the film, of course, throwing

a lot of figures back and forth. On and on. There was a new name I caught, Collinson, that sounded vaguely familiar—but I didn't get much more of that.

I finished "Murder as One of the Fine Arts" and was a few pages into "Confessions of an English Opium Eater" when I suddenly realized they were talking about something different. I distinctly heard Hans-Dieter say, *"Bayerischer Landpolizei"*—Bavarian state police—and I was all ears.

"Sein Name war Potter, nicht? der Englander?"

A pause, then Ursula answered, *"Potter. Ja."*

I leaned toward the door and strained to hear more, but the rest of what they had to say, which wasn't much, was said in whispers.

But having heard what I did, I wasn't exactly surprised a little later when Hans-Dieter took me aside. Ursula was powdering her nose or something. He looked at me very seriously. "I should tell you something," he said.

"What's that?"

"Today, very early, we got a telephone call from Munich—the police there."

"So?"

"The man I told you about, the bodyguard, they found him."

"Dead, of course."

He nodded. "The body was in a shallow grave in the forest. A dog dug him up."

"Nice." I looked at him, waiting. "Well, what did the cops say?"

"They wanted to know if he was an employee."

"Only that?"

Again I waited. "They wanted Ursula and Otto to come back to Munich to give their account of the events of that night."

"Is that what's going to happen?"

"No," he said emphatically. "I told them it was impossible. Fräulein Toller is completely involved in finishing this film. We—" He hesitated. "We worked it out so that she could give a statement to the German consul here."

"And Otto? What about him?"

"They said he would have to return. We put him on a flight at noon."

"Didn't I tell you it was dumb not to report it?"

He didn't answer. But as Ursula appeared, ready to leave, he said suddenly, "I suppose this means you'll want more money." He sounded pretty hostile.

"We made a deal," I said. "It sticks."

I remembered having said that as I was driving over to the Intertel office. I knew I had said it. I knew I meant it. So why was I heading over there to listen to this guy Wallace pitch me on a job? With the call to him behind me, I knew I was committed to listen—but why? Just to have my ego massaged? Probably that was partly the reason. And maybe I had it in mind I could keep this guy on the string for a month or until I finished up with the Tollers. Maybe I could. That was probably the only reason I was listening to him at all.

But ever since I had left the LAPD, I had operated on my own and liked it that way. Why now was I suddenly considering drawing a steady paycheck, maybe even working in an office? Too many lean times lately? Being forced to take jobs like that last one down in Mexico that were way outside my operating range? Jesus, I was lucky to come out of that one—lucky to come out of it in one piece.

Or was I in two pieces now? Soon to be three? Yeah, there was Alicia and the kid she was carrying. They were what was different, maybe they were why I had decided to go and see this guy at Intertel. The thing about it was, I hadn't worked all this out in my mind yet. I didn't know where this thing with Alicia was going—or really if it was going anywhere at all.

One thing I did know. I couldn't just drop her off on

some street corner in East LA and wish her good luck—not after the way she had saved my skin up in the sierra among the *amapolas*. We were together at least until after the baby was born and Alicia got the green card the Feds had promised her after I'd delivered them five contrabandistas and a load of heroin. After that? Well, we'd have to work that out.

All right, Chico, admit it—I said to myself—you wish the kid was yours. To tell the truth, I never thought Saint Joseph got anything like the credit he had coming to him.

Shit! I hit the steering wheel in anger and frustration, realizing that I had just passed Twenty-sixth Street and was rolling into Santa Monica. I had overshot my destination by a good ten blocks. So I pulled over to the side and waited a full minute for traffic to break on both sides. Then, hoping there were no cops around to see me do it, I made a U turn on Wilshire.

Keep your eye on the ball, Chico.

Intertel was located in one of the new high-rises near Bundy. Not much was going on around there at night, so parking was no problem. The building guard was also no problem. I told him, "Intertel," and he told me "fourteenth floor." I signed in and took the elevator up.

It was when I got off that the fun began.

There was a big, broad guy in a business suit sitting behind the receptionist's desk. I bet he didn't sit there during the daytime. Over on his left—my right—was another one just as big who threw down his copy of the *LA Weekly* and walked over to me quickly and pushed me over to the desk. I didn't like that.

"Okay," he said, "hands on the desk. You know the drill."

"Hey, I'm here to see Mr. Wallace."

"Hands on the desk."

He gave me a shove hard enough to put me off balance. I put my hands out and caught myself on the desk—right where he wanted me. The other guy sat with his hands folded, smirking at me from a couple of feet away. I was patted down professionally, all the way down to my socks. The .38 got handed over my shoulder to the guy behind the desk, who took it with a grin.

"Hey, Artie," he said, "I didn't know they made these things anymore." He opened a drawer and put it inside. Then to me he said, "I'll keep it right here for you."

Artie kept me in that position about seven seconds too long, then he gave me a pat on the ass to indicate he was satisfied. I pushed up to an erect position, adjusted my jacket and tried to regain what little dignity I had left.

"Now, who was it you wanted to see?" asked the guy behind the desk.

"Wallace."

"*Mister* Wallace," he corrected me. He looked down at a stapled couple of sheets on the blotter in front of him. "You're not on the list. If you're not on the list, it means you're not expected."

"How do you know I'm not on the list if you don't know my name?"

"All right, what's your name?"

"Antonio Cervantes."

"I thought it'd be something like that. No names like that on this list."

"Call him," I said.

He shrugged, picked up the phone, and dialed. Artie was still hovering behind me. From what I gathered from the brief conversation on the phone, Wallace was giving me a safe conduct. By this time I didn't much care whether I saw him or not.

The guy behind the desk hung up. "It's okay," he said, "but buddy, you weren't on the sheet. Next time get on the sheet." He motioned with his head over to the left. "Artie, bring him back there."

Artie took me by the elbow. I shook off his hand. "You lead," I said to him. "I'll follow."

He looked at me and shrugged, then led me down the hall. "In there," he said, pointing at a closed door.

I knocked. He waited until the door opened and left me facing Wallace.

A firm handshake to go with the strong voice: "Bill Wallace, Mr. Cervantes. *Awfully* glad to meet you. Come in, come in and sit down." He indicated a chair and closed the door after me.

Across the desk from Wallace, I sized him up. About fifty, in good shape—probably played a lot of tennis. His brown hair was going gray at the temples, just enough so that he looked distinguished. Or maybe not quite. There was something a little too bright and quick for distinction. He seemed sort of like a sales executive. But yes, I decided, I would buy a used car from this man.

"Did the boys give you a hard time out there?" he asked apologetically.

"Well, it wasn't quite the reception I expected, Mr. Wallace."

"Call me Bill. And you're . . ."

He knew who I was. I decided he'd probably never know me well enough to call me Chico. "Tony," I said.

"Well, Tony, they're really just security guards in mufti. We keep a lot of sensitive documents around here, and our client files are *absolutely* confidential, so we do feel it necessary to maintain pretty strict office security. I'm sure you understand."

I shrugged. "Sure."

"I'm glad." A quick smile, then he launched into a heavy, long-winded rap on intelligence and its importance in the business world today. First he went on and on about global markets, and how political boundaries don't mean anything anymore: the failure of a crop in, say, Uruguay, can put a company in Chicago out of business; the closely guarded projections on the gross national product in a nation like China can provide American companies with tremendous marketing opportunities.

40

He really had me convinced, but he hadn't half started. "And communications!" he exclaimed suddenly. "Do you realize, Tony, that there are something like ten thousand data banks in operation in the world today. And we have access to most of them. Let me ask you something, Tony."

"What's that?"

"Are you computer literate?"

"Well, I—"

"Do you know the basic computer languages—FOR-TRAN and so on?"

"No, but I guess I could learn."

He frowned and nodded. "Sure you could." He looked down at a file folder on his desk—mine?—and made a notation. Then he went on to explain that raw information in and of itself wasn't worth much, that it was what you did with it that counted. "Analysis!" he shot at me. "That's the key!"

Then more minutes passed as he explained the importance of analysis from every angle: quantitative, qualitative, political, geopolitical, economic, you name it. He talked generally, and then gave specific examples.

It was expansive, far-reaching, impressive. It was also pretty boring. And it sure didn't sound like me.

Maybe he sensed my interest flagging, for he came directly at me. "This is where you come in, Tony."

"Yeah, I was wondering about that," I said.

"We don't, believe me, depend on other sources entirely for our information. Oh, no. We have our own data bank—accessible only to us for our clients—and they include some of the top corporations not just in this country, but in the world, Tony. To get the special information they require we have a trained and experienced staff of field investigators. We have an opening right here in Los Angeles for someone with your background. The pay starts at sixty-thousand per annum. With the usual perks and benefits—car, hospitalization, and so on. How does that sound?"

"Well, it sounds pretty good. But I was wondering—you remember I asked how you happened to hear about me?"

"Now, that's—"

The telephone on his desk rang.

He frowned his annoyance at the interruption, excused himself, and picked up. There were murmurs of "Yes, yes, I understand," and "Of course, we'll probably have to look into that," and so on. And then he hung up.

"Tony," he said to me then, "I'm sorry for this inconvenience, but something's come up. One of our field investigators has come in with a very important piece of intelligence. He has to be debriefed immediately, and since it's my file, I'm afraid I'm elected."

I shrugged and nodded. "I understand."

"Wait right here in my office, why don't you? This shouldn't take long. Here—" He tossed a loose-leaf notebook with Intertel embossed on the cover over to my side of the desk. It made a pretty heavy clunk. "This may answer some of your questions about our operation. I'll be back just as soon as I can." As he left he scooped up the file folder on his desk—my file?—and took it with him.

As it happened, he was gone half an hour, almost to the minute. The notebook wasn't of much interest. It was the source for a lot that he had laid on me. Figures, examples, even a lot of the same phrases were repeated in it. I didn't need to get it all twice. I thumbed on and saw that, yes, they really were international—offices in Paris, Hong Kong, and Bogota. (Bogota?) Plus five more in the US and one in Toronto. Impressive.

I'll admit the money sounded good. Sixty-thousand was about what I'd made in my best year, back when I bought the Alfa and came up with the downpayment on the condo. To get that kind of money coming in at nice, regular, predictable intervals—that was worth thinking about. So I thought about it. I fantasized about it. I thought about it long and hard. And I'll admit that Alicia figured in my calculations. Was this what I wanted? Well, I'd always thought

42

I was a good snoop—and that was what they wanted, wasn't it? They must have thought I was good, too, or they wouldn't have brought me in to talk.

By the time Wallace returned, I was getting pretty restless. But he evidently hadn't come to stay. Although he went to his desk, he didn't sit down. Instead he opened a drawer and pulled out a sheaf of papers about a quarter-inch thick and put them before me.

"Tony, I'm sorry," he said. "This is taking much longer than I anticipated. Take a look at this. It's a battery of tests that our personnel department insists every applicant complete. You're probably familiar with some of them—Kuder Preference, and so on. All pretty much standard. Why don't you get started on these while I wind things up?"

Then I stood up, and he looked disappointed, like I was a live one, and he didn't want to lose me. "Maybe I could take them with me," I suggested. "I've really got to get back home. My wife—well, she's not really my wife, but the woman I live with—she's pregnant, in her ninth month, and, well, I don't like to leave her for too long." As soon as I said it I found myself wishing I hadn't. Maybe living with somebody I wasn't married to would count against me. He had his hook into me pretty deep, didn't he?

"That would be the lady I spoke with on the phone," suggested Wallace.

"Yeah, she's just learning English."

"And very charmingly, too."

I laughed. "She makes a lot of mistakes. I hope she wasn't too hard to understand. But—oh, yeah, she said you spoke Spanish Spanish."

"A little. Enough to get by." He sighed. "Look, Tony, how're we going to solve this little problem? Why don't we do this—?" He took a few more papers out of the drawer. "This is the employment application form. Why don't you sit right down and fill it out. It shouldn't take too long. And if I'm not back, just leave it on my desk here. This way we'll have something to work on."

"And the tests?"

He shrugged. "Well, take them along. They'd cry bloody murder if they knew I let you do them away from here, but that'll be our little secret, right?" A wink, then he said, "I don't put much faith in them, and I'm sure you don't either." He stepped forward and shook my hand again. "Experience and can-do know-how—that's what we go by here at Intertel."

"Well, I've had plenty of experience."

"I know you have. We'll set up another meeting and talk about that." At the door, he turned and gave me the thumbs-up sign. "I like your style, Tony." Then he was gone.

I could have probably taken a couple of the psych tests in the time it took me to fill out the employment app. Talk about detailed! It was three full pages, both sides, of questions like, "What was the name and rank of your last commanding officer during your military service?" Well, I struggled to come up with that and others like it. All in all, it took me another hour to finish. I hate filling out forms of any kind. I hated this one more than most.

Finally, I laid it on the desk and left, finding my way back the way I had come with Artie. He and his buddy were there where I had first seen them, but Artie was asleep, and the guy behind the desk was nearly out. He roused himself enough to open the drawer and hand me back my .38. I pushed the button for the elevator and waited.

You could hear them talking and laughing inside the elevator car before the doors opened. It was the cleaning crew—three *paisanos,* talking the gutter Spanish of northern Mexico—*chinga* this and *chinga* that. They could have been me—without the father and mother I had, and without the education I got. Does that make any sense? It did to me at that moment. They pushed past, with their mops and brooms in a big waste container on wheels, taking no interest in me. I saw how little interest the security team took in them. Artie didn't even stir. The invisible men of Los Angeles.

44

On the drive home it occurred to me that I never did find out from Wallace who passed my name on to them. I knocked that around in my mind for a few blocks—and got a zero. Then, about the time I hit Westwood, it came to me that if they were as high-powered as Wallace claimed they were, then the good word could have come from Silverstein in Washington. He was State Department. I liked that idea, so I hung onto it.

Walking up the stairs, I found myself looking forward to a nice big Cuervo Gold on the rocks. And then I remembered I was supposed to lay down the law to Pilar. Inwardly, I groaned at the thought, but I kept trudging upward.

Again I only got my key in the door when it flew open. But there was no " 'Eeeeere's Chico!" this time. Instead, a flood of words from the two women, mixed Spanish and English, as they flew at me, wide-eyed and excited.

Pilar—around fifty, solid and motherly, about as I had expected. "Mr. Cervantes, you gotta call your clients right away. Something terrible happen."

"*Si! Pronto, Chico, pronto! Que desastre! Un homicidio!*"

"Oh, *Jesus, Maria y Jose,* I prayed, no! No! No! No! I pushed through them and ran to the telephone. Dialing the Toller place, I got through right away to Hans-Dieter.

"Where have you been?" he demanded. "We have been calling you for each five minutes for almost an hour."

"Never mind that now. What happened?"

"There was an invader. He got inside the grounds but not into the house. The guard shot him."

"Is he. . . ?"

"Of course. He's dead."

What did he mean, "Of course?" "Who was the guy? What do the cops say? Let me talk to one of them."

"There are no police here. We're . . . we're still talking about that."

"Well, stop talking and call the fucking cops."

45

The cops were still coming by the time I arrived at the Toller place. I was relieved to see them, dome lights flashing. They were coming down the hill, rather than up—meaning they were LAPD and not Beverly Hills cops. This place was right on the line. And nobody, not even Eddie Murphy, wants to deal with those guys from Beverly Hills. It's not that they're mean. It's just that they're so . . . pissy.

I pulled over to the side in a hurry and let the cruiser pass. He blew through the open gate. I swung out and followed him cautiously. The gate stayed open, but an LA cop came out and stopped me on the spot.

He came over and leaned in my window. "Sorry, sir. Place is closed to visitors."

"I know. There's been a shooting."

"How—may I see your ID?"

Out of my wallet I dug my PI license and handed it over. "I work for these people," I said. "Have the gate guard call the house. I'm expected."

The cop handed it back and looked me over. "The guard's up there at the house now." He turned back and called out, "Al, hey Al!" Another cop stuck his head out of the gate house door. "Call up there and see if it's okay to let this guy—"

"Cervantes."

"—this guy Cervantes in." Then back to me: "Maybe you'd better back up and pull over to the side. Until we find out. There's going to be some more traffic through here."

I did as I was told, but no sooner was I in place than the cop at the gate waved me forward.

"Park near the house," he called as I crept by.

"I know where."

On the way up there, I flashed on the scene back home. I had to let Pilar leave. I knew I might be here most of the night. The woman left, promising to be back by eight-thirty or nine in the morning. Would Alicia be okay? I could only assume she would. She had a month to go, and there was no reason to think her labor might start early. Of course there wasn't. But she'd never been through this before, and neither had I. So what did we know?

The front door was open. Literally. But a cop stood there, leaning against the doorjamb, daring me to try to get past him. But before we could settle down and discuss this like two intelligent human beings, somebody called from inside to him. He looked around, shrugged, and threw the door open wide enough so I could get past.

"Tony Cervantes," I said. "I'm a PI working for them."

"I know that. I'm Sergeant Gulbransen," he said. He didn't offer his hand. I didn't expect him to. "Just go in there and wait. We're talking to people one at a time."

"I wasn't here when it happened."

"I know that, too. Just wait in there."

Going in ahead of him, I looked around a large room I hadn't been in before. They were all in there—the old man, Ursula, Hans-Dieter, the maid, another woman I figured for the cook, two security guards, one of whom I remembered from the night before—but of course no Otto.

It was funny, looking at them there in that fancy room with paintings on the wall and sculpture in the corners, I was reminded of those old-fashioned Agatha Christie mysteries I used to read when I was a kid. Here were all the suspects sitting around, waiting to be called for questioning by the inspector. The role of the inspector was played by Sergeant Gulbransen. Maybe he'd talked to one or two of them already.

Hans-Dieter got the nod from Gulbransen, and the big blond guy got up and, with an unhappy face, followed the detective sergeant to who knew where. Taking a chair in the corner, I sat down and studied the others in the room. They sat in pairs. From opposite ends of a big couch, Ursula gave me a nod and Heinrich Toller waved a sober greeting. Then he muttered something to her. The two women, the maid and the one I assumed was the cook, were sitting close together, whispering. The two security guards sat solemnly, not saying a word, not even looking at each other. I wondered which of the two had done the shooting. Or maybe there was a third. Maybe Gulbransen's partner, whoever he was, was talking to him right now. I decided to go over and find out.

Kneeling down between the two guards, I looked from one to the other. Neither of them gave me much eye contact. "Okay," I said, "what happened?"

One of them, staring straight ahead, said, "We don't have to tell you nothin'."

"Yeah, well, I guess that's right," I agreed. "But it might help to run through your stories once before you tell it to the cops."

They looked at each other as if they were trying to decide about that.

"Which of you two shot the guy?"

"Neither one of us," said the talkative one. "Eckerman did."

I was right. There was a third guard. "And he's with the cops now?"

"Yeah."

"Then you guys don't have anything to be scared of. Why don't you just relax and tell me what happened?"

With a little more encouragement, they did just that. The one who hadn't said a word—Newell, the gate guard from the night before—opened up at last and gave me his version of what had happened. The other one chimed in from time to time.

Eckerman, who was going off duty, had brought Newell down a thermos of coffee from the house at about eight o'clock or maybe a little after. They stood around watching a movie on TV for a little while, then the gate man happened to notice that one of the lights on the big board had lit up red. That meant that the circuit on one of the sensors had been broken. Then the dogs started barking. Eckerman said he'd go out and take a look around. Then they heard a shot and a little later another one. The two of them had run out to see what had happened—one of them from the gate house and the other one from the kennel, where he was getting the dogs ready for their first round of the night. Eckerman was way over in the far corner of the Toller property, just past that bend in the road. They found him bending over the body of a guy who was lying face-down behind some bushes.

Eckerman's account of it was that he had spotted two figures moving among the bushes at the far end of the property. He'd called out quietly for them to freeze. One of them took a shot at him, then dropped out of sight. Eckerman waited, under cover, and when they tried sneaking back to the fence, he got his shot at the one with the gun. The other one got away.

"Over the fence?" I asked the gate guard.

"Yeah, over the fence. Where else?"

I nodded. "Okay. Did you hear a car start up and drive away?"

49

The two looked at each other and shrugged.

"No car?"

"Maybe not," said the gate guard.

"We were pretty fucking excited," the other one said.

"Sure you were," I said sympathetically. "There's just one more thing. What's the time frame on this? I mean, how long was Eckerman gone before you heard the first shot?"

"I dunno. I was watching the movie on TV. Maybe five minutes. Maybe a little longer. He was, you know, looking around."

"And how long between the shots?"

"A minute?" guessed the dog handler.

"So if you were running over there, you must have been pretty close when the second shot was fired. Did you see the other guy go over the fence?"

The two of them glanced at each other, just a quick shift of their eyes, and then the gate guard said, "No, I, personally, didn't see anyone."

The other one said, "I may have seen something. I'm not sure."

I turned to the gate guard then. "All you saw was Eckerman bending over the body?"

"Uh . . . yeah."

Something was funny there. I'd leave it to Sergeant Gulbransen to pursue it.

I said, "Thanks, you guys." Then I stood up and went over to the couch. I took a place between Ursula and her father.

Heinrich Toller looked over at me and then down at his hands folded in his lap. "It's a very serious business, De Quincey," he said to me. "Two men have now been killed—in Munich and now here."

I agreed it was serious and asked him where he had been when he heard the shots.

"In the library," he said, "talking with Mr. Geisel. We heard them. He went out to find out what had happened. He came back and said a man had been shot."

"Then you didn't go out there at all?"

"I have no wish to look at dead people."

I turned to Ursula. "How about you?"

She shook her head. "I did not hear the shots."

"At all?"

"No. I was in my bedroom watching a video with an actor in it who is considered for a film we plan. It was noisy, a gangster film. Maybe I hear them and think it is the movie."

"Well, when did you find out what happened?"

"Just before the police got here."

"Not until then?"

"No. Hans-Dieter came to my room, and he told me. He said the police would probably ask me questions. So I come down here to wait with everyone."

I nodded. They were really protecting her, weren't they? I noticed then that she was staring at me in a funny way. "What is it?" I asked.

"You like this, don't you?"

"Like it? What do you mean?"

"I mean what I say to you. You make a movie of this in your head. You play the detective."

"Lady, I *am* a detective," I said, more than a little annoyed. "I did this on the LAPD for ten years, and now I do it on my own. This is how I make my living. I ask questions."

"Well, you do not ask more questions from me," she declared. "You work for me."

Not for long, baby, I promised myself, not for long. I glanced over at the old man. His hands were still folded in his lap. He was staring straight ahead. He wanted no part of this.

Then, just as I was turning back to Ursula, trying to form an emphatic phrase or two that would put her in her place, Hans-Dieter returned with Gulbransen close behind.

The sergeant wiggled a finger at me. I got up, surprised. I expected to be called last of all—if at all. But I went over, ready to tell him whatever he wanted to know.

"Come on," he said. "Let's take a walk."

So we walked—down the hall and out the front door, the cop posted there holding it open for us.

We got outside, and he lit up a cigar. Once that was accomplished, he turned to me and said, "Cervantes—that's your name, right? Cervantes?"

"That's right."

"Tell me what the fuck is going on here, anyway."

"Well, it's kind of complicated."

He looked annoyed. "Don't give me that shit. I'm a cop—and you used to be."

I looked at Gulbransen closely. Had I known him before? I didn't think so. "Where'd you hear that? From that guy you just talked to?"

"Nah, I didn't get nothin' from him but a bunch of bullshit. I just heard, that's all."

"Good or bad?"

"Neither one. I just heard you were a cop before. So don't try to bullshit me, too." He started out onto the flagstone, turned, and waved me forward. "Come on," he said. "We walk. You talk."

And that's what we did—across the driveway, and then diagonally across the big lawn. I had an idea where we were headed. I could see a set of headlights out there and flashlights bobbing in the dark.

"I wasn't here, remember," I said.

"Yeah. Just tell me what you know."

I did—more or less all of it—and I realized it wasn't much. I gave him what I had heard from the two security guards. I left my doubts out of it. He could form his own.

"Well," said Gulbransen, "that pretty much tallies with what the shooter is saying. My guy Wayne Chang is taking him over it a time or two just to make sure there's nothing he left out."

And probably a time or two after that, I thought.

"What about the others?" he asked.

"Well, yeah, I didn't talk to the maid and the other

52

woman," I said. "But the other ones, the old man and his daughter, they were out of it. She didn't even hear the shots. That guy you talked to, Hans-Dieter, he handled it for them."

"Yeah, Hans-Dieter." Gulbransen repeated the name with some distaste. "These are movie people, aren't they?"

"Right."

"But they're Germans."

"Right again."

"Jesus, I hate dealing with movie people," he sighed. "They're such a pain in the ass."

"Right again again." I thought a minute about this next bit as we walked on. You know how it is. You weigh what you should tell the cops against your duty to the client, and you come up with something like this: "Listen, there's a couple of things I ought to tell you because they're going to come out eventually, anyway."

"Okay," he said. "Shoot."

Then I told him what had happened in the mountains up above Munich, and how one man had been killed there. "Only this is the weird part," I said. "They didn't report it."

"What? Why not?"

"They didn't say so exactly, but I get the idea they had a pretty good idea who those almost-kidnappers were. Only, like I say, they're not too specific about that. Anyway the German cops found out about it, and they brought the chauffeur back for a friendly get-together."

"Ve haff vays uff making you talk," Gulbransen put in.

"Maybe. We'll see," I said. "Which brings me to the second thing I should tell you. When you talk to the neighbors, you'll probably hear that this business took place around an hour and something ago."

"And they waited half an hour or forty-five minutes to call it in?"

"Something like that. Remember? I wasn't here."

"Well, why did they take so long?"

"I haven't talked to them about that yet."

"Yeah, well, I will."

"Do me a favor when you do. Tell them you got it from a canvass of the neighborhood."

Gulbransen drew on his cigar, like he was thinking about it, then he glanced over at me. "Okay," he said.

We were there. A couple of forensic guys were beating the bushes looking for whatever they could find. They moved in and out of the twin beams of light provided by the coroner's meat wagon, which was pulled up on the lawn near the fence. The coroner's men were at the back of the van, pulling a stretcher out through the open doors. There was a black plastic bag on the ground. A body bag.

There was a lot of activity. But in the middle of it all was the figure of a man in the state of ultimate relaxation. He was stretched out facedown behind some shrubbery. In the light from the van he seemed to be sleeping peacefully. I hoped he was. I took a step back from Gulbransen and surreptitiously blessed myself.

I followed the sergeant over to the body and gave it a look. It was a man in his twenties with dark straight hair, about my height. He was wearing black, top and bottom, dressed for night moves. His hands were empty.

"Who was he?" I asked.

"No ID," said Gulbransen. "Nothing at all."

"They said he had a piece. He took a shot at the guard."

"Yeah, he did." Gulbransen turned and called over to one of the forensic guys. "Miller, you got the piece he had in his hand?"

Miller came over, dug deep into his jacket pocket and produced a big glassene envelope with a small revolver inside. "It's not much," he said.

He was right. It was snub-nosed, probably a .32, the kind that would fit easily into a pocket. It looked old. Maybe that's why it also looked unfamiliar. "What kind is it?" I asked.

Miller shrugged. "I don't recognize it. Probably South American manufacture. There's Spanish writing on it."

Colombians? Maybe. I didn't much like that idea, so I put it out of my head, instructing myself that it was unprofessional to jump to conclusions that were presently unprovable.

"Sergeant, if you're through with him, we'd like to get him out of here." It was the coroner's men, both of them, one holding the stretcher like it was a couple of tent poles, and the other with the body bag in his hand.

"Miller?" Gulbransen asked. "How about it?"

Miller nodded.

"Okay. Take him away."

The two came forward, knelt down and got to work. The one who had the body bag opened it up and unzipped it. The other guy put down the stretcher poles and flopped it open.

It was only as they moved the body around that I noticed the entry wound—high on the right side of the neck—directly into the medulla oblongata, and that's all she wrote.

They got him onto the stretcher and were working him feetfirst into the body bag. You couldn't miss the exit wound. Most of his throat was blown out. The guard must have used a magnum on him. They go for those big blasters.

I studied his dead face. Could be a Colombian, all right, or an Arab, or an Iranian, or . . .

I turned to Miller who was there beside me, looking down at the body, like I was. "Hey," I said, "you got a flashlight?"

"Yeah." He produced one from another pocket of his jacket.

"Shine it down on his face, will you?"

He did, and we both moved forward to take a closer look. The two from the coroner stopped and waited.

I looked closely at the features, round faced but with thin lips, already setting in the mask of rigor mortis. My mind strained as I stared down.

Standing up then, I turned to Gulbransen. "You know," I said. "I think I know this guy."

Yeah, but who was he? Everybody stood around for a couple of minutes looking at me looking at him. Finally, I just shook my head, unable to squeeze more from my raddled memory than a vague notion that I'd had some contact with the guy when I was on the LAPD myself, probably back at the Rampart division. That was the best I could do, and that was what I told Sergeant Gulbransen.

"Well, that's okay," he said with a shrug. "Maybe you'll be able to do better tomorrow at the autopsy."

"You want me there?"

"Sure I want you there. It would definitely help to know who this guy is. If you can figure it out, we want to know." It was practically an order the way he said it. I could have ignored it, but if I did that, I'd lose whatever cooperation I might otherwise have gotten from him. He could make things a lot harder for me. "You know where to go, don't you?" he added.

I knew where to go. The LA county morgue was located among the warehouses and loading docks, on the east side of downtown, on Los Angeles Street. There wasn't much to it, really—a long, low building with a fenced parking lot around it big enough to accommodate a steady stream of traffic in and out.

I pulled in around eleven, when I was told to be there, found a space and made my way inside the building. Inquiring at the reception desk, I was directed to Examination Room 3 and told where to find it. The cop leaning up against the desk exchanged a glance with the black receptionist that somehow excluded me. It made me realize that I really was an outsider. I hadn't been here inside the morgue for ten years—way back when I was a cop. And that ten years' absence was all right with me.

There used to be a show on TV where the medical examiner was the detective. I watched it a couple of times. It wasn't bad. I liked the guy who played the lead. But in a way it was just as phony as everything else they had on the tube. It couldn't help but be phony because there were all these scenes in the LA county morgue—and you couldn't smell it. You could watch the show for a whole season and never know that the morgue smells like dead people.

You walked in, and it was there—not overpowering, simply present, a light, high, almost sweet odor, like perfume going sour. And the funny thing is, when you smell it for the first time, you recognize it immediately and know its origin. Revulsion from death and decomposition, the corruption of the body, seems to rest deep in us all like a primeval memory, some ancient taboo.

Rounding the corner on the way to Examination Room 3, I nearly bumped into a gurney on which a corpse lay under a sheet—an old woman, gray haired, pale, apparently dead from natural causes. She seemed as if she were sleeping there in the hallway. In spite of myself I had paused a moment to look. But then I hurried on through the double doors at the end of the hall.

They already had him out on the table and were washing him down. The two morgue attendants went about it casually enough, but I could tell that Gulbransen and his partner, Wayne Chang, were no happier to be there than I was.

57

I went over to them, and they turned to me, apparently glad to have contact with someone or something besides the naked male body on the table. I noticed that Gulbransen had a cigar in his mouth.

"Is it okay if I smoke?" I asked.

"Maybe," he said. "I don't know. Ask them." Meaning the attendants. Then I noticed that Gulbransen's cigar was unlit. He was just chewing on it.

One of the attendants looked up. "Sure. Go ahead. It's up to the ME anyway. He'll tell you to put it out if he wants you to."

I lit up. I didn't smoke that much, a couple of packs a week. But at least it was something to do here and now. No, it was more than that. It was a peculiar way of dealing with my sense of mortality, which at that moment was very strong.

"Had any thoughts?" asked Chang. His narrow face wore a nervous smile. "About who he is, I mean."

I shook my head, no.

"Take another look," Gulbransen ordered.

I shrugged and walked over to the table, keeping back so that the attendants could continue with their work. I didn't know; stretched out like that, naked, he looked deader, somehow, than he did the night before. That big exit wound in his throat looked just as nasty then as it did now, but there was fresh blood around it before. That made it seem less final, like he could be patched up or something. Well, he was beyond that now.

Then I saw something that interested me. On his chest, over each nipple there was a crude tattoo of a snake. They were meant to be identical, but they weren't. The one on the right was coiled tighter than the one on the left. I pushed in or a closer look.

"Hey," I called over to Gulbransen, "did you see these? This guy's done time. These are jail tattoos."

The two came over, and the attendants stepped aside.

Gulbransen nodded. "Oh sure. I've seen those before. San Quentin."

Chang looked up curiously. "How can you tell he got them there?"

"Not professional," I said. "I'd bet it was done with a sewing needle, and then each punch filled in with ink. Look how this one's raised here and in this area here." I pointed to the snake image on his right breast. "Probably got infected."

Chang nodded. "Oh yeah."

The attendant on my side gave me a nudge. "You want professional?" he said, "take a look at this." He raised the guy's right arm, revealing another tattoo on the inner part of the bicep.

He was right. It was professional work, all right, and of a high quality. It had to be, because the design was executed almost in miniature. The grinning skull was only about two inches high, but the details on it were beautiful, precise and perfect. And the lettering beneath was very surely executed. It said *Compañeros.*

"You got a Polaroid here?" I asked the attendant.

"Sure."

"Could you give me a shot of that?"

He shrugged. "I guess so," he said. "Why not?"

He went into a cabinet and pulled out a Polaroid camera. While his partner held up the arm, he sighted from close in, and then snapped. We waited.

"Why do you want that?" Gulbransen asked.

"It looks familiar," I said.

"So does his face. That's what you said last night."

"That's right. His face and now the tattoo. Now we got two things to go on. Or three. The snake tattoos say he did time. And according to you, it was probably in San Quentin."

"Okay," said Gulbransen. "Now we got three. Only if he did time in the state of California, then we can get an ID from his fingerprints."

"But that's going to take a day, maybe two or three," I said. "You know how they work. I thought I'd get a jump on them."

The attendant tore off the film frame and handed it over. It was good, coming in clearer and clearer. "Maybe you could give me another one of his face."

He nodded and set about to take it. It wasn't so easy. He couldn't focus straight down on the table, so in the end, they had to lift the guy up from the shoulders. The other attendant held him up, but I could see he needed some help, so fighting back my squeamishness, I ditched my cigarette—went around, and lent him a hand. Two hands.

"Wait a minute," I said.

The morgue attendant looked up from the camera. "Yeah? What is it?"

"Could we put something around his neck, you know, to cover up that hole in his throat?"

They rummaged around and came up with a towel. We held down the ends on either side, and as we propped the corpse up, the picture was taken. He went down with a bump, and again we waited for the picture.

Detective Chang was fascinated by all this. A nervous smile played on his face as he watched. Then, finally, he said, "He'll still look dead. His eyes."

"Yeah," I said, "but not quite as dead as before."

"Come on," sad Gulbransen, "what is this, anyway, Cervantes?"

The photographer ripped off the picture and handed it to me. I looked at it. The image was coming in loud and clear. But Chang was right. The eyes were a problem.

"This," I said, waving the photo at Sergeant Gulbransen, "is my ticket out of here. I got all I need with these two pictures. You can stick around and watch the ME do the butterfly cut and pull the organs out and weigh them—but not me. On the off chance you should come up with something else, you can reach me over at Rampart in the youth division. That's where I'm going to find out who this guy is."

It was a pretty good exit speech, if I said so myself. But as I headed for the door, Gulbransen grabbed me by the

60

sleeve. "Cervantes, you son of a bitch," he said, "it's a good thing you're not a cop anymore, or I'd—"

"I couldn't agree with you more, Sergeant. It's a good thing I'm not a cop."

I pulled away from him as he was about to say something else, but just then the medical examiner walked in, beaming sunshine at everyone in the room. "Good morning, gentlemen," said the ME to the cops. "I trust your stomachs are settled. This won't take any longer than it has to, Sergeant, if you can just control yourself. No messes on the floor like last time, eh?"

I tried to slip around him unnoticed. Fat chance.

He looked at me, almost hurt. "Oh? Leaving us?"

"Just visiting," I said, and I was out of there like a shot.

There was a pay phone just off the lobby. I went straight to it and called the Toller office in West Hollywood. After getting switched around a bit, following Ursula Toller around the building, I finally managed to hook up with Casimir Urbanski.

That's right. The pride of Hamtramck, Michigan, the LAPD patrolman whose cherished ambition it was to guard the beautiful body of Raquel Welch, had joined the Toller team that very morning.

"So?" I said to him. "How's it going? No problems?"

"No, hey, no problems at all." There was a moment's hesitation, then, "No shit, she can really drive that Porsche"—he said it *Por-shee*—"can't she?"

"A thrill a minute."

"And hey, listen Cervantes, she's not bad, you know? I mean, she's no Raquel, but by me she's okay. I gotta thank you, you know?"

"Don't mention it. No trouble getting off for this then?"

"Nah. I phoned in sicking out today. The department owes me so much time already it'll be a week before they even notice."

"It shouldn't take that long. Just stick close to her, okay?"

A low laugh rumbled in his throat. "You don't need to worry about *that.*"

We said our good-byes, and I got off the line—then out the door, headed for my car.

The night before, after the meat wagon hauled the corpse away, I went back into the house and settled a few things. Before I parted company with Gulbransen, I went back into the kitchen with him and listened to Detective Chang take the security guard through his story, probably for the twelfth time. I wasn't really surprised to find out that the guy who did the shooting was the one who had given me a hard time at the gate that morning. He took his job a little too seriously. Out in the hall, Gulbransen told me they weren't booking him but were of course holding it open pending further investigation. There'd be the coroner's inquest and so on. None of that surprised me, either. You let these guys carry guns, and you had to face the fact that in certain situations they were going to use them.

Then I got the Tollers and Hans-Dieter and brought them into the library. "We have to talk," I told them. So we talked. The first thing I asked them was why in hell they had waited so long to call the cops.

Hans-Dieter sat up abruptly at that. I could tell he was offended at my diction and tone. Let him be.

"Well!" he said—it was kind of a *hrrumph*—"we couldn't get you on the telephone."

"What did that have to do with it? You have a shooting on the premises, you call the cops."

"Also, we had trouble at first reaching Ted Gittelson."

"Who's he?"

"Our lawyer. The one who gave us your name."

"Oh yeah. Okay, you got him. What did he tell you to do?"

Hans-Dieter sighed, deflated. "He told us to call the police. We talked about it."

I held up both my hands, resting my case. "Look," I said, "that kind of delay only makes the cops think there's more going on here than just a prowler getting shot." I paused then and looked at each one of them. "Is there?"

Ursula jumped up. "This is wrong!" She snarled it out gutturally and stamped her foot. If she'd had her tote bag handy she would probably have hit me over the head with it. "You do not talk to us this way. You work for us!"

She looked to Hans-Dieter and her father for support. The young man rose in her support; the old man motioned them both to sit down. They sat.

"I want you to know," I said to them very seriously, "that I'm willing to change that right now or any time in the future when I think I'm not getting the straight dope from you. You can't pay me enough to get blindsided." Would they understand that? I wasn't sure, so I translated. "If I'm going to get shot at, I have to know where to look. You got that?"

Heinrich Toller nodded. "We understand that, Mr. Cervantes. You make your position very clear." Maybe I had an ally.

"Okay. Good. Now listen, there's some very funny stuff going on here. If the guy who got shot tonight was just a prowler, which I doubt, then it doesn't relate to what happened back in Munich. Chances are, it does. Right?"

I got no reaction from either of the Tollers. Hans-Dieter shrugged.

So I continued. "What I'm saying is that it's time to go on the offensive instead of just reacting. I mean, who are these people? What are they trying to do? Kidnap Ursula? Why? What the fuck is this all about?"

I was pretty charged by that time, and there wasn't much to add to that, and so I just waited. I was sweating. I sweated a lot when I got excited.

"What is it you want to do?" asked Toller.

"There's a good chance I can find out who that man was who got shot tonight," I said. I was talking directly to him. "Now what I'm saying is that we'd be a lot better off following up on that, trying to discover who's behind all this, than we would be just sitting around and waiting for them to make their next move."

"*Ja*, sure," said Hans-Dieter, "and what if they make their next move while you're out playing detective?" Had he been talking to Ursula? Had she told him what she said to me?

"That's a problem," I admitted. "The digging around I have to do is going to take me a couple of days, maybe longer. I think you're going to have to hire somebody to cover Miss Toller while I'm out on this."

"Then you should pay him," put in Hans-Dieter, pointing his finger at me. I could have done without that.

"You could argue that," I said. "You're saying I should subcontract it. But you hired me as a bodyguard, and now you're getting me as a detective. I'd say that's a pretty good deal. You said you wanted somebody who knew LA. Well, I know it well enough to think I can find out who the guy is who got shot and who hired him. Which is what you want, whether you know it or not."

Hans-Dieter lifted his hand again and started to say something more. But suddenly a great bellow filled the room. *"We should not argue about this!"*

It was the old man. The two others turned to him in surprise. I guess that's how I looked, too. He had so far showed such a calm exterior that I didn't think he had it in him.

He looked at them and finally at me. "How much money are we talking about?"

I shrugged. "I don't know. Anywhere from fifteen hundred to five thousand dollars—if I can get the guy I want."

"There? You see? For five thousand dollars you would gamble with a life," he said to Hans-Dieter. "Her life. Mr. Cervantes' idea is a good one. We fight back. I spend my life fighting back, and most of the time I win." Then he added with a half smile, "Most of the time. Hans-Dieter, bring me my checkbook."

Obediently, without a word, the big guy got up and

walked around to the desk. With a key he opened one of the drawers and brought out a big, square executive checkbook and took it over to Toller.

Holding it on his lap, Heinrich Toller wrote out a check and dutifully entered the details on the check stub. He tore the check out carefully and offered it to me. I walked over and took it from him. He had made it out for ten thousand dollars. I noticed it was on his personal account.

"Find us a good man, De Quincey."

I found them Casimir Urbanski. It wasn't so hard. He had called me once after I got back from Mexico, asking if I'd heard anything from "the people around Raquel." I had to tell him not yet and felt guilty about it. Anyway, he made it clear he was available. He didn't even mind that it was around midnight when I called him back that night and offered him five hundred a day to babysit Ursula Toller—if he could show up bright and early the next morning. He said he'd be there.

Just one more thing about that night. As we were leaving the library, I took Hans-Dieter aside and asked him about the security guards. "Who are they, anyway?"

"What do you mean?" He said it like he didn't understand the question.

"I mean, who are they? I noticed they don't wear any company insignia or anything. Did you hire them directly or do they work for some security outfit?"

"They work for a company, of course," he said. "We said no insignia. It didn't seem . . . right for us here." That made the guards a little like the Tollers' private army.

"Well, okay. Which company?"

"I have no idea. You'll have to ask the accountant at the office. He handles all those bills." He shrugged, like he couldn't be bothered and started to walk away.

"Hey, Hans-Dieter," I said, a little louder than I needed to, "come back here." He turned back to me but stood his ground. "*You'll* have to ask the accountant. If I'm going to conduct an investigation, you're going to cooperate in it. In other words, I need all the help I can get. Is that clear?"

He tried to stare me down, but it didn't work. Finally, he just nodded and left the library.

So now the pressure was on me. I had more or less promised I could find out the identity of the dead man and take it from there. Maybe I could. Maybe I couldn't. But I had the feeling that the first answer might be found in the files they kept in the youth division down at Rampart. So that's where I was headed.

My last year on the force I put in a few months as a youth officer. That was back when there weren't so many Spanish-speaking cops down there. And since the youth division's work there at Rampart was ninety percent Hispanic gangs, I got asked and said okay. But I didn't find the work rewarding. What can I say? They were lousy kids.

It was only when I saw that tattoo on the inner bicep that I placed the guy on the morgue table with the gangs. His face looked familiar. But that tattoo—I was sure I'd seen it before and reasonably certain it had to do with my short stint as a youth officer. So I'd called ahead and told Carlos Colon that I used to work in his office, and if it was okay, I'd be dropping by in the early afternoon to talk to him. He was head of the youth division there at Rampart.

When I gave my name to the duty sergeant, he phoned ahead and waved me through. He started to give me directions. I told him I knew the way. The place hadn't changed much.

Colon seemed pretty young. He looked like he couldn't be much older than some of his "clients"—which I guess is what they call them now. When I walked into his office, he gave me a shake and offered me a chair, then sat back down behind his desk.

"When you say early afternoon," he said, "you mean early." He pointed to the clock on the wall. It was one minute after twelve.

"Yeah, well, I got away sooner than I expected."

"You almost missed me. I was about to head out for lunch—beat the crowd. Wanta go?"

"In a minute, maybe. Let me show you a couple of pictures first."

He nodded, and I tossed the Polaroid of the tattoo onto the desk. A slight smile moved across his mouth, and he nodded again.

"Look familiar?" I asked.

"Sure. It's a gang emblem, of course."

"Yeah, but which one?"

"It's right there—the death's head, and underneath, see, *Compañeros.* Meaning, *Compañeros de la Muerte.*"

"Yeah, that sounds right." I frowned, concentrating. "They were a kid gang, right?"

"Not anymore."

"Well, tell me about them."

"That may take a while. Let's see your other picture."

I handed it across to him. "Can you put an ID on this guy?"

He studied it for a long time. No sly smile this time. Finally, he handed it back with a frown. "Can't say I recognize him. Sorry."

"I am, too. He's done time. Maybe in Quentin. That help?"

"No." Colon hesitated, then he asked, "He's dead, huh?"

"I guess it shows."

"The eyes. You know. He's either dead or not very wide awake."

"He's asleep at the morgue right now. I just came from there."

"You still want to eat?"

I shrugged. "Sure. I got out of there before they started on him."

"Then let's go."

We drove up to El Chavo on Sunset. Carlos Colon didn't seem to mind the trip. On the way, he told me what I al-

67

ready knew from reading the papers and watching the eleven o'clock news: that the gangs weren't into grand-theft auto and breaking and entering anymore; they were drug running and dealing, some of them working directly for the big guys.

"Don't get me wrong," he said. "Silverlake isn't South Central Los Angeles, and it isn't East LA. And with a little luck, and a lot of hard work it won't be. But there's definitely a gang problem here. Which shouldn't surprise you."

"I worked in youth for a while, remember?"

"Well, that was ten years ago. Things have gotten a lot heavier since then. There was a drive-by last week over on Alvarado—the Santos took out one of the Soldados with a shotgun, a fifteen year old. We're trying to bring them together for a sit-down now. I don't think it's going to work."

He went on and told me why, and who, and where the lines were drawn. It was territorial. It was always territorial. My barrio against your barrio, the honor of the neighborhood.

He really got into it. By the time we were drinking beer and eating the Combinacion, I had to remind him that he had promised to tell me about the Compañeros de la Muerte.

"They're out of my league now. Like you said, they were a kid gang ten years ago."

"Yeah, that's the way I remember. Sort of."

"Well, the Mafia was a kid gang in Brooklyn in the beginning."

"These guys are the Mafia?"

"No, not really. But see, there were never very many of them, even when they started out—twenty, maybe less. You remember that?"

"Sort of."

"And they never expanded much or organized vertically. I mean, they never had any auxiliary down in junior high—just twenty guys who stuck together in high school and afterward. Nobody messed with them, though. They got the first Uzi in Silverlake, and one night they used it. That was about six years ago."

"Oh yeah," I said, "I remember that. Up against a wall. Just like the Saint Valentine's Day Massacre. I didn't know that was them, though. I thought they never got the guys who did it."

"They didn't. But it was them."

"Are the Compañeros the big guys the kids are working for?"

"I'm not the one to answer that," said Colon. "From my end, I'd say no. But you should talk to the guys in narcotics."

"When we get back maybe." I paused, hesitated, then said, "Back in the office you acted like there was a lot to tell about these guys. Now there doesn't seem to be so much?" Yeah, I put a question mark at the end of it. I expected an answer.

He took a swig of beer, sat back in his chair and looked at me. "Well, this is all street talk, understand. These guys are all twenty-five, twenty-six now. Adult. Very. And what they're into is out of my jurisdiction, if that's the right word. But, you know, you hear stuff around the station."

"What're they into?"

"Coke. Coke and crack."

"They must have a Colombian connection then." I was trying to put this together with Hans-Dieter's admission that Toller used "unorthodox" sources of finance. Did it fit? Then I noticed Colon was smiling again, that same sly smile.

"Right," he said. "They have a connection, a very good one." It was his turn to pause. I waited. "The guy in charge is Jaime Fernandez. He's half Colombian, by his mother, and she raised him. It's a family connection."

"The strongest kind."

He nodded. "Jaime is a pretty smart guy. He's even got some college, I hear—a business administration major."

"It figures."

"The Compañeros don't even try to move their stuff in Silverlake," he continued. "There's not much market. They deal in West Hollywood mostly, maybe a little bit in Beverly Hills, maybe not so little there. Who knows? In fact, most of the Compañeros don't even live in Silverlake, or anywhere around here anymore. I hear Jaime has a place in West Hollywood, on Burton Way or someplace like that."

Just a couple of blocks from the Toller building—right then I was beginning to feel pretty uncomfortable. It was beginning to sound more and more like the Colombians really were involved. They were international. They could certainly have managed that operation in Munich. And now I find out that the guy shot inside the grounds of the Toller place wasn't just a prowler, as I'd hoped, he was in a gang with strong Colombian connections. Maybe the Medellín was laundering money through Toller. Maybe he was skimming from them. Who knows? I had some hard questions to put to Hans-Dieter and the old man.

Then something occurred to me. "Wait a minute," I said to Colon. "If the operation is on the west side, and these guys don't live down here anymore, what's the Silverlake connection?"

"Esperanza," he answered.

"How's that?"

"Esperanza. It's a kind of combination disco-sports bar farther down on Sunset. We passed it on the way here. The Compañeros own it, or maybe it's Jaime's and they all hang out there. I don't know. Anyway, that's where they are most nights. It figures in their operation somehow. I don't really know how. That's another thing they might be able to tell you up in narcotics."

Again I thought about it, and again I came up with the same questions that needed answers. I looked across the table at Carlos Colon. He had dumped a lot into my lap in about five minutes worth of talk. At last I forced a smile. "Well, like you said, the Mafia started out as a kid gang in Brooklyn."

70

"That's what I said, all right," he replied. Then he was silent for a moment as he took another swig of beer from the bottle. "Just one more thing, Cervantes—that's your name, right? Cervantes?"

"Right."

"If you decide you've absolutely got to go to Esperanza, just watch your ass when you do."

By the time I headed back home, it was mid afternoon, and I was exhausted. I had been up most of the night before with Gulbransen and the Tollers. The rest of it I spent trying to figure out just what I was going to do, now that I had managed to sell them on upgrading my professional services. What would I do? More or less what I had always done—play it by ear. These days, however, I know enough to dignify this nonmethod of mine by describing it as "drawing on the right side of my brain"—giving free rein to my instincts (i.e., playing it by ear). They go for that kind of talk out here.

I was running on empty when I returned with Colon to Rampart station. What held me up there was a lucky break. I took Colon's advice and looked in at records and showed the officer behind the desk there the picture taken in the morgue. He looked at it, and then at me, and shrugged.

"So?"

"Any chance of getting an ID on him?" I asked.

"With this?"

"Well . . . it's a good likeness."

"The guy's obviously dead."

"I'd still like to know who he is."

He looked at the picture again. "He's at the morgue, right?"

"Ah," I said, "you're acquainted with their work. Personally, I think the lighting's a bit harsh, myself."

He didn't think it was funny. He pushed the picture across the desk to me. I took it. "Go back and get fingerprints," he said. "They fingerprint stiffs all the time down there. I might be able to do something for you with a set of prints. But not with any picture."

He was right, of course. That was how the system worked. "They'll be coming," I said. "I just thought you might recognize him." I slunk out the door. No lucky break there.

That came on the way out, when, acting on Colon's recommendation and an unfulfilled obligation, I stopped in at narcotics division and asked if Billy Johnson still worked there.

The kid with the long hair and wispy yellow beard looked up from the typewriter, where he was hunting and pecking a report. "You mean Sergeant Johnson?"

"Yeah," I said, "I guess I do."

He nodded toward a row of offices in back. Then he looked me over appraisingly. "What's, uh, what's your business with him?"

"Nothing official. I used to work with him is all."

"Here?"

"Here and at Wilshire."

He got up and pointed, indicating I was to stay right where I was. "Who should I say. . . ?"

"Cervantes," I told him. "Just tell him Chico."

He nodded and headed down the hall.

A half minute later, Johnson appeared, just as black as ever, but even bigger now that he'd added about thirty

73

pounds to his large frame. He said nothing at all, just looked at me across the squad room and threw a long looping gesture in my direction—beckoning me forward. Then he disappeared down that same hall.

I followed him. About halfway to his office I passed the bearded, long-haired kid. He flashed me a smile. This guy not only looked like one of the street people, he smelled like them, too. These undercover cops really get into it today.

I stepped into the glass-walled office. Johnson waited for me there, his fists on his hips. "So you finally showed up," he said.

"Yeah."

"This means, of course, you're looking for a job." At this point I started saying no, emphatically shaking my head, and making other negative signs. But he kept right on. "Yeah, when you left, everybody said you'd be back, couldn't make it on the outside, never cope with civilian life, won't even begin to—"

Johnson suddenly broke up, doubling over, his deep laughter filling the little office space. He grabbed at me, still laughing, encircling my neck with his big arm, giving me a playful squeeze.

"Hey," I gasped, "hey, Billy Jay, why're you doin' the dozens on me?"

"'Cause you never come to see me, you little wetback. Why'd you stay away so long?" He released me then and pushed me down in a chair.

I hesitated, trying to think of a good answer. Finally, I decided the truth would have to do. "I guess it was because I was afraid I'd hear something like that rap you just laid on me—only for real."

"Not from me."

"No, not from you, I guess. But, as we both know, there were others . . ."

"Ah, yes, there were others . . . Murphy, Tucker . . ."

"It was widely predicted I'd fall on my face."

"Only you didn't. Doin' pretty good, I hear."

I shrugged and wiggled my hand. "Oh, up and down. You know."

"Tell me about it."

And so I did, giving about an hour of my time and taking an hour of his. And why did I do that, when I had places to go and people to see? For friendship, I guess—for the hours we'd spent together one summer on stakeout, and for the time he saved my life by pulling me back one night when I seemed determined to jump out into the path of a bullet. That, I guess, was something you never forgot—and never should forget.

Anyway, we talked. I gave him an overview of the PI hustle, told him how I fit in, and what kind of cases I was working. He never once asked how much money I made, which was all right with me because I wouldn't have told him.

On his side, Billy Johnson told me how he had at last managed to get himself moved up to sergeant just a year ago. It was in the nature of a battlefield promotion. Sergeant Leszek, who I never knew, had a coronary on the job. Billy Jay, as senior detective, was made acting sergeant. LAPD failed to supply anyone else with anything like his experience, and so he was at last given what was long overdue—his three stripes.

"You know what?" I said to him. "It would have taken an act of God like that to get me mine."

He looked at me seriously. "Maybe not. Your minority's in style. Mine's not."

"That's not something I want to argue with you about," I said.

There it hung between us for a moment. Finally, he slapped the top of his desk and said, "Well, what brings you here—really?"

I tossed the tattoo photo down in front of him.

He glanced at it. "Okay. Compañeros. Bad bunch. What about them?"

I tossed the other photo to him. "He's one of them—or was. Who is he?"

Billy Jay studied the picture for about a minute. Then he shrugged and shook his head. "No," he said at last. "I can't help you. You took that Compañero tattoo off him?"

I nodded.

"Well, he doesn't look familiar. I thought I knew them all. But not this guy." He hesitated, then: "Of course, it might help if he was alive when you took this picture . . . but not that much." He took another look, then shook his head. "No, I don't know him."

"I was afraid of that," I said. "Tell me about the Compañeros de la Muerte then."

"What do you want to hear about? Silverlake's own little Valentine's Day massacre? You want a rundown on Jaime Fernandez? You looking for—"

Just then the scruffy-looking kid from the squad room came in the open door and without a word tossed a pile of papers into Billy Jay's in box. As he turned to go, he glanced down at the photos on the desk in front of Johnson. He stopped and looked again.

"Who is that?" he asked. "Julio? Wow, he looks terrible."

That stopped me cold. Billy Jay and I exchanged looks. "Who's Julio?" I asked the kid.

He pointed at the picture. "Well . . . that is, I guess. Only he looks—"

"He's dead. But who was he?"

The kid glanced at Billy Jay, as if to ask whether it was all right to talk to me. He must have gotten an okay because he turned back to me then and said, "Julio Robles. He just got out of San Quentin a couple of months ago. Did five for armed robbery."

"How did you know him?" I asked.

"He was the bar boy at the Dos Mundos. I was in a lot of nights when it was slow, and we talked."

"Did he know you were a cop?"

76

The kid laughed and shook his long locks, like it was still fun thinking about it even if Julio *was* dead. "Yeah, sure. I didn't tell him, but he knew. Everybody there knows. I think he got off on it, having these long conversations with a cop."

"What did you talk about?"

"The slammer. San Quentin. He let me know what it was like. He was out to convince me I'd never make it on the inside. Probably right, too." He laughed again, kind of inappropriately, you might say, and we looked at each other.

I hadn't noticed much before except the thin blond beard and the long hair. But now it was his eyes that struck me. They were that weird-looking, nearly colorless blue for which a certain actor is famous. A funny thing about eyes like that: they make people who've got them look a little bit crazy. This guy was no exception.

"Chico Cervantes meet Ray Jorgensen," said Billy Jay by way of introduction.

The kid stretched a long arm across the space between us, and I half rose to shake his hand. I must have mumbled something, but I was certain Ray Jorgensen said nothing— just looked at me intently and nodded.

"Ray's got more arrests and arrests leading to conviction than anybody in this division," BJ continued.

"Yeah," said Jorgensen. "I'm terrific."

"Modest, too."

"Just your average, run-of-the-mill supercop." And then that laugh again. Sudden—and almost embarrassing to hear, there in that office. I glanced at Billy Jay a bit uneasily. He was just shaking his head at the kid like an uncle at his favorite nephew.

"Now go on," Johnson said to him. "Get out on the street like a good cop."

Jorgensen didn't exactly say anything—just gave me a kind of two-fingered salute and left, laughing.

"Is he always like that?" I asked.

"Yeah. More or less. He says he's going to quit when it stops being fun."

"I guess he's not going to quit for a while then."

"I sure as hell hope not," said Billy Jay.

Driving back to West Hollywood, I felt pretty good, and then again, I didn't. I mean, I'd made a little progress, hadn't I? There was a name for the guy in the morgue and some known associates. There were things to find out, questions to ask. At least I knew what my next move would be and where I'd make it. So that wasn't so bad.

The thing was, I was flying blind, and I knew it. I still had no real theory to go on. I was just turning over rocks to see what would pop out. And from what I'd been told about the Compañeros, that might prove to be a dangerous method. If I could just catch a little sleep, I told myself, then I might be able to come up with something.

Sleep. That's what I was thinking about when I stuck my key in the door and walked into my apartment. Surprise! Nobody home. I called out to Alicia. Then to Pilar. No response—and that at first was quite all right with me. Here was a chance to get in bed and get to sleep before they could involve me in their angry games. And so I headed straight for the bedroom, tossing off clothes as I went—tie and jacket in the living room, pants and shirt on the bedpost. I dove under the covers and then began to worry.

Why weren't they around? Where had they gone? Was this the day Alicia was supposed to go to the obstetrician? It was on the calendar in the kitchen. Maybe I should get up and check it out. Yeah, but if today wasn't her day at the doctor's then I'd worry about her even more. Labor pains maybe? Well, it was possible, of course—any time from now until the estimated time of arrival. That's why I asked Pancho to send me someone who had a car and could drive it. Well, that was Pilar, wasn't it? Sure, and with all

78

her grandchildren—five, was it?—she would know just what to do. So why was I worrying, anyway? Women have been having babies for centuries, millennia, maybe millions of years. It was just the first time for me—that was all.

Just try to get to sleep with your mind running along like that. I tried both sides of the pillow, belly down and belly up, but still it was no use. I was wide-awake—and exhausted, wiped out from the sleep I'd missed the night before, scared I wouldn't be able to make it through the night coming up unless I got some rest.

So I felt almost relieved when, ten or fifteen minutes after I laid down, I heard the door open, and the bickering that began the day before was carried along by them into the living room. I sat up in bed and waited for Alicia to make her appearance.

The door creaked slowly open. I looked up and saw her head poke through the gap.

"Ah!" she said, relieved. "You're awake, Chico."

"I am now."

She came inside and sat down at the end of the bed. "Did she wake you up? That woman?" She meant Pilar, of course.

I couldn't lie. "No. I was awake. I couldn't sleep."

"You want me to lie down with you?"

"The way *mamacita* used to do?"

"No," she said, clearly annoyed, "the way *I* do."

I threw off the covers and swung my feet down to the floor. "Right now I'd like a cigarette," I said. "Toss me my shirt."

She did, letting me have it full in the face. I dug out the pack and a book of matches from my pocket, fished one out and lit up.

"You shouldn't do that," she said.

I am that rarity, a three-a-day smoker, occasionally more and usually less. Toward the end of a pack they get stale, so I throw out what's left and buy a fresh one. It's the only bad habit I have that doesn't worry me. Nevertheless I gave her the benefit of the doubt. "Maybe you're right. Maybe I shouldn't."

"That's what the doctor says. She says it's bad for me."

"But you don't smoke."

"Yes, but you do. And she says that's bad for me."

I sat, steadfastly puffing, looking her straight in the eye. "What else did she say? Is that where you went with Pilar?"

"No. The doctor said that before. A month ago." She looked away evasively. "That woman and I, we took a walk. She says I'm too fat. The doctor says so, too. Every day I should take a walk. It's for the baby and for me the doctor says."

"Come here," I said. She bounced over a couple of feet on the bed and I pulled her toward me. One arm around her shoulder, I gave her a kiss. She responded weakly. She was being consoled, and she knew it. I kissed her again, then leaned over and put out my cigarette. Then I shrugged. "It's true," I said. "You've put on a few pounds. So maybe a walk every day isn't such a bad idea."

"But Chico, she made me walk all the way to Sunset."

"That's just two blocks."

"But uphill!" She groaned.

I got this picture of her struggling up to Sunset from Fountain, Pilar beside her, urging her onward—no, commanding her, demanding. You know what? That picture looked pretty good to me.

That's when I realized that deep down I thought she'd been hanging around the apartment too much. Watching too much TV. Eating too many taco chips. I decided Pilar definitely had the right idea—get Alicia out, get her walking, take some of that weight off. What was it the obstetrician had said? Twelve pounds overweight—and that was a month ago. Since then she must have put on five or ten pounds over and above baby weight. On her—she was barely five feet tall—that was an awful lot.

Just then she turned on me suddenly. "You're smiling,"

she wailed. "You want me to suffer don't you? You thinl that's funny!"

"I don't think it's funny. I do think it's a good idea fo you to get out and walk. I mean, it wouldn't hurt i you . . ."

"Okay, *sí*. If I want?"

I sighed. "Oh, it's nothing. Never mind." Why go into it? In another few months she'd look like half the women over twenty on Whittier Boulevard—short, solid, no waist to speak of, prettier than most. But what did I expect? What was I hoping for? Some kind of animated blonde Barbie doll off TV? A Heather? A Vanna? No, Chico, this was the real world. And Alicia Ramirez y Sandoval was a real woman.

She waited, studying me almost suspiciously.

"Look, Chiquita," I said to her, "I should take a nap."

"Go ahead." She shrugged. "You're always tired—like you were the one having the baby." Then she looked away and began studying a picture of my grandmother on the far wall quite intently.

"Aw, stop that," I told her. "You remember how it was—how late I came in last night?"

"This morning."

"Exactly. Then I had to get up early and go see the police."

"You're not in trouble?" Suddenly, unmistakably worried.

"Nothing like that, no. Just business. I have to go out again tonight."

She was on me then, grabbing me, almost shaking me. "Take me with you," she demanded.

"I can't, Chiquita. It's business."

"Business! Always business! Maybe you have another woman out there somewhere."

"If I do, then she must be pretty lonesome by now." I looked at Alicia and let her see the irritation I felt.

"Another woman."

"Only you."

"That's nice to hear. I hope it's true." She flashed me another look with those dark eyes of hers. Then, with a flourish, like she was playing her last card, she said, "A man was following us."

Just that. She said it and watched for my reaction, which was slow coming. First I studied her, trying to decide if what she said was true—literally true. I knew she could have made it up consciously and completely just for the effect it might have on me. She was capable of that. Then, too, she could have imagined it. Or spotted some guy half a block behind and assumed the worst. Or, on the other hand . . .

We stared at each other a full minute. Finally, I jumped up, went to the closet and pulled on my robe. "Pilar," I called out. "Let's talk!"

Coming through the door, I found her leaving it, walking off hurriedly into the living room. She'd been listening to us in the bedroom, of course.

"Pilar!"

"Oh, yes sir, Señor Cervantes?" More polite than usual. Guilt? She stood in the center of the living room, the palm of her hand just above her bosom, her fingers twisting a button at her neck.

"Alicia just told me there was a man following you today, just now while you were out walking."

"*Sí?*" A definite question mark there.

"Well"—slightly exasperated—"was there?"

She seemed flustered, uneasy. "Of course," she said, "it's very hard to tell sometimes. By accident, people often go your way. You turn, they turn, and it's all just—"

"I know all that. It's understood. Do *you* think you were being followed?"

She looked around the room, as if the answer were written on the walls somewhere. Then at last, giving me no more than a glance she said, *"Sí, señor."*

H ere I was sitting in this so-called sports bar down on
Sunset Boulevard in the heart of Silverlake, the place
they called Esperanza. Hope. Somehow, in these circumstances, the name seemed appropriate. I didn't have much
more than that for backup here. And hope was all I had
that I could make good on the assurances I'd given to the
Tollers.

This was the kind of place I wouldn't go to on a bet if I
wasn't on a job. Not that it was crummy or run-down or
anything. No, every item in it looked like it was on display,
just as shiny and new as it must have been the day the place
opened, which was (as I recalled) two years ago. But it was
all chrome and plastic, a monument to the high-tacky
rococo that the world outside associated with Los Angeles.
Maybe the world was right, and I was wrong—who knows?
But I could remember when this town had some real style.
What about Spanish colonial? And there were all these
great old Victorian houses left over from the last century,
like the big one at the end of my block in Boyle Heights

when I was a kid. And there were a couple of blocks of them only about a mile from where I was sitting just then. That was real LA style, not this Melrose Avenue–Johnny Rocket put-on that half the people around here seemed to take seriously.

And sports bar? What made this a sports bar? Nothing more or less than the eight or ten television sets placed around the big room, all of them turned on and tuned in to the Dodgers' game. The funny thing was, the place was practically empty. Unoccupied tables were arranged in tight formation around a good-sized dance floor where nobody danced. A waitress tracked indifferently on a path between the tables, slapping them lightly with a towel as she went. She ignored the Dodgers.

Only two of the sets were watched, and both of them were behind the bar. From them Vin Scully crowed loudly, gabbing about Valenzuela's comeback season, as if it was something already proven, while up there on the screen Fernando himself was working hard against the Cubs, trying to make that comeback happen. In the closeups on the mound he looked worried. Maybe he was bearing down a little too hard. *Cuidase, 'mano!*

There I sat watching the game about halfway down the bar, trying my best to give the impression that the only thing that stood between me and the television set about six feet away was the bottle of Dos Equis that stood on the bar. At regular intervals I reached out and slugged down a mouthful of the dark brew as I pretended to stare fixedly at the glass screen.

What I was really doing most of that time was keeping an eye on the group at the end of the bar. There were four of them, three who were plump and prosperous, prematurely gone into early middle age; with them it was a state of mind as much as their physical condition. They surrounded the fourth man. He was still young, although perhaps chronologically older than one or two of the others. The thing was, he still looked lean and hungry, a state of mind as much as his physical condition; him I took to be Jaime Fernandez, the leader, the half-Colombian *caudillo*. The others looked like they were trying to entertain him, to keep him happy. And he, well, he was playing it cool. His attention was directed toward the television and the Dodgers. Occasionally he would turn and smile at his companions—at a *broma*—a wisecrack, tossed out by one of them. And I saw Jaime wink a couple of times at the barmaid who attended the group; she was silent except for a remark now and then to the others. Did they want this? Did they want that? *Su servidor.* What they spoke among themselves wasn't Spanish or English, exactly, but a brand of disc jockey Spanglish in which words from both languages collided at high speeds, with no apparent damage on either side.

So these were the Compañeros—death's companions—or some of them, anyway. Except for Jaime, they didn't seem to me like such heavy dudes. But looks, I knew, deceived.

What surprised me about this place of theirs was that it was so empty. Sure, it was early in the evening, but after all, this was a Friday night—and you'd have normally expected a little drop-in business from the neighborhood. But maybe they didn't want it. Maybe they liked Esperanza just the way it was—their private club, a place for parties when they wanted to give them, a front for whatever they happened to be into this week or the next.

I began to wonder about that. What was the physical setup here? If the place was bigger than it needed to be, maybe there was a reason for that. Was there a basement? You couldn't tell from the outside. Was there even more to the flat one-story structure out in back? I decided to take a look around. Waiting until Fernando had retired the side, I called the barmaid over and asked for the location of the "caballeros." She gave me directions—quite unnecessarily, for there was only one direction to go, but it seemed like a good idea to establish my destination beforehand. I pushed away from the bar and landed flat-footed on the carpeted floor. Without making a big show of it, I tried to give the impression I'd had more to drink than the beer I'd been nursing in front of the TV set.

As I turned a corner and passed out of sight of the bar, what I found was a corridor about twenty feet long— CABALLEROS and DAMAS on one side and two unmarked doors directly across from them. I tried the knob on the first one then the other and found both locked. That didn't surprise me.

What did surprise me was the sudden appearance of one of the Compañeros from the bar. He didn't exactly catch me red-handed, testing the locked doors, but he did find me still hanging outside the men's room when, by rights, I should have been inside it. I thought fast, pulled out a cigarette, and asked him for a light.

I could sense the guy giving me the once-over as he held out a silver-cased cigarette lighter to me and then suddenly shot a butane flame a full four inches in my direction. I recoiled instinctively to save my nose from incineration. As I took the light, I caught a glimpse of him—heavy black brows, a mustache, and an evil smile. I mumbled my thanks, and he simply laughed.

He followed me into the men's room then, and as I managed to squeeze something into the urinal, he stood whistling before the mirror, combing his thick black hair, patting it first this way and then that.

I stumbled out of the place, catching one last glimpse of his eyes following me in the mirror. It seemed like a good time to leave. I stopped off at the bar, tossed a few singles out next to the bottle of Dos Equis, and headed for the door. Conversation at the end of the bar stopped, but nobody followed as I marched out the door and made it to my car.

So that was Esperanza. My visit hadn't told me much. It had given me a look at Jaime Fernandez and three of his friends, and that might come in handy sometime soon. But it had also given them a look at me—a bad trade.

86

I glanced into the rearview mirror as I pulled away, leav- ing the club behind. No other car started up after me. No- body even came out the door to look where I had gone. That suited me fine.

All of a sudden I seemed to be living my life looking over my shoulder or peeking into the rearview. I didn't like that. If I was doing the detecting, then why did I feel like I was the one being watched? Either I or maybe Alicia. What was that all about, anyway? Why would somebody follow a pregnant woman and her middle-aged companion down the street, and do it so openly that both were aware they were being tailed? Of course it could have been some loony tune who had a thing for Latin women in their ninth month. But I didn't think so—not from what I had heard from Alicia and Pilar.

What had I heard, exactly?

The two women seemed to agree that whoever the guy was, he was pretty well dressed—not the kind who wore a suit and tie, but he did have on a sport jacket and slacks— "and one of those shirts with an alligator on it," as Pilar had said.

"He got close enough for you to see that?" I had asked her.

"How not?" She shrugged. "He crossed the street with us up at Sunset. Then, when we started back down here, he let us get ahead—but not too far ahead. He wanted us to know he was there."

"Are you sure? Did he say anything? Make any re- marks?" At this point I was still entertaining the loony-tune theory.

"No, but when we went into the building, he waited out- side for a while—like maybe he thought we'd come outside again."

"Well, don't," I said. "Don't go outside again. I think it was a good idea to get Alicia to take a walk, but this changes things, don't you think?"

Pilar looked at me solemnly and nodded.

Alicia, who had left the bedroom to listen, crowed forth a single triumphant *"ha!"*

I had turned at her then, annoyed, irritable, ready for a fight. "I'll get you an exercycle!" It was a threat.

"What is this 'exercycle'?"

"You ride a bicycle, but you stay in one place."

"Just like America," she said scornfully. "You work hard, but you stay in one place."

"Oh, now you know all about America and you want to go back to Mexico, huh?"

"I'm thinking it over." Then she turned to Pilar, as if to direct the threat to her, too. Why should Pilar care?

"Well," I said, "suit yourself."

She glowered at me. But that lasted just a mini moment. Then her face altered, visibly changing the subject. Her eyes narrowed. "Hey! You know something?" Suddenly sharp, playing detective. "This guy who was following us? He seemed like a cop to me."

"A cop? A *policeman*? Why do you say that?"

"Why not? That's how he seem to me."

Woman's intuition.

"You think I can't tell a gringo cop?" she persisted. "He was like that guy Keeney you bring to see me that one time in Mexico."

Pilar looked from her to me, suddenly interested, wanting more of the story.

Alicia must have noticed, too, because she changed her line of argument. "Besides, a cop is a cop. They are fundamentally the same all over the world. They walk like this—" She took a few rolling steps, managing to swagger in spite of her big belly. "They try to show how much man they are."

"That's how he walked?"

She hesitated. Then, almost pugnaciously: "Sí!"

I looked to Pilar. She nodded her agreement.

Well, why not? It didn't add up, but nothing else did, either. As I drove the few blocks from Esperanza to the

Dos Mundos I thought over the conversation with Alicia and Pilar and tried to factor it in. Here was the problem: An open shadow of that kind was meant as a threat. Sort of saying, "We know how we can get to you." Yeah, but who was "we"? Cops? I doubted it. But every time I tried to imagine that peculiar scene—the two women walking down the street, throwing puzzled, worried glances over their shoulders—all I could come up with, trying to visualize their pursuer, was a kind of identikit version of an all-purpose cop dressed in civvies; he was about equal parts Frank Keeney and those two clowns, obviously rent-a-cops, who had hassled me at the Intertel office. It was funny that nobody, obviously not Alicia, thought of me as a cop. I guess that was my problem when I was one.

The Club Dos Mundos is more than just a barrio night club. It's kind of an institution down there in Silverlake. There are bigger places and louder and hotter locations downtown and out in East LA, but the Dos Mundos offers its own brand of excitement, something more in the nature of innocent fun. The fact that Julio Robles had been working there as bar boy struck me as odd right from the start. I was glad to get the word from Jorgensen, of course, and I never doubted that he had given me good information. Nevertheless, I couldn't figure out why one of the Compañeros, right out of jail, should have been reduced to such a lowly state. Well, maybe I'd find out.

I pulled into the parking lot next door to the club, feeling a little perplexed by all these open questions but confident I'd get the right answers. I had to think that. A detective is a professional optimist, the last pure believer in truth.

As I pulled to a halt just inside the gate, the lot attendant, a young kid with a hopeful moustache, ran up to the car.

"How you doin' tonight, Señor?" He held the door open for me.

I unbuckled and hopped out. "Not bad," I said. Then, slipping him a couple of singles: "Look, don't bury it too deep, okay? I may want to leave in a little while."

"A car like this? Not a chance. I'll put it right up front with me. Keep an eye on it myself." He didn't seem to mind the patch of gray primer on the fender.

Satisfied, I headed for the entrance to the club, paid the admission, and marched upstairs.

The Dos Mundos is a big room. You can tell that even from the outside, where the little Christmas tree lights surround the upper floor, flashing on and off, making it look more like a wedding cake than a nightclub. Who knows? Maybe that's truth in advertising. It was a long time since I had been there, maybe the first year of my marriage when my wife said she wanted to see some Mexican nightlife. Well, I wasn't about to take her downtown where the sharks swim. I thought the Dos Mundos might be all right—a neighborhood club, a slightly older and more respectable clientele—and really, it was all right. But here's what happened: Those old guys (old? most of them were about the age I am now) took one look at this *gringa* with the long legs and blond hair and decided she must have been born to dance. And you know? I think they got that right. Anyway, they kept her busy the whole night—and she loved it. Mambo (this was back when they still did the mambo), salsa, bossa nova—you name it, she did it with style and grace. Me, I never have been much of a dancer, as I'd proved on innumerable occasions. She had a great time, and so did her many partners. I got drunk. She had to drive us home, and we had a fight. Subsequently, we went back a couple of times with just about the same results.

So I guess you could say that my memories of the Dos Mundos were more or less mixed. Still, I don't blame the place or the people who frequent it for the bad times I had there. They didn't make the trouble. We brought it in with us.

As I took a place at the far end of the bar and looked out

on the dance floor, I thought about it again, of course, but the ten years or so that had passed made it possible for me to smile, if a little crookedly. I was proud of that smile.

The bartender came over, and I asked for a Dos Equis. As he busied himself icing the glass and uncapping the bottle, I sized the guy up. He was in his fifties, gray haired, black mustached, something contained, consciously macho about him, as if he'd been around and wouldn't shock easily. I decided to test him.

As he poured the beer and the white cap rose above the brown liquid to the top of the pilsner glass, I said the name, "Julio Robles." Just that.

He stopped pouring and looked at me curiously. "Sí, Señor?" he said. "He works here."

"Not any more."

"Oh?"

"They have him down in the morgue—his body. He was shot last night up in Benedict Canyon."

The bartender didn't blink an eye. "What were the circumstances?" he asked.

"It may be he was trying to break into a house up there. That's what they are saying, anyway."

The bartender nodded and made a sour face. "He was not a good worker," he said and walked away.

Some epitaph. *R-I-P.*

Over at the service bar he busied himself cutting lemons and making himself generally useful. Meanwhile the younger bartender whipped back and forth, in and out, filling drink orders for the waitresses. I saw the older guy whisper something to the younger one, probably telling him that Julio was dead. Anyway, the service bartender stopped suddenly and looked down the bar at me. He stared for a moment, as if asking a question. But he got no answer from me.

I turned away and looked over the crowd at the tables surrounding the dance floor. The place was less than half full, but it was early, and they were still coming in, arriving

91

from all parts of Silverlake and Hollywood, and as far away as Santa Monica. This was *the* place on the west side.

It was a little jazzier than I remembered. Literally—for the music that stuttered out from the bandstand in short repetitious phrases could only be categorized as Latin jazz. Dave Valentine and Poncho Sanchez had happened to the music in the decade or so since I'd been gone. A driving trombone solo now squawked and soared over the steady irregularity of the driving drumbeat. Now it was an alto sax taking his turn, making like Paquito de Rivera for all the world to hear. I found myself wishing I wasn't working, so I could just settle back and enjoy the band.

Out on the floor the dancers were just getting warmed up, most of them over thirty—well over thirty. They dipped and twirled with well-practiced grace. It was funny, but most of the women and some of the men seemed to defy the laws of physics—the bigger and rounder and heavier they were, the lighter they seemed to be on their feet. They called the little guys with the big women "truck drivers." I guess that made the women *camiones,* some of them eighteen-wheelers.

I looked back at the two bartenders working the service bar. The older guy, the one I had talked to, was pouring a bucket of ice into the bin, having a little trouble with it. It occurred to me then that he must have been doing Julio's job. There was no bar boy in sight, and both men seemed to be working away at double speed. I waited until things slowed down a little and beckoned my barman over with a twenty dollar bill.

I held it out to him.

"You want another?" he asked, topping the nearly full pilsener glass with a finger.

"No," I said, "I'd like to talk about Julio—when you've got time."

He took the twenty. "I've got time."

"He'd been in jail," I said.

"You have the answers. Maybe I should ask the questions." He began rubbing at the bar with the towel he had carried over his shoulder. All of a sudden I wasn't getting eye contact from him.

"All right," I said, "go ahead and ask them."

"You're not with the police? You haven't shown me a shield."

"No. I'm private."

"Then I don't have to tell you anything."

"That's true. But you will."

"Why? How do you know this?"

"Because you took my money."

He did at last take a look at me then and nodded.

I leaned forward. "Listen," I said, "how long had Julio been working here?"

He shrugged. "About a month. The boss gave him a break. Julio just got out of jail."

I nodded. "San Quentin. Did anyone come to visit him here?"

"Many. His old friends, some new friends. He never had time to do his work he was talking to his friends so much. I complained to the boss. The boss said give him a chance. Well, Julio had his chance, eh?"

He was an unforgiving so-and-so, wasn't he?

"These friends of his," I said, "these people he talked to—did any of them seem unusual to you? Out of the ordinary?"

He thought about that a moment. "Two," he said with a sense of certainty. "There was a young one, a gringo, blond with white eyes. Julio said he was from the police."

"I know about him."

"You know a lot." He paused, then gestured gimme-gimme. I pulled out another twenty and put it on the bar. This was the payoff, and he knew it. "So," he went on at last, "Night before last there was one who came in to see Julio, even asked for him by name. He didn't know him, but he had his name. He was gringo—Anglo—what do they say?"

93

"WASP?"

"Yes, WASP. Like it sting you, huh?" He frowned, remembering. "He was about my age, but tall the way they are. He looked like he never had a sick day in his life."

"So?"

"So Julio came out to talk to him. It was pretty slow, so they had a long talk. I let him, you know? I never really gave him a hard time. Anyway, I didn't listen in on them, but I passed by a couple of times, you know, doing business behind the bar, and I can tell they're making some kind of plan together. The guy is drawing a map on a napkin."

"What was on the map?" I asked.

He shrugged. "Nothing you could notice—a road, a fence. I heard them talking about dogs. That's all."

"That's *all*?" I didn't think I was getting my forty bucks worth.

"Oh, one more thing. After the guy left, Julio turned to me, and he said, 'You see that guy I was talking to? He just gave me my ticket out of here.'"

"I guess he was right about that, wasn't he?"

"*Claro.*"

"But wait a minute. Tell me more about this man who talked to Julio. How was he dressed?"

The bartender made a couple of gestures—stretching imaginary lapels, straightening an invisible necktie. "*Bien vestido*! The works—suit, tie, white shirt. He looked like a lawyer—a gringo lawyer. A—how do you say it again?—a WASP. No mustache—gray in the hair, but mostly brown. And his Spanish . . ."

"He spoke Spanish?" Why didn't he say so in the first place?

"Ah, *sí*. Of course. Anyway, his Spanish was good, but it was that funny Castilian kind. You know, with all the lisping. His Spanish was *too* good, if you understand me."

"Out of a book."

"*Sí.*"

Satisfied, I let him go at last. The bartender had just described Bill Wallace of Intertel right down to his accent in Spanish.

A couple of minutes later I was on my way out of there. Big news. If this wasn't an intrusion of a new element in the picture, then it was the most remarkable coincidence since Lee Harvey Oswald was in exactly the right place to squeeze off three perfect shots at a moving target with a fifteen dollar rifle.

Wallace was something to think about, all right, and I was thinking about him when, doing a turn on the stairs out of there, I almost bumped into Ray Jorgensen coming up. I started to speak, but something in those weird blue-white eyes of his warned me not to. Then I saw he was being followed by an honor guard of local heavies. I recognized one of the group from Esperanza among them. Was Jorgensen in trouble? No, but his look said that he might be if I spoke to him. We passed without a word. The Compañero didn't seem to notice me at all.

I was glad to be out of there and on the street but a little disappointed when I saw that the kid at the parking lot hadn't kept his word. My Alfa was up near the front of the lot, all right, but there was another car parked in front of it, a Cadillac, blocking my way out. I looked around for the kid to move that big truck.

Nowhere. The only sounds were the cars passing on Sunset and the ghostly salsa rhythm floating down from the second floor.

I waited a minute or two, then started over to the car, thinking I could raise him by honking my horn. I was just at the door, about to reach in the open window, when a figure loomed up in front of me. I hadn't heard a thing and had no idea where he had come from. An arm was extended toward me.

"You want a light, amigo?"

Just as I was turning to get out of there, a four-inch jet of flame shot out toward me, and I heard that same nasty laugh again. I fell back. Somebody grabbed me from behind.

I started to yell. A hand was clamped tight over my mouth. Before I could bite it away, I felt the prick of something sharp on my wrist. A needle. It became a bit difficult to move.

That was all I felt. That's all I remember.

I think that in a way the worst part of what followed was my complete loss of any sense of time. Well, maybe not the worst. Of course it might have been the drug they hyped me with. It probably was. I mean, a lot of downers will short-circuit those little synapses in your brain that inform you when approximately fifteen minutes has passed, or fifteen hours.

Or maybe it was that complete blackout I endured from the time they grabbed me in the parking lot beside the Dos Mundos and brought me to—well, wherever this was. How could my brain keep count of the passage of time when it had lost count so profoundly and completely during such a crucial period? This could have been the result of a kind of neurological crisis of confidence.

But okay, I'll admit it. The big problem for me, the thing that practically drove me literally crazy, was the total darkness I found when I woke up. Woke up? How could you tell you were awake when what you saw when you opened your eyes was exactly what you saw when they were closed? That is—nothing. It was probably the way the drug worked, but there was what seemed like a long period of time when I was going from unconsciousness to consciousness and then back again. It seemed like it lasted a long time. But how was I to know?

Anyway, that's how it was. Without knowing where I was or where I'd been, and remembering only gradually what had happened there in the parking lot, I began to have some sense of how I'd come to be here. But where was here? I was aware that I was lying down on some kind of cot—no sheets, no blankets, just a mattress. I could feel the stitching and the buttons. I knew it was just a mattress, so I must have been awake, right? But when I did the little muscular twitch that you do to make your eyelids raise, there was no change at all. I did it again, and then a third time—but nothing happened. No change. I began to panic. Could they have blinded me? Maybe that guy with the blowtorch cigarette lighter had leaned over and let me have it in each eye while I was under. No, of course not. My eyes would hurt. That would be unimaginably painful. But no, nothing like that. No pain at all. Still, just to make sure, I touched my eyelids carefully, tentatively. My eyeballs were still there.

The pain I had was not exactly physical, not localized anyway. There was just this tremendous lassitude, an awful physical dullness—as if I was going to slip right back into unconsciousness at any moment. And who knew? Maybe I did. Like I say, it was hard to tell.

Anyway, I finally got hold of myself enough to pull up to a sitting position on the cot. I groped around and measured it out at not much more than a yard wide. It was pushed against a wall. "Well," I thought (did I say it out loud?), "maybe I can't see anything, but I'm going to explore this place by touch." That took about two seconds. I took a step forward, put out my hands, and met a solid wall. Was it brick? I rubbed a palm over it—hard and unyielding but smoother than brick. Cinder block. Well, there was no breaking through that.

98

I turned and counted off nearly three strides—well, about two and a half—before coming up against a wall, and in it, a door. The door was big and thick, and locked, of course. There was no rattling the doorknob to find out, because there wasn't any doorknob. I had to dig my nails into the edge of it and tug, just to be sure.

So the place I was in was about eight by eight—a little smaller than a living-room rug. There was just enough room in it for the cot. And me.

The place—call it a cell; that's what it was—seemed totally bare except for the cot. Not even any pipes or fixtures coming out of the wall. Just a cinder block square box, eight by eight, and about eight feet high. They couldn't keep me in here very long, could they? I'd go nuts. Maybe that was the idea.

I sank down on the cot. My head drooped and I stared down at the deep darkness, unable even to see my feet beneath me. I may have sat there like that an hour or just a matter of minutes. Maybe I was listening, but there was nothing to hear, just the sound of my own breathing. I waited. I had no choice.

"HEY! I'M AWAKE! YOU WANT TO TALK, I'LL TALK!"

I yelled it out as loud as I could, and found myself screaming hoarsely at the end. Everything I had went into it—but it didn't do any good. There was nothing, only silence beyond the cinder block and the door. Or maybe I couldn't have heard if there was anything out there because my ears were suddenly filled with the sound of my own loud breathing. No, I was panting. My lungs filled and refilled at a frightening rate, like I'd just tried to run a mile or something. Was I hyperventilating? Well, if I wasn't I would be soon. I forced down my rate of breathing, pulling in great scoops of stale air and pushing them out slowly, until at last I had it under control. But did I really? No. I needed something to concentrate on, something . . .

Without quite knowing when I'd begun I found myself reciting the Our Father in Spanish, the way I'd learned it:

"Padre nuestro que estas en los cielos . . ." And on and on, over and over again. I don't know how many times I repeated it, but it worked. I calmed down to the point that I could begin to think. And the first thing that occurred to me was that even if the air I was breathing was pretty stale, I was still breathing. That meant the air had to be coming in from somewhere. There had to be a vent or a hole or something in here.

Not because I thought it would help me out much, but because I thought it was important for me to keep busy, I began looking for the air source. Moving the cot around, standing on it, feeling my way along the walls, I found one of the cinder blocks missing above the door, and in its place a screen. I dug at it with my nails. It wouldn't budge. There had to be something I could use to pry off that screen. Maybe some piece of the bed. I threw off the bare mattress and started feeling around the flat steel springs where it had been. I was looking for something loose—long and flat enough to do the job.

I found it—a blade about a foot long up near the top, holding together some key pieces of the webbing. And yes, it was a little bit loose. I ran my hands over it and got some idea how it could be worked loose—and out. The only trouble was that it meant moving the cot around and banging the springs. Well, there was nobody around anyway and no reason I could see not to make noise, so I started in on it.

And I did make some noise. Rasping the legs of the cot over the cement floor, shaking the steel-spring webbing, I managed to work one end of the blade free. I was concentrating so hard on what I was doing—or maybe just making such a racket—that I never heard the footsteps that must have sounded just outside, not even the pull of a big bolt on the door. No, the first thing I knew, the door was flung open and a great big industrial-strength flashlight was beamed right into my face. I couldn't tell for sure, but I think there were two of them. I couldn't tell because I

100

couldn't see anything for a minute or more. My eyes were shut tight, then blinking. I was trying to keep from going blind. By that time one of them had shoved something into my hand and said, "Here. Put this over your head," in English—barrio accent.

It was cloth, a hood. I did as I was told. One of them grabbed me, turned me around, and tied my hands behind my back very efficiently. Then I was pushed out of the cell—propelled with such force that I stumbled, nearly fell, and wound up flattened against a wall opposite the cell door. One of them chuckled.

A hand clamped my shoulder. I was pulled back and pushed forward, marched roughly down a hall, probably about thirty feet long. A light came on at the end of it, that much I could tell through the thick cloth over my head. When the light was strong, they stopped me, and I was given another shove. This time I kept my balance and passed through a doorway into a well-lighted room. There were people inside. I could smell sweat, cigarette smoke, and . . . perfume? I heard a low murmur from a corner on my left. No words—just a grunt and a whisper. There was something about that whispering voice. What was it?

Before I could work that out, another voice came, loud and clear. "Put him up there." It was a light voice, a tenor, but assured, the voice of authority. It had to belong to Jaime Fernandez.

Grabbed on each side, I was hustled forward until I bumped up against something hard, wooden, something that moved. A chair?

"Up," said a voice beside me. "Up, up, up!"

My foot explored the air and then the object in front of me, which was most definitely a chair.

"*Cabrón!*" A hand grasped my ankle and jammed my foot down on the seat of the chair. I had to hop on the other foot to keep my balance. "Now, up."

And up I went—pushed, prodded, hardly under my own

power at all. The top of my head brushed something. It moved away, then came back and brushed me again.

My God! It was a rope!

I tried to jump off the chair, but another pair of arms grabbed me at the knees and held me. I struggled, ducking my head, throwing my shoulders back and forth. But they got the noose over the hood and around my neck, then pulled it tight.

Then I was still, rigid, waiting. If you want to know what was going through my head at the time it was the Act of Contrition. I didn't know if this was a game they were playing, but if it wasn't . . .

That voice, Jaime: "Now. Take the chair away."

It wasn't a game.

The chair tipped out from beneath my feet. The rope cut into my throat. The muscles of my neck tightened reflexively against it, then collapsed against my need for air. But there was no air, just the searing, burning pain in my throat as my whole body fought to breathe. I realized I was going to die.

"Okay. That's enough. Put it back."

Miraculously—it seemed like a miracle at the time—my feet were hauled up and planted firmly on the seat of the chair. My knees straightened, and I was suddenly back from the dead. The rope still cut into my neck, but I was able, just able, to breathe.

"Take it off."

The noose was loosened, and pulled back over my head. I could open my windpipe wide then—but God, what torture it was to breathe. I took it just as easy as I could, filling my lungs a little more with each breath, letting life flow back into them.

"Sit down. Sit down on the chair."

Shakily, afraid I might collapse at the end of that long step down, I took it, then pulled down the other foot. All this was kind of tricky with my hands tied behind me—just try it sometime—but I managed, I managed. Both feet firmly on the floor, I sat. And waited.

"That's just to show you we're serious people."

I nodded. I wasn't sure I could speak.

"We don't like the story you tell us, then up you go. Understood?"

Again, I nodded.

"Say something. Say, 'I understand.'"

"I'm not sure I can talk." I managed to croak it out. Then, realizing that had been more or less comprehensible, I added, "I understand."

"Maybe we left you up there a little too long. You know, a few seconds can make a big difference when you're at the end of a rope. Hey, somebody. Get our guest—Señor Cervantes—get him a glass of water. That'll help you talk, eh? Sure it will."

A chair scraped on the floor. Someone moved across the room. I heard water running.

But the voice—Jaime—continued. "I gotta give you credit, though. A lotta guys, they would piss their pants as soon as they feel that rope around their neck, you know. But hey, not you, Cervantes. You got some *huevos,* you know?"

He seemed to want a response. "Thanks" was all I could manage.

"You know how it is, though. We hadn't taken you down, you would have pissed your pants for sure, shit them, too. They all do that, you know?"

After some hesitation, I said, "I know."

The glass of water arrived. The hand that held it raised the hood slightly and began pouring it in my mouth. I spluttered, choked, began to drown in it.

"Hey, take it easy. Take it easy," said Jaime. "You want to kill the poor guy?" He played it for a laugh, and he got it. From the response I judged that there were maybe seven or eight other people in the room, and one of them—the perfume, the whispering voice, and now the laugh—was a woman. I didn't think it was the barmaid, either.

The water came slowly then. I took it in as well as I could. It helped. The fire in my throat was still burning—

but not quite as fiercely as it was before. Could I talk? Well, I could try.

"You're a private detective."

I nodded, yes.

"You had a picture in your pocket, a picture of a friend of ours named Julio Robles. From the way he looks, I think he's dead. You tell us how he got that way."

So I told them. Gasping and croaking, never managing to raise my voice much above a whisper, I gave them the whole story. I said I'd been called to the Toller place because a man had been shot on the grounds by one of the security guards. The cops took me out to have a look at him, and I told the cops he looked familiar.

"Hey, okay, wait a minute," said Jaime. "You tell me. Why did he look familiar?"

"How about some more water?"

There was a moment's hesitation. Then, as if a signal had been given, there was movement, steps across the floor and the sound of the faucet and running water. I waited.

"I warn you, Cervantes. I gotta very sensitive shit detector. You start talking shit, and I'll know it."

I nodded.

This time when the guy raised the hood over my head to give me the water, he was a little careless, and I got a glimpse of my interrogator. It was Jaime, all right—knife thin, hair slicked back like a model.

The water helped. I began again, explaining that I had been a cop ten years ago, and that for about a month I had been in the youth division at Rampart. There was a murmur in the room at that. I tried to put a fix on it. Hostile? Not really. More like a murmur of anticipation.

"And you remembered Julio from then? You bust him or something?"

"I don't think so. No, I would have remembered him if I did. Just the face. What made me sure was the tattoo I saw in the morgue."

"Oh, he had a tattoo?" Very innocent, ironic. "What

104

kind of tattoo? Maybe you should describe it for us, Cervantes."

"You saw the picture of that, too. It's just like the one you've got on the inside of your right arm."

Sudden silence, waiting.

Then, just as suddenly, Jaime laughed—and then a few others joined in with him. "Oh, I like that! I like that! You're a tough little *maricón,* huh? You gonna show us how much you know, huh?" He paused for dramatic effect. Then: "Listen, *pendejo,* I don' care what you know. We put that noose around you and stretch your neck, and then you don' know nothin'. *Entiende?* It's all gone. You're dead. But okay. You know about Julio, and you know maybe a little bit you heard from the cops about the Compañeros. So you come up to look us over. You watch the ball game. You drink your beer. And you sneak these little glances at us like we're not supposed to notice. Then you go to the Dos Mundos, and you talk to the bartender. Now, we talked to the bartender, too, and we know what you asked him and what he told you. We don' have to give him money. He told us because he likes us. We got lots of friends here."

He paused for just a moment, then plunged on, as if summarizing the case for the prosecution: "So we know all that. We know who you are, why you come down here to bother us. We even know what you got out of your little trip to Silverlake. Everything the bartender told you, he told us. We know it all, Mr. Detective, except what *you* think of it, what you make of all this shit. That you gotta tell us."

If I hadn't had the hood on, I would have stared him down. I did the next best thing. I waited.

He jumped up. I heard it, sensed it. *"Cabrón!"* he shouted into my face, then, to the others, "Okay, put him back up."

"I think Julio was set up," I said at last.

"So. Now we get somewhere. You think he was set up.

105

Sure. We think so, too. But who did it? Who was the guy who talked to Julio a long time at the bar? Was he trying to get at us through Julio? See, that's what we gotta know, Cervantes."

By the time he finished, Jaime was almost panting. And he was close, very close. I had the feeling that if I leaned forward we'd bump noses.

"No," I said, "I don't think it had anything to do with you—with the Compañeros."

"Keep going."

"I think they picked Julio out because he was just out of the joint and needed bread. He was expendable. They wanted somebody to make a feint at the Tollers and get put down in the bargain. They wanted somebody nobody would miss."

Jaime didn't say anything. I got the message he'd gone back and sat down to think. Then he spoke up: "The Compañeros miss him. He was a Compañero."

A rumble of approval at this. I caught a quiet call, *"Compañeros hasta la muerte!"* Like a slogan. And a response, *"Que viva!"* Then some whispering. It was like a vote taken there on the floor. Jaime was quiet, polling the membership.

Satisfied, he picked up where he had left off. "Okay, Mr. Detective, I tell you something about our friend, Julio. He was a Compañero from the beginning. He was one of us. But Julio, he had a problem. He was dumb, *estúpido,* you know? Couldn't follow orders. Always off doing little things on his own. That's how he took that fall, making his own move, trying to rob a fucking bank by himself! So he did five, and he gets out—when was it? two months ago— and he wants back in. Since then we got big. We're doing business. We're computerized and everything. He comes to us, he rolls up his sleeve, and he shows us what he's got on his arm, and he says we owe him. So what I say to him is this, I say, 'Julio, you're on parole, right?' 'Right, sure, *claro,*' he says. 'Well,' I tell him, 'you're on parole with us,

106

too. You get a job. You show us you think the right way. You do what we tell you, and you're back in. Hundred percent just like before.'

"So now you come and tell us he was off doing something on the side, and he got whacked. Up to his old tricks. I believe you. I think you're right. It's very tempting just to walk away and say he got what he deserved. *But!*"

Jaime came to a full stop and waited. It was easy to see how this guy got to be boss. He was an orator.

"But he was a Compañero. He wore the tattoo—and nobody dumps on the fucking Compañeros!"

A cheer. Applause. Angry laughter.

"So," he resumed, "we gotta do something. Make a show. So the thing we gotta figure is, what kind of show. Hey, I got it! Maybe we do a drive-by on this place up in Benedict Canyon. We shoot the place up. Make a, you know, memorial to Julio. You like that idea, Mr. Detective?"

The skinny bastard had me. It was a threat, but one I knew he would make good on. What could I say? "Uh, I don't think that's such a good idea."

"Speak up, Cervantes. We can't hear you so good under that hood."

"I said, I don't think that's such a good idea."

"Oh, that's right, you're the *bodyguard.* You're supposed to keep people like us away from the people in the big house. Well, maybe in that case, you tell us who is this man who talked to Julio for a long time at the Dos Mundos."

"I don't know." I said it a little too fast. Well, I didn't know—not for sure, anyway.

"Oh. You don't know. Then, tell us who you *think* he is."

That was the deal. Either I gave him Wallace, or they'd shoot out all the windows at the Tollers'. Maybe worse—take out the gate guard, the chauffeur, anybody who shot back.

107

"Hey, come on, Cervantes. You're a pretty good detective, I think. I'll bet you got a pretty good idea who is this guy. All you gotta do is tell us, and you're outa here. Otherwise . . ."

I sighed and said, "I'm not sure who he is."

"Well, we want you to be sure. We're serious, but we're reasonable. We could put the rope around your neck again, but I think a better way is we let you think about it just to be sure. Go back in the little room, and do some more detecting in your head. We'll talk again tomorrow."

So there I was, staring into the dark again, rubbing the rope burn on my neck. No, I didn't go back to the project I had underway when they came for me. There was really no point in dislodging the screen. I couldn't squeeze through a hole the size of a single cinder block. It had just been make-work, something to keep me from going bananas. So once inside, the bolt on the big door thrown behind me, I simply wrestled the mattress back onto the cot and sat down on it.

The darkness didn't matter much now. The worst had already happened—I'd had my interrogation. But I survived it. They even gave me back my wallet before they took the hood off and pushed me back into the cell. I knew what they wanted and what they would do if they didn't get it: either/or.

The funny thing was, the more I thought about it, the more attractive the deal seemed to me. They wanted Wallace. I wanted to give him to them. This was the guy who had hustled me away for a bullshit job interview that, with travel time, had taken nearly three hours. In that time they had put Julio inside the Toller compound, gotten him killed, and scared the shit out of the Tollers. Was that all they wanted? Or was Julio dropped inside to do some damage? What kind?

And what about this: I had a pretty good idea why they

had picked out Julio, but at this point I couldn't figure out how. Wallace knew about Julio. It had to be Wallace at the bar that night—he certainly wasn't a regular at the Dos Mundos. The bartender had obviously never seen him there before. There was no way that Wallace could have known Julio's background—that he was the perfect expendable—unless someone had told him, someone who knew him from before, knew he'd done time and was just out of the joint. Who knew that? Well, the Compañeros did—but who else?

And okay, here was another one: Why did Wallace have to pull me away and keep me busy if I wasn't going to be there at the Toller's anyway? Answer: He didn't know that. He had a man on the inside, so he knew who I was and how to get hold of me, but that man on the inside hadn't gotten close enough to know the terms of the arrangement I had worked out with Hans-Dieter. As far as Wallace knew, I'd be staying at the Toller place.

It was all kind of tentative and circumstantial. I knew that. But as far as I was concerned, it was enough to tie Wallace to Julio, and that was reason enough to hand him to the Compañeros. What was the old saying? "My enemy's enemy is my friend." I didn't have to like Jaime Fernandez to hook up with him. I mean, did Roosevelt like Stalin? Did Churchill?

So there I was, thinking dark thoughts of revenge. I'd been back in the cell maybe an hour, maybe less, when something completely unexpected happened. I heard the bolt on the door drawn back. I was apprehensive, not quite afraid, already thinking like a prisoner. Jaime said we'd talk tomorrow. That was the order that had been established, and now it was interrupted. I knew I didn't want to go back into that room and stand up on that chair again. Maybe if there was just one of them this time I could rush him and get past him, maybe even if there were two. The thing was to hit him hard as soon as that door swung open. After that? I didn't have time to think about after that. I backed up to the far end of the cell. Eight feet wasn't much of a start, but as soon as that door swung open, and I saw that flashlight . . .

It didn't swing open. I heard it pull back just a couple of inches. There was no flashlight, just a voice, whispering. "Cervantes. Are you in there?"

Who was it? I couldn't tell, but it sounded friendly, so I risked a response. "Yeah. I'm here. Who is it?"

"It's me. Jorgensen. From narcotics."

The door swung open all the way, and I couldn't exactly see him, just a faint shape against the wall, but Jesus, Mary and Joseph, I was glad he was there. I stumbled forward in the darkness and through the open door.

"How did you find me?"

"I knew where you were. I just couldn't get to you. Come on. Let's get out of here."

He took firm hold of my arm and half pushed, half guided me along down that corridor I had walked with the hood over my head. Then we took a right and moved along a shorter distance. "Careful," he whispered. "There's some stairs here."

We went up, just feeling our way in the dark. Then there was a door, and on the other side of that, a low night light. It was enough to show me the men's room directly across the way. I glanced off to the right and saw dimly that it was the main room of Esperanza. I started off in that direction.

Jorgensen grabbed me and pulled me back. "No," he said. "This way."

I followed him out the back and through a door. There was an alley there. "The car's down here, just off the street," he said.

It was a ten-year-old Toyota. Once inside, I began shaking uncontrollably, suddenly close to tears. "Jesus," I said, "I'm sure glad to be out of there."

He started the car and backed it out of the alley. "That guy from the Compañeros at the Dos Mundos kept me there with some bullshit story about one of the kid gangs distributing for the Crips. I figured they'd taken you—and that had to be to Esperanza. So I drove over, but there were all these cars there, so I knew they were inside. There was nothing I could do but wait until they left." He paused. "Where's your car? Back at the Dos Mundos?"

"I guess so."

"Can you drive?"

I was breathing better now. The shaking had stopped. "Yeah, sure," I said.

He roared off down Sunset in the direction of the club. Traffic was light, but the street wasn't exactly empty. "Look," I said, "how long did you wait? How long was I in there?"

"About four hours."

"Only four hours? It felt like twenty-four." I looked out the window and saw a drunk reeling along, concentrating on the sidewalk beneath his feet. "Time sure goes fast when you're having fun."

10

There was a surprise waiting for me next morning when I pulled up to the gates of the Toller place: they were open.

I looked around, called out, but saw no one and got no response. Pulling inside, I parked just beyond the gate house, jumped out of the car and went to the door of the little stone structure. I tried the knob. It clicked open, and the door swung wide. There was nobody inside. I expected that. What I didn't expect was that all the sophisticated surveillance equipment that had crowded the room was also gone. Where the big board with all the colored lights had been, where the row of television monitors were placed, there was now just a bare table and an empty rack. Wires had been pulled. The place was swept clean.

I didn't like what I saw.

Outside, I took a look at the house. The only thing different was that there were two cars I couldn't identify parked out in front beside the Porsche and the limo. I jumped into my Alfa and accelerated up the circular drive.

Well, at least the front door was locked. I banged on it insistently and rang the bell a couple of times. Nothing. I hit the bell three more times. I could hear great cathedral chimes gonging away somewhere inside and at last the sound of steps on the tiled hallway.

The big door swung open, and a tall figure filled the frame. It was Derek Denison, the director. It took a moment to place him, though—not because I didn't recall his raw, red face but because of the way he was dressed. He was wearing jeans and a Porter Waggoner shirt, all rhinestones and silver studs. He teetered uncertainly on high-heel boots as he shifted, looking down at me. And on top of all this he had a big, wide-brimmed sombrero pushed back on his head. The guy had seen too many John Wayne movies.

We didn't move for nearly a minute. Finally, he said, "Bloody hell."

I started to step forward and had my foot on the doorstep, but he didn't move.

"You must be the gardener," he said. "Go around to the back." He gestured. "Comprendo? Around in el backo, mate."

I looked him in the eye. "Don't give me that shit," I said. "Do I look like the gardener?" Maybe I wasn't wearing a suit and tie, but I had on a jacket and suntans and even wore an ascot around my neck to cover up the rope burn.

He frowned, then his eyes finally lit in recognition. "Oh, you're the bodyguard, the little fella who was around the other day with Ursoola."

I didn't like his description much, but I said, "Yeah. I'm the bodyguard."

"Well, we've a new fella now, and he's working out most satisfactorily. Damned heroically, if you ask me. I'm sure you'll be paid off promptly. Good-bye." And he began to inch the door closed on me.

I hit it with my shoulder as hard as I could. It hurt, but it got results. The door flew back, banging him in the face and knocking his Stetson down to the floor. I walked past him as he bent to retrieve it, a hand clapped to his forehead.

"Do you know who I am?" he called after me.

"Right," I yelled back, "and now you know who I am."

Little fella, huh? It may have given him a headache, but it did me a lot of good. I'd been pushed around and hung from a rope, and now I felt like fighting back.

I strode down the hall, stretching my legs in long steps, my heels ringing loudly on the tile. Pushing open the double doors, I checked the library. Nobody there. I slammed them shut and continued on my way.

"Hey, where is everybody?"

There was no answer to that, but a little farther down the hall I came to another set of double doors, flung them open, and found the Tollers and Hans-Dieter at breakfast. The maid was serving them.

"Ah, De Quincy," said the old man with that ironic smile of his. "Was that you at the door? Sit down. Have something to eat. Eggs? A croissant, at least."

"I've eaten."

Hans-Dieter eyed me critically. He leaned toward Ursula and muttered something to her in German. She nodded.

"Then coffee," said Toller.

"Okay," I said, "I'll have some coffee."

"Ilse," he said to the maid, "coffee for Mr. Cervantes." So he did know my name, after all. I'd begun to wonder about that.

I sat down. She poured. "Where are the guards?" I asked. "The gate was wide open."

Hans-Dieter leaned across the table and slapped his hand down on it. "I fired them," he said. "Sent them packing." He was in command mode, as he usually was around Ursula.

I glanced over at Toller. "Well, do you think that was wise? I mean, after the other night you must know you're a target here. That guy who got shot did have a gun."

"Exactly!" he crowed. "They get us into trouble with the police then, and last night when they *should* shoot, they do nothing!"

"Wait a minute. What happened last night?"

"Well, as you would know if you phoned us, as you were ordered, last night we were again attacked."

Toller nodded confirmation. He looked like he was about to say something, but Ursula broke in. "If it had not been for Casimir, we would all be dead and the film destroyed."

"What film?" I asked, a little stupidly.

"The film! Our film! *Faust!*" She fairly shouted it. "We were attacked by agents of the military-industrial complex, enemies of disarmament! They don't want our message to get out to the world!" By the end of that she was pounding the table.

"Let's take it by the numbers," I said. "Without making a speech, just tell me exactly what happened."

She rolled her eyes in exasperation. *"Aber mein Gott!"*

I stood up. "All right, forget it. Where's Urbanski? I'll get it from him."

"Casimir is upstairs sleeping," she said almost primly, "unless you woke him with all your shouting and slamming doors."

"Thanks." I stood up and started for the door. Then it opened and Derek Denison stood there, looking at me accusingly. He was holding a lumpy wet towel to his head— ice cubes inside. He'd left his sombrero somewhere. "You know what this bloke did to me?" he asked them all.

Before he could answer himself, I pushed past him with a muttered, *"Tu madre, pendejo."* I love it when I talk dirty.

As I took the stairs up two at a time, I began to wonder about Urbanski. Some bodyguard, sleeping on the job! Ursula seemed satisfied, though. More than she ever was with me.

"Hey, Urbanski! Where are you? Wake up!"

In answer, a door popped open about halfway down the long upstairs hall and Urbanski stuck his head out. "Oh, yeah, it's you, Cervantes. Come on in."

He was just stepping into his jeans and zipping up. I was amazed. Bare chested, the guy had muscles on the muscles. He must have been pumping iron the last ten years to look like that.

"Sorry," he said, "I just woke myself up." He pulled on a light cotton sweater, then went over and got a plainclothesman's holster rig from the back of a chair. As he squeezed into it, he explained, "I told Ursula to get me going just as soon as she got up, but you know how she is, real sweet hearted, I guess she thought I needed my sleep after last night."

Casimir? Ursula? Real sweet hearted? Something was happening here I never expected. It was then that I looked around and realized that there was a definite, though restrained, feminine touch to the room's decor and furnishings. I mean, that was definitely a vanity table over in the corner with a whole lot of tubes and bottles scattered on it. And there was a bra dangling from the bedpost. By ingenious deduction, I came to the conclusion that this was Ursula's bedroom. We detectives are more clever than mere mortal men. Sometimes it takes us a while, though.

"Yeah," I said at last, "I want to hear about last night."

"Sure thing." He grinned like a kid and nodded eagerly. "See, last night we was by the, like, poster-production place."

"You mean postproduction. Over on Bundy?"

"Yeah, right. Everybody was working real hard, and I was just, like, hanging around."

"Telefon! Telefon! Ein Anruf für Sie. Es ist die Polizei." It was a woman's voice from down the hall. *"Herr Cervantes, Telefon für Sie. Polizei!"*

I knew enough German from the army to understand that. I shrugged at Urbanski and went out into the hall. He grabbed his windbreaker and followed.

It was the maid, Ilse, of course, panting slightly from her trip up the stairs, fingering her white apron and nodding at me emphatically. *"D'runter,"* she pointed, *"bei der Tür."*

116

I nodded that I had understood and took off down the stairs with Urbanski close behind. I knew where the telephone was—on a little stand in the hall. I picked up the receiver. "Yeah. This is Cervantes."

"Gulbransen. We got some trouble."

"What kind?"

"Chang and I went to talk to this guy Eckerman, the shooter from night before last. You remember?"

"Are you kidding? Of course I remember."

"Yeah, well, anyway, we went over to this place in Van Nuys, only a couple of blocks from the station, and he's not there. Not only that, but the place has been cleared out completely. He skipped."

"Why would he do that? You said yourself—he'd get a pass."

"I know what I said. But he showed up on the computer."

"How?"

"Did time at San Quentin for armed robbery. Got out twenty months ago."

I thought a moment, then I said, "Check and see if he had anything to do with somebody named Julio Robles while he was at San Quentin, cell mates or anything."

"Who's Julio Robles?"

"That's the guy who bought it in the bushes."

"Jesus Christ, Cervantes!" The receiver crackled so loudly that I held it away from my ear.

I happened to glance around then and saw that I had gathered an audience there in the hall. Behind Urbanski stood Ursula and Denison, arms folded, looking on suspiciously. I turned my back to them, hunched over slightly, and lowered my voice. "Yeah, I know I was supposed to let you know if I found out who he was. I got hung up, though." As soon as I said it I wanted to take it back. Did Freud have a category for unconscious puns? Yeah, I guess he did.

"And what about that tattoo?"

"A kid gang in Silverlake he used to belong to." Well, that wasn't a lie, anyway.

"I expected better cooperation from you."

"You'll get it."

"I better. Oh, just one more thing. There was blood on the floor of the bathroom and in the sink. It was smeared. Somebody made a pass at cleaning it up. We're having it checked for Eckerman's blood type now. We've got a bulletin out on him, too."

There was silence at his end. "Uh . . . is that all?" I asked.

"Yeah, that's all. Stay in touch, will you?"

"I will," I promised.

He hung up without a good-bye. I stood for a moment, staring at the receiver in my hand, trying to think. Then I heard another click. Somebody had been listening in. In this house, of course. I hung up and turned back to the three in the hall. Hans-Dieter was absent. It had to be him on the extension. Ursula took a step forward, about to say something. I motioned to Urbanski. "Let's go outside," I said. "I want to take a look at the gate house." There was nothing to see there I hadn't seen already. I just wanted to get him away from the rest of them.

He shrugged and started after me to the door.

"We don't need you now," Ursula shouted after me. "We have good protection!"

I didn't say a word, didn't bother to look back.

Outside, on the porch, Urbanski gave me a reassuring pat on the shoulder. "Don't worry," he said. "I'll talk to her."

I looked at him and shook my head. This was a hell of a situation, wasn't it? "Come on. I want to hear about last night."

West Side Postproduction was a big, low building near the corner of Bundy and Olympic. It has a good-sized parking lot in back. There is no front door. You enter from the parking lot, or you don't get in at all. Considering the trouble they had been having, Hans-Dieter thought it would be a good idea to put a guard right there at that door. He got in touch with this high-tech security outfit, the one that hired trigger-happy ex-cons, and told them he wanted an extra man assigned to the postproduction house. Well, it probably was a good idea. It certainly wasn't a bad idea. It's just that in the long run it wouldn't have mattered if they had left the door wide open and put up an electric sign out on the street pointing the way. It would have happened, anyway.

One thing that surprised Casimir was that movie people really worked. He seemed genuinely impressed by that. I guess he thought, as most people outside the Industry seem to think, that making movies is a big game where people are paid huge amounts of money for goofing around. He confessed that he didn't even know that this part of the process—postproduction in all its ramifications and thousand details—even existed. So for the first hour or two he was pretty interested in what was going on. He followed Ursula around to the editing rooms—there were three of them—looking over her shoulder at various bits and pieces of *Faust* on the editing screens, listening to her argue with Denison about which takes to use. He'd never dreamed it was so complicated.

Somebody said, or I guess I read it someplace, that your first day on a movie set is the most exciting day of your life, and your second day on a movie set is the most boring day of your life. Well, in postproduction it doesn't take that long, or at least it didn't for Casimir. He went from pretty interested to indifferent to bored out of his skull, all in the space of hours. About the only thing that kept him alert was his interest in Ursula's body and hers in his. He found himself exchanging glances with her, then little smiles, and finally comments. A couple of times she asked his opinion on one take or another—or rather, she asked him to back up her own. He agreed with her wholeheartedly, vo-

119

ciferously, and soon found himself receiving annoyed looks from Denison. That didn't bother Casimir.

But eventually, even his fantasies about the delights that pulsed beneath Ursula's loose slacks and tight T-shirt were exhausted—and so was Casimir, fallen into that state of mental stupor that only caffeine or more expensive drugs could cure. He settled for coffee. Promising to be back in a minute, he took five or six in the little makeshift kitchen just down the hall from the editing rooms. He found plenty of coffee in a cabinet over the sink, and there was a brand-shining-new Braun coffeemaker waiting to be filled up and plugged in.

The coffee had just come down—in fact, Casimir had the glass pot in one hand and the dripping filter top in the other—when he heard a commotion out in the hall. The second or two it took him to get rid of the coffee makings may have proved the difference between success and failure, life and death, in what followed. There were men yelling loudly about nobody getting hurt as Casimir ditched the pot and top in the sink. He turned, wrestled the Colt Python out of the holster underneath his windbreaker, and as he took the two steps to the door, a woman started screaming.

He was there in the hall, pistol extended, and in a mini second he took it all in. The woman screaming about twelve feet away was Ursula. About five feet beyond her, and on his side of the hall, a man in a ski mask was pointing a big, strange-looking something at her, shouting at her to shut up.

Casimir fired once, twice. The second shot missed, but the first hit the guy in the ski mask in the arm, above the elbow, knocking him off balance and then to the floor. As he went down, he dropped what he held, and it began making funky, *phut-phut* noises as it clattered to the floor. Slugs whizzed all around for an instant, ricocheting off the floor tile and then past Casimir down the hall. Two other guys in ski masks popped their heads out of one of the editing

120

rooms farther down. One of them was waving an automatic. Casimir fired at him first, then at the other one. They dove back into the room. But like any good cop, Casimir had been walking around all day with five rounds in the cylinder—an empty chamber under the hammer—and now he'd shot off all of them.

As he ducked back into the kitchen to reload, he saw that Ursula was still in the hall, staring wide-eyed at him. He yelled at her to get back into the room behind her. He pulled a full-moon clip out of his jacket pocket, shook the cylinder empty. Brass scattered on the floor. He fumbled the quick-load in, lost a second or so that way, and snapped the cylinder shut. Then, delaying just long enough to bless himself, he poised at the doorway, leaped across the hall, and came down flat on his belly.

The three of them were there, but in retreat. The guy with the automatic fired at him three times. All three went high. The other one had a snub-nosed pistol in his hand but was helping the third one along, the one who had been hit. Casimir looked for a shot at the shooter. Couldn't find it. He took his chances and jumped up from the floor. They were at the end of the hall by this time, sixty feet away. He shot twice—in a hurry—and missed, and then they were gone, disappeared around a bend.

He stopped just long enough to make sure that Ursula was all right, then took off after them. He was smart. He stopped at all the blind spots, and he jumped around the corners in the shooter's crouch. But that slowed him down. The security guard in the lobby slowed him down, too. When he stepped forward suddenly and asked what the fuck was going on around here, Casimir almost put a bullet in his chest.

So by the time Casimir pushed through the glass doors to the parking lot, all he saw was a van pulling away, then at the lot exit, then turning onto the street. There was no possibility of a shot without running the chance of hitting one of the houses across the way.

121

"Jesus," I said, after Casimir had told his story, "no wonder she said they had all the protection they needed."

"Aw, well, yeah. But I only hit one of them."

"What did the cops say? Did they send out the shooting team?"

"That's just it, see, Cervantes. Like, we decided not to report it."

"*We* decided?" It was Hans-Dieter and Ursula all over again, I was sure.

"Okay, it was their idea, but it was all right by me because, look, I phoned in sick yesterday to take this job. I could get in trouble by personnel. You know? Besides, nobody got killed."

"You sure? What about the guy you hit?"

"Well . . ." Casimir shrugged. "The round I put into him prob'ly broke his arm. And if he was dumb enough not to put a turnkey by it, he coulda bled to death. But that's his fault."

"Turnkey?"

"Yeah. You know. You put on a, like, bandage, and twist it until it's so tight it stops the blood so it won't bleed out the hole. You know?"

"Tourniquet."

"Yeah. What I say. Turnkey."

By this time we had made a complete tour of the grounds in front of the house. We were near the front door, walking up the circular drive. Casimir gave me a playful punch on the shoulder. It hurt. He was like a big kid, eager and friendly. "Hey, come on," he said, "I'll show you something."

He led the way over to one of the two unfamiliar cars parked out in front, a five-year-old green Chevy, badly in need of a wash. He pulled out his keys and opened up the trunk.

"Take a look at this," he said. There, lying on a beach

122

blanket, was an Ingram M-11 machine pistol with a silencer barrel. "That's what the guy had I shot." He flashed a grin. "Neat-O, huh?"

"Uh, yeah, I guess."

"You want it? I ain't supposed to have stuff like this by me."

"I'm not either. But . . ." Thinking about the Compañeros and their threat to do a drive-by. "You better hold onto it for a while," I said.

"Okay." He banged down the trunk lid. I noticed he didn't need much persuading.

"What about the guard at the door?" I asked.

"Yeah, well, what about him? He said he was in the john taking a shit, didn't hear a thing."

I looked at him then. We both knew it was bullshit. "Just one more thing," I said.

"What's that?"

"What were they after? The guys in the ski masks. Not Ursula?"

"Naw, not this time. They were gonna steal the movie."

He made it sound like plagiarism. "Whatta you mean?" I asked.

"What I say? I mean they even brought in a dolly with them and everything. They had the thing halfway loaded up with film cans."

I thought about this. Ursula said these guys were agents of the military-industrial complex. More likely they were agents of Pauline Kael. I followed that line of reasoning for a moment. Was *Faust* too flossy? Too disheartening? The ultimate bad review—steal the film.

But then I thought about it some more. Finally, I said to Casimir, "Whoever's doing all this is out to put Toller under."

"Whatta ya mean?" He looked at me like I was crazy. "Put 'em under? Look at this house. They're rich."

"Casimir, they got problems."

Just about that time the maid poked her head out of the

123

front door and found me there by Casimir's car. *"Herr Cervantes!"* She beckoned me in. *"Komme mal, bitte. Noch mal Telefon."*

I nodded that I understood and said to Casimir, "Come on in. I've got more to talk about."

Inside, I picked up the telephone, expecting Gulbransen at the other end. But what I got was the excited, almost hysterical voice of a woman babbling at me in Spanish. It was Pilar. She was speaking in a jumble about the man who had followed them on the street yesterday. He was big, she said, and looked like a criminal type. Not a policeman.

"Pues, sí," I said, trying to calm her down. "I understand that. But what about him?"

"Alicia!" she fairly screamed it into my ear.

"Alicia what?"

"She went downstairs to chase him away. She took your gun."

Oh Jesus, this was all we needed. "Call the police," I yelled into the receiver. "Nine-one-one. Tell them—tell them . . . just call them."

I turned to Casimir, who was standing close by. "Tell the Tollers I had to go. Something came up."

"But they're—"

I interrupted him. "I'll be back as quick as I can."

"But—"

I spun around then and started for the door. But who should I find blocking my way but Hans-Dieter, looking sour, and Old Man Toller, smiling in amusement at my sudden crazy state.

Hans-Dieter opened his mouth. He looked like he was about to lecture me.

I cut him off before he could say a word. I pounded my index finger into his chest. "Listen," I said, "all I want from you is just two things. One—you get some security guards here by nightfall. Don't shop around. Buy a standard brand, Pinkerton, Global, one of them. Two—and this is important—I want to see the bills from the other bunch."

"But they're at the office." He looked terribly offended and glanced over at Toller.

"Then go to the office."

By that time I was past him and had my hand on the knob of the big door. I was just swinging it open when I heard, "De Quincey, one moment please."

With a sigh I turned back. "Yes, sir."

"Be back in an hour. I need you to drive me to the airport."

"But can't you get—"

"I need *you* for this. We must talk."

"Yes, sir."

And I was gone.

11

I f Ursula had been along on that drive back to my place, I
would have scared her the way she scared me with her
Porsche. What the Alfa lacks in brute power, it makes up
for in high revs and the best gearbox known to man. In the
five minutes or less it took me to get home, I was up and
down from first through fourth more times than I could
count. I never did make it into fifth, but I know I hit eighty
on one straightaway. My eye strayed from the tach to the
speedometer—and there it was. I gulped but sat on it like a
man until I hit traffic—then geared down and picked my
way through at sixty.

You don't exactly think about other things at a time like
that, but I remember promising myself never to leave Alicia alone with my Smith & Wesson .38 Police Special
again. I had caught her holding it and aiming it around the
living room one day. Sure, it was unloaded, but I took it
away from her and gave her the standard lecture about how
many people get killed each year with unloaded guns. After
that battle up in the Sierra she thought she was a real

pistolera. I didn't remind her how she had collapsed into a quivering hysterical heap after she had done her shooting. Maybe I should have.

As I turned down my block, I suddenly panicked trying to remember if I had unloaded the .38. I mean, I always did that. It was routine. But I couldn't specifically remember emptying it the last time I had it with me. When was that? It was . . .

There was a black-and-white double-parked at the end of the block. Thank God for that—unless, of course, there was a bleeding body in the gutter. Then—well, one thing at a time.

Pulling up behind the black-and-white, I counted noses and decided that all were present and accounted for. There were the cops, two of them, out on the sidewalk. One held my .38 in his hand by the barrel. The other was shaking his finger at Alicia. She was standing so close her distended belly almost touched him and up on her tiptoes—the guy towered over her—yelling back at him. Pilar stood off to one side, about as faraway from the action as she could get, one hand cupped over her mouth in apprehension. Back in her part of town, neighborhood beefs like this were common but cause for concern; somebody usually wound up in jail. And there, too, in the middle of it all, was Alicia's intended victim. He was big, taller and wider than anyone else in that group on the curb. He was wearing a badly fitting suit but no tie. The cop holding my .38 was keeping an eye on him.

As I hopped out of the car, I was assaulted by a stream of gutter Spanish aimed at the taller of the two cops who stood glowering down at her. Thank God neither of them could understand—or maybe they could. I ran up to them and used the oldest line in the peacemaker's vocabulary. "Is there anything I can do to help, Officer?" And to Alicia, a muttered but threatening, *"Callate!"* She shut up.

The cop turned to me, looked me up and down, and said, "Who're you?"

"I'm, uh, the owner of the pistol."

"Yeah, you can help. You can tell me what the fuck's going on around here."

Alicia: "I told him, Chico. I told him in *English*. And then I told him in Spanish, and he didn't understand that, either. You tell me. What language does he speak?"

"*Callate!*"

She glared at me and then turned away.

Me, to the cop: "Well, as I understand it, this person"— pointing to the big guy in the tight suit—"has been annoying these ladies the past couple of days by following them.

"Hey, I told you," the big guy exploded. "That's bullshit. I never followed anybody. Just walked along behind them is all."

"And then"—I moved on to the second count of the indictment—"he loitered around over here across from the building and stared up at our apartment in a threatening manner."

"I wasn't . . . loitering. I was just . . . thinking."

The guy was annoying me. I turned and looked at him directly for the first time. He was even uglier than I expected. "Yeah," I said to him, "that must be a real challenge—thinking and making your feet move at the same time."

He tensed, and his hand curled into a fist, but he looked from me to the two cops and didn't say a word. It was pretty hard playing tough and innocent at the same time.

"What did you tell him?" Alicia asked in stage-whisper Spanish.

"*Callate!*"

"So," said the cop, "go on. Your wife, or whoever she is, Mr.—Mr. . . ."

"Cervantes."

"Mr. Cervantes, she came down to threaten this, uh, gentleman with your gun. Is that correct?"

"That's my understanding, yes."

"You know him?" asked the cop, nodding at the big guy.

128

"No," I said quite honestly.

"Any idea why he'd do this—if he was doing it like they say."

"No," I said, not quite so honestly.

"You got a permit for this, I assume," said the cop who was holding the .38.

"Certainly. Certainly." I dove into my back pocket and came out with my wallet. After a bit of fumbling I produced my gun permit in its little plastic case and handed it over. To the other cop I offered my private investigator's license.

As they glanced over them, I looked at Alicia. She seemed like she was about to say something. I shook my head—no!

"You're a PI, huh?" asked the first cop.

"That's right."

"You do any time on the force?"

"LAPD, ten years."

"Where?"

"Most of it at Rampart. The rest in Wilshire."

He nodded approvingly. It was respectable duty.

"This your service revolver?" asked the other cop.

"Yeah."

He handed it back to me along with the permit. "Keep it away from her."

"Oh, I will. Believe me." When I took the .38 from him, the weight of it told me that it was loaded—five rounds, an empty chamber under the hammer.

The first cop returned my PI license. "That's a pretty old piece," he said. "You might want to shop around for something new. They got better stuff now." He patted the butt of the magnum on his hip.

"Yeah. So I hear."

"Well," he continued, "the way I look at this, we don't book this guy for loitering or a public nuisance or whatever, and we don't book this lady on a gun offense, and everybody goes away happy, right?"

129

"Sounds good to me," I said.

"Hey, wait a minute," said the big guy. "I told you guys I wasn't loitering."

He didn't know when to let up, did he? The two cops turned to him and gave him the same sour look.

That's when I said as innocently as I could, "Hey, I was wondering if one of you two officers happened to pat this guy down."

And then I got the sour look. "I don't think we have to do that," said the first cop. If he had a piece, I'm sure he would have blown her away." Then he added with a wry smile, "That's what I would have done."

I nodded and looked away, and where I looked there was a big Lincoln limo double-parked. I hadn't noticed it pull up. I had a good idea who was inside.

"So?" said the cop, "everybody happy?"

"Yeah," I said, "sure."

Tight-lipped, the big guy nodded.

"Then let's be on our way, people." The cops started back to their car.

I turned to Alicia who was wearing a big triumphant smile. "Hey," I said to her, *"Digale."* In English I said, "Thank you. I'm sorry I caused you trouble."

"Como?"

I said it again slowly.

Her lips moved silently for a moment as she practiced it to herself. Then: "Zanc iu. Aim sori Ai caust iu troebl."

The cops turned back, frowning. "What did she say?" asked the first cop.

"She said thank you and that she was sorry she caused you trouble."

"Oh." Then he glanced over at the cause of it all, who was still hanging around about a dozen feet away. He called over to him, "Hey, buddy, take a walk."

The big guy mouthed a silent "shit" and began hiking for the corner, straining the seams of his suit with each step he took.

The cops got into the car and started away.

"See," said Alicia, "I told you the policeman doesn't understand English."

"Come on," I said, grabbing her arm and starting her across the street.

Pilar came running over. "Oh, Señor Cervantes, you handled that beautifully. Very polite. I always tell them in the neighborhood, it's better to be polite."

"He wasn't polite," said Alicia.

"What? Who?"

"The policeman. When I say 'Zanc iu,' he's supposed to say, 'Iur uelcoem.' That's how it is in the book."

"Terrific."

"*Que quiere decir*, 'terrific'? *Como terrífico?*"

"Take her upstairs, Pilar. I have to talk to these men in the car."

"But Chico!"

"Upstairs!"

I watched them go until they were inside the building. Then I crossed the street and walked over to the black limo. I had the .38 tucked in my belt in plain sight.

There behind the wheel was the pyromaniac who had tried twice to burn my nose off.

One of the dark back windows rolled down silently. Jaime Fernandez was there. "Get in," he said, "we'll talk."

"No, thanks," I said, "I'll stay here."

"Oh, you got a gun. Look, Carlos, he's got a gun. He's wearing it right out where we can see it."

Carlos looked and laughed. Well, at least I didn't have a noose around my neck this time.

"Well, see? I got a knife." He held it up, hefting it in his hand. It was one of those weighted throwing knives they advertised in *Soldier of Fortune*. "That makes me one up on you. You make a move for that thing you got tucked in your middle, and you're dead before you can shoot your *huevos* off. One thing I know how to do is use this, *'mano*."

131

I believed him.

"So. Might as well come inside. We can watch TV, have a drink . . ."

I thought it over. Maybe he was right. My enemy's enemy is my friend. The door swung open. I ducked down and stepped inside. Shutting the limo door behind me, I settled into the seat beside Jaime.

"You got trouble with the cops?" Jaime's hands were empty. The knife had disappeared somewhere into his clothing.

"I handled it." Trying to sound a lot more confident than I was.

"Who's the woman?"

"A friend."

"You got her big with a baby. Be nice if you were around for the birthday."

"Oh, cut the shit," I said, exasperated at last. "Did I come in here to talk or to hear more of this stuff?"

He gave me a long, flat stare. Then he suddenly smiled and slapped me on the knee. "I like you, Cervantes. You got sand, and you're—*como se dice*?—resourceful. Yeah, resourceful. Pretty good word, huh?"

"How do you mean?"

"The way you got out of the little guest room in the basement. Big bolt lock. You were in, and then you were out. How'd you do that, *'mano*?"

I'd been wondering about that myself.

"We think you had outside help."

"Come on." I said, "Let's put it on the table."

"Okay, okay," he shrugged. "You're right. Enough. We talk now like serious people. You know our offer. You heard it last night."

"You shoot up the place?"

"That's right. Never know what we might hit or who. Went by earlier today, and the gate was standing wide open. We could get pretty close, Cervantes. Might be tonight, or maybe next week when they're not expecting us or maybe the week after that. We don' forget about it. Believe me, it'll happen—unless . . ."

"Unless what?"

"You give us a better target."

This was it. "Okay, listen," I said. "I think the immediate cause of the problem is an outfit known as Intertel. They've got this front as a big high-tech commercial intelligence agency—you know, industrial espionage, all that stuff. Sort of a CIA for the private sector. Right?"

"Okay, right." I had him interested.

"Only, like the CIA, too, they do some dirty stuff. Maybe that's all Intertel does. Maybe the high-tech stuff is all bullshit. Maybe it's just Murder, Incorporated, with a classy logo. Now . . . when—"

"Wait a minute," he interrupted. "What's this Murder, Incorporated? Tell me about that."

Jeez, I thought, crooks today, they got no sense of history. But what I said was, "Later, okay? That was a long time ago, anyway—over fifty years ago."

"Oh. Yeah. Right." His hand rose, maybe involuntarily, like he was tossing Lepke Buchhalter and his boys back on the trash heap.

I pressed on. "So, anyway, Intertel is involved in something with the Tollers. I don't know exactly what, and I don't know for who. But the *what* got Julio killed. They set him up, I don't know, for bait, or for some kind of attention grabber or something."

"They got our attention." The way he said it, it was a threat.

"Yeah, but they don't know that."

"They find out when we blow the place up."

"You do that, and you might get the right guys and you might not."

"So we get some somebodies. How do we know who's the right guys?"

"We have to get inside to find out."

"You mean, we kick ass, huh?" He made the fingers of

133

his two hands into a machine pistol and went, *eh-eh-eh-eh-eh*. "How 'bout it, Carlos?" he called up to the driver. "You like to do some ass kicking tonight?"

Carlos laughed again on cue. It sounded like the idea appealed to him.

"No. Listen," I said. "I've got a better idea."

After I hollered and raged and stamped my foot, after I had told Alicia that she must never, never, never so much as touch my pistol again, after I had told her that if she got in trouble like that again, they would surely send her back to Mexico—and that she could count on that—after I had done and said all that, she looked up at me with her big dark eyes and said, "I feel funny."

She had sat in a chair there in the living room. Well, her head wasn't exactly bowed, but she took it all humbly enough, without giving me her usual brand of tough back talk. Every once in a while, when I tossed an *"entiende?"* at her, she would purse her lips and nod. Pilar, who was standing on the sidelines through this, all but cheered me on. She shook her finger at Alicia's back. She waved her fist. At one point she even applauded me. That was too much for Alicia. She turned around and gave her a hot, vicious look. But when she came back to me, she seemed contrite enough. And now that I stood over her, fists on my hips, panting with righteous anger and feeling like a bully, she said she felt funny.

It didn't quite get through to me for a moment. I tried to assess what she had said. Was this more dramatics? She was a great little actress. Finally, I said, "What do you mean, 'You feel funny'?"

"Just funny. That's all. The baby's been moving around a lot."

Pilar came around and looked at her. "You think it's your time?" Then to me: "It could be the excitement."

I knelt down beside Alicia. "What about it, *chica*? You feel pains the way the doctor said?"

She looked at me seriously and shook her head, no. "I just don't feel so good now. I'd like to lie down for a while."

I didn't know exactly what to do or say. Should I call the doctor? Should I stick around? It was a good twenty days before the baby was due. Finally, I said, "Sure. Come on. I'll help you into the bedroom."

And that's what I did, hauling her out of the chair, wrapping my arm around her, letting her lean on me as we made it into the room together. Pilar hovered at the door, looking concerned. I gestured for her to beat it. Then Alicia tumbled into bed like the large, round object she was.

"Are you okay?" I asked.

"Yes. Really I am, Chico. I'll just sleep for a little while, and I'll feel better. I think you should go and do what you have to do."

"I'm not so sure."

"The baby is a long way off. I can tell."

She probably could. "Well . . ."

I leaned over and kissed her, and she surprised me by suddenly throwing an arm around my neck and almost smothering me for a moment as she drew out the kiss and thrust her tongue into my mouth. Finally, she pushed me away.

"You're good to me, Chico. I'm sorry for the trouble I caused. It's just that I got angry, and I felt like I was in prison here, and that big man down on the street was the guard. I felt like I was breaking out of prison when I went downstairs to chase him away. You understand?"

"I understand."

"Leave now. Go."

I sighed. "Okay."

Giving her a pat on the thigh, I turned for the door, but she called after me.

"Chico."

"Yes."

"You're a good man. I hope you find a good woman—one better than me."

135

By the time I pulled up in front of the Toller place, the old man was outside waiting, with two soft-leather suitcases of modest size at his feet and Ursula beside him. I wasn't late. He was early.

The two were heavy into it. But the old man was doing all the talking—in a quick, precise German, not angrily but stern and direct. I only caught a word here and there—*ich* and *du,* mostly, but another, *gefährlich,* came through: "dangerous." She made an earnest reply, but shrugging, as if she was trying to justify herself. He came back at her tough, shaking his finger. His voice rose, but I couldn't get any of it. And then, my God! Ursula hung her head and nodded apologetically. Standing a good three inches above her father in heels and Gloria Vanderbilt jeans, she was suddenly a kid who'd been soundly scolded by her father. He might be down, but he wasn't out.

I was standing off to one side by my car at a discreet distance from all this. He had glanced over in my direction once or twice. He certainly knew I was there, but he wasn't ready to go. He gave her a pat on the shoulder, murmured something to her, and she nodded again. Then he was ready to go.

Not hesitating for a moment, he picked up his bags and started over toward me and the car. I hustled over to help him. Then Ursula surprised me again. She let out a wail— "*Vati!*"—and ran after him. *Daddy*? From her? She caught up with him in three long strides, scrunched down and plastered two or three big kisses on his face. Even he looked surprised and didn't resist when I took the bags from him. I walked over to my car, opened up the hatchback and tossed them inside. He was right behind me and had climbed into the passenger seat before I could come around and open the door for him. I would have done that for him.

I jumped in behind the steering wheel. "Where to?" I asked. "Long Beach?"

"No. Just drive. Let's get out of here." He turned in his seat as I started the car. Looking back, he gave a half-hearted wave to Ursula, who was standing back a few steps from where he had left her in the driveway. She looked almost forlorn.

I jammed the car into gear. Seconds later we were through the gate, headed toward Sunset.

Toller shook his head and sighed. "That one," he said, "she goes from trying to be a man to being a child so quickly that I myself find it quite confusing. But . . ."

I glanced over at him. He was staring straight ahead through the windshield. He seemed to be talking to himself rather than to me.

"Well, it's to be expected, of course. The girl had no proper upbringing. The child of my second marriage—my *only* child. *Aber mein Gott!* I had forgotten about her completely. A few years ago—well, nearly ten—I was going through bills I had been paying automatically, and I said to my secretary, 'What are all these bills for this school in Klosters?' And she said, 'For your daughter, of course.' And I had to pretend that I remembered. Embarrassing,

137

disgusting really, to be so egoistic to forget your own daughter. But—that is how I am—or was.

"I went to visit her. I found her practically as she is now—willful, angry. But I asked her what she wanted to do with her life, and she said she planned to join my organization—not a request, you understand. Well, I had been looking for an heir—someone to teach—and I had one."

"So," I said, "has she been a good pupil?"

He looked over at me, a sly expression on his face. "Good intelligence, bad judgment. She still has much to learn."

We were on Benedict Canyon by then, nearly to Sunset.

He kept on talking. "Ilse, the maid, she said you understood German."

"Some," I said. "Enough to know she wants me to come to the telephone. Well . . . maybe more than that. I was in the MPs in Frankfurt during my army time."

"Did you understand any of my conversation with Ursula?"

"No. My German's pretty rusty. Besides, I wasn't really trying to listen."

"*Ach,* De Quincey, you are unique in your profession!" He laughed. Then, a moment later, he said, "You will have no more trouble from Ursula. But *should* you have trouble with her, or with Hans-Dieter, or with anyone, then you are to call Herr Klemper." He repeated the name. "Herr Klemper. Do you have that?"

"Yeah. I've got it."

"His official title is treasurer. He is my bookkeeper. He reports directly to me. You can always reach me through him."

We had reached Sunset and were waiting at the light.

"Look," I said, "where are we headed? You said we weren't going to Long Beach . . ."

"No. That private plane is Uschi's egoism. I fly Lufthansa."

"LAX then."

138

"Yes, but it is two hours before the flight. We go someplace and talk, eh?" He thought a moment. "I know. We go to the beach. Take Sunset to the end, and we will look at the ocean."

And so that was where we went, following that twisting ribbon of concrete uphill and down, above and across the 405, through a couple of little canyons, then into and out of Pacific Palisades. The Alfa liked the road. We hung low on the curves, swung up to meet each rise, and shot along the straightaways with a sweet ease that made me smile. As long as the Alfa was happy, so was I. I kept quiet and just let myself enjoy the road.

The moment I turned west on Sunset, Toller had lapsed into silence. He maintained it for miles and miles. Maybe he was enjoying the ride. More likely he had his mind on things other than the rolling road and the unreeling scenery. About the only remark I remember him making during those long minutes was something derogatory about Frankfurt—how he pitied me for having spent time there. How long was it? A little over a year, I told him. Then came his gloomy lament: "Terrible city, De Quincey, terrible people. They want only to grasp, to get, to have." He sighed deeply. The phlegm in his throat made it sound almost like a death rattle. "Frankfurt is where I must fly today."

There was one last twisting descent with the smell of the ocean now in the air, and then there it was before us, blue the way it seldom really is, with flickering glints of silver from the sun shining down on it. I took the left onto Pacific Coast Highway and drove a little in the right-hand lane. I looked over at him. It was a question.

"Anywhere along here," he said.

And so I signaled, slowed, pulled over and stopped near an unused lifeguard tower.

It was beautiful out, but the beach was nearly empty. The ocean was too smooth that day and hour for the surfers. As for the sunbathers, well, this was a weekday and school was in. And anyway, it's a funny thing about South-

139

ern Californians: even though the weather doesn't change much from season to season, people sort of pretend that it does. Most of them wouldn't think of heading for the beach except on summer days.

Toller and I got out, and I helped him scramble over the rocks that provided a barrier between the road and the sand. He didn't need much assistance—gimpy leg and all, he was still pretty good on his feet.

"Let's walk down by the water," he said, tossing out a quick, boyish gesture.

We headed down to the tide line and began walking south along that ribbon of sand where it was just damp enough to support us without sinking into the wet or getting our shoes soaked by the rush of the ocean. He knew the way. I could tell the old man was an experienced beach walker.

"You've been on your own for two days now," he said. "Tell me what you've been up to."

I gave him a full report, sticking pretty much to the facts. I wanted him to know that I'd found out a few things. Well, I did throw in a pretty lurid account of that necktie party— that was what they called them in the old westerns I saw as a kid—down in the basement of Esperanza. Then I took off the ascot and showed him the rope burn. He looked. He was impressed. I wanted him to know I'd suffered for the cause.

But he wanted to know if the Compañeros would come and shoot up the place while he was away.

Then I told him as reassuringly as I could about the deal I'd made in the backseat of Jaime's limo. He listened closely and noted that I had ordered Hans-Dieter to have guards on duty starting tonight.

"He'll do it, won't he?" I asked.

"Oh yes. I told him to do it just as you said—how was it? 'Don't shop around.' He doesn't like to follow orders, but he'll follow mine. You make sure that he does."

"I will."

140

He stopped then and looked me in the eye. "But be honest, De Quincey. You don't really trust these people, these . . . Compañeros, do you?"

"Not a hundred percent, no."

"But you gamble with my people—with my daughter."

"I think the odds are good."

He stared at me, assessing me and maybe calculating the odds. Then at last he nodded and started walking again. His head was down as he shuffled along. He didn't even notice the pair of eighteen-year-old California blonds who passed us by.

Finally: "All right, you get inside this place, this Intertel, and what do you look for?"

"You tell me."

"What do you mean?" he asked with a sharp, almost suspicious look at me—then looked off beyond at the ocean.

I was annoyed, and I'm afraid that it showed. Anyway, it was there in my voice when I said, "Come on, Mr. Toller. Don't make me work in the dark. You must have a pretty good idea who's paying these people to give you all this trouble. Give me a hint, a name, something."

I glowered at him. He glowered back at me. Then he said, "You are the detective, De Quincey. You find out."

I'd expected better of him.

We stood like that, not exactly nose to nose because he was about four inches shorter than me, but close enough and kind of intense.

"Then look," I said, "why don't I just go to the cops with what I've got so far? It'll save me risking my neck tonight. And if the Compañeros come by, the cops can handle them better than Casimir and I can."

He made a short, dismissive gesture with his hand: "No police," he said. Just like that. Then he turned and trudged a few steps on down the beach. He waved me forward. "Come. We walk some more."

I sighed and caught up with him. We went along the

shore for a few minutes without saying anything. There wasn't much to say.

We had come a long way. He pointed ahead into Santa Monica Canyon—the hills beyond the long cliff that overhung the highway. "Up there," he said, "you know who lived up there?"

I said nothing.

"Salka Viertel. You never heard of her, and if you did you couldn't know what she meant, who she really was. She was Europe, De Quincey. During the war, when we ran here from every country like stray dogs, she kept us alive. She fed us. She found jobs for us. But she kept our hearts alive. That was more important. Every Sunday she brought us together—such gatherings. You can't imagine! Stravinsky would come. Marcuse was there—Mann *und* Brecht, but never at the same time, they hated each other—and Lorre and Laughton and Huxley. *Ach, Gott!* what times those were!

"Why do you think I keep coming back here? All right, yes, for the money, for the deals. But deals I can make in Europe now. It's the history, those years, those people, the only history this God-forsaken city will ever have that is worth anything."

He had stopped and stood rooted in the sand. He was sort of making a speech. By the time he finished, he was jabbing a forefinger up into the air and practically shouting. He routed a bunch of gulls and sent them into flight.

I watched them go, then looked at my watch. "Come on," I said, "we'd better get you to the airport."

The trip to LAX started quietly enough. I was able to take Lincoln and avoid the freeway. It really wasn't very far at all—through Santa Monica and on to Venice, then through the marshlands that end out there somewhere around Playa del Rey.

It was about there that he began a monologue, not a

speech this time but a kind of lesson he had to teach me, a lecture he had to deliver. He was turned away, staring out the open window of the car through most of it.

"You know what it's like to be a producer?" he began. "To be a producer is to spend your whole life chasing money. You have a script. You have commitments from actors, the right director. But it is all shit without the money to begin the production, to put it before the camera. Who can get that money? I can. It get it in places nobody else looks. It's the one talent I have that surprises them all—getting money—maybe my only talent." He paused, hesitated, then added, "No. That's not true. I can also read a script. Not many in the business know how to do that."

We were at the top of the hill now, just starting into Westchester. I sped up, weaving my way through traffic, cutting right and left, spurting out ahead, playing road games with all the less-nimble cars. Toller had lapsed into silence for about a minute, but then he picked up where he had left off.

"De Quincey, I'll tell you something. There is one rule in financing a film that must never be broken. You get your money from wherever you can. In the end, it doesn't matter. All that matters is the quality of the film. But one thing that you must never do—never, never, never. You must never put your own money into a production. Sure, maybe a little bit in the beginning for development. You option something. You buy a script. But the big money to make the film—the big gamble, the millions—that must always be somebody else's money.

"That's the rule—and I broke it. Everything I have is in that stupid movie."

I eased off on the accelerator and looked at him. "You mean *Faust*?"

"Naturally! *Faust*! What else? It didn't make a nickel for Goethe—and he was a genius. There are no geniuses on this *Faust*."

"Hans-Dieter says it's going to be a hit."

143

"Hans-Dieter knows nothing."

"Then why did you put money into it?"

He sighed. "Yes. Why? I'm an old man, De Quincey. I did it to please my daughter. It was a gift to Ursula—total control of a production from start to finish, what she's been asking for ever since she joined my organization."

"Respect?"

"Oh? You heard that, too?" He laughed a dry, bitter laugh. "Yes, respect. Well, it's true I—my organization—face total destruction because of this boring monstrosity they are now putting together. There are those who want my destruction, who want it badly. But we shall see. I have one last card to play. I go now to play it."

With that he shut up. I glanced over at him, half expecting him to go on, to tell me just what he planned to do. But he had said all that he was going to say.

I swung into the lane that would take us to the upper-deck level of the horseshoe drive and on to the departing flights. Then, knowing just where I was headed, I buzzed around the slow traffic and squeezed in right in front of the Tom Bradley International Terminal. There I pulled to a halt and, leaving the motor running, popped open the trunk and jumped out of the car to give Old Man Toller a hand. But he was back there before I was, motioning over a skycap to take his two bags, slipping him ten, turning to shake hands with me.

"So. De Quincey. We wish each other luck, eh?"

"Yeah, right," I said, sort of lukewarm. "Good luck."

He gave me the same sort of stiff little bow I got from Hans-Dieter the first time I met him, and then we separated.

I jumped into the Alfa and craned back, hands on the wheel, looking for a break in traffic. Then suddenly Toller was back, beating at the window on the passenger side. I leaned far over and rolled it down.

"Okay," De Quincey," he said, "You wanted a name, I give you a name. It is Collinson—Norman Collinson."

144

With that, he pulled his head out of the window, turned, and headed into the terminal. I called after him, trying to get him to come back and tell me more—tell me something. But he was gone, a little man wearing an expensive suit and sand-dusted shoes, walking with a slight limp. He disappeared into the crowd.

I decided not to bother with Hans-Dieter. Now I had a man on the inside, and it seemed like a good idea to make myself known to him. And so I dropped in a quarter, dialed quickly, and waited, tapping my foot, waiting, waiting.

On the fourth ring I got, "Toller Entertainment."

"Mr. Klemper, please."

Another couple of rings and, "Office of the Treasurer."

"I'd like to speak to Mr. Klemper."

"And what is this regarding?" Why do they always say that?

"I'll tell that to him."

"*What?*" She sounded shocked—just like I'd said something obscene.

"Give him my name—Antonio Cervantes. He'll know who I am and in general what it's about."

"Well . . . just a moment." She sounded pretty uncertain when she put me on hold. I stayed there for about a minute.

146

Then: "Klemper." It was a dry, nasal voice, just right for a bookkeeper. I pictured a small, thin bald man wearing rimless glasses.

"You know who I am."

"Yes, yes," he said. "The one he calls De Quincey." He was telling me to get to the point. "If you wish to contact Herr Toller, it's out of the question. He's just now taken off on a flight to Europe."

"I know," I said. "I dropped him off at the airport."

"What then?"

"I was wondering. I asked Hans-Dieter to check some bills for me. It occurred to me he'd probably have to go through you to get them. Has he asked to see them yet?"

"How do I know that until you tell me what they are for?"

"It's the bills for the security system at the house."

"What about them? A new company has just been hired." Well, I thought, thank God for that.

"Yeah, well, I'd still like to get some information off the old bills."

Without a word he put me on hold. I waited. And waited. At last he came back on the line. "Yes," he said, "so. I have them here now in front of me. What is it you want to know? They were sent out monthly on the twenty-fifth. There are four. All but the last one was paid. You want the amount?"

"No. I want to know what it says up on top."

"What do you mean?"

"The name of the company, the address, all of it, line by line, just the way it is on the bill."

He gave a light hoot of annoyance but did as I wanted him to do. "All right," he said, "it says, 'Watchdog Security,' then on the next line, 'A Division of Intertel, Incorporated.' And on the next li—"

"You can stop right there," I said.

"What?" He sounded confused. For the first time, probably, in weeks.

147

"I've got all I needed. Thanks." And I hung up on him. I stood for a moment, my hand still resting on the telephone receiver, considering the situation. Yes, I'd gotten all I needed—but it was just confirmation of what I'd already guessed. I had to know more about Intertel, but the only way I was going to do that was to get inside.

Getting inside wasn't the problem. It was what happened afterward that tore things apart.

I had scouted out the building ahead of time, and I knew that the entrance we wanted certainly wasn't the front one, but rather the utility dock, off a sidestreet and up a short alley in the rear. That was where the trucks made deliveries and where the garbage got picked up. There were a couple of empty dumpsters out there on the dock. But there were no trucks of any kind and no cars in the little alley.

I was early. I made my way up the short stairs on one side of the dock, past the dumpsters and over to the big, wide double back door. There I stood for a moment uneasily, trying to decide whether I should get things under way or wait for Jaime and the Compañeros. I glanced down at my watch. It was five-fifty, or would be in about a minute. It had been agreed that we would gather here on the dock at six sharp. So why was I early? In order to make sure they wouldn't start the party without me. And here I was, being tempted to duck inside on my own.

Well, I'd just resist temptation. That's what I'd do. I looked at my watch again—five-fifty on the button. I checked the dumpsters out—they were clean, all right, empty down to the bottom. I decided it was pointless and probably suspicious looking for me to hang around the back door like this, so I headed back down the steps and out the alley. There on the sidestreet I waited, checking my watch every minute or so, then taking a hike in the direction of Santa Monica.

But wait a minute. About half a block down that sidestreet that ran perpendicular to the alley, what I saw parked inconspicuously behind a pickup truck was a big black Lincoln limo. It was just like the one in which Jaime and I had had our discussion right around noon that same day. I checked the license plate. In fact, it was the same car. He and the gang had arrived even earlier than I had. They were probably inside already. I ran back to the loading dock, retracing my steps precisely. Up the stairs again, then to the back double door. I put my hand inside my windbreaker and grasped the handle of my .38.

I tried the door. It was locked. I wiggled the doorknob a bit, then gave that up and banged hard on the metal surface. No response. I found a bell and rang it. Then I banged again, making the thing rattle on its hinges. That got some results. I heard a lock thrown back on the other side. The door came open about six inches, and in the half light on the other side I made out the face of Carlos, Jaime's driver, the guy with the cigarette lighter. He reached out, grabbed me by the arm and pulled me inside. I bumped my shoulder on the door on the way in.

I stood there blinking, trying to adjust my eyes from light to dark. The door slammed behind me, and the lock clicked loudly back into place.

Carlos nudged me at the elbow. "Come on," he said.

He led me through the big gallery-sized back room, down a fairly well-lit hall, and through a door into a kind of locker room. Jaime was there and another guy who had to be a Compañero. He had to be because he was busy tying up one of the Mexican cleaning crew. He had tied up one of them already. Two more were waiting their turn. But they were joking about it.

"Hey, *'mano*," said one of them, "not too tight, okay? We gotta get loose from this sometime, you know."

The others laughed.

Jaime looked up and winked. He came over and said quietly to me, "I gave them money, like you suggested, but

149

they said, 'Hey, you better tie us up, too, or we don't have no job to come back to tomorrow.'"

"Solid citizens," I said. "They think of the future."

"*Claro*. They supplied the rope. Emilio does the job. He's very good with rope. You met him last night."

I frowned at Jaime, puzzled, then he grinned, and I understood. Emilio was my hangman. He didn't look like a hangman. He looked like a nerd.

Yes, I had to admit he was very good with rope. Methodical but reasonably quick, his small hands moved over the knots he had made, adjusting them, moving one so that it would be within reach of the fingers of one tightly tied hand. It would take a while, but yes, this one would be able to work his way loose when it was time.

Emilio looked up at me and smiled a surprisingly gentle smile, then he went on to the next man.

In that way, all the cleaning crew were tied up and moved off into one corner of the room. I helped haul two of them myself. The funny thing was, after all that they were pretty quiet. No laughs and no jokes. They just watched us get ready, pulling on clothes that roughly approximated what they were wearing: blue chinos, chambray shirts—janitor clothes. And they just watched, hardly a word between them. Maybe they were having second thoughts about the hundred-dollar-a-man deal they had made with Jaime. Or maybe they were feeling particularly vulnerable, tied hand and foot the way they were. They knew we could do anything to them. And there was a moment when I caught Jaime staring at the four as he buttoned up his work shirt when I wondered just what he might have in mind. But that moment passed, and minutes later we were out of there.

Jaime sent Carlos off to the limo with their clothes. We stood around looking at each other for a minute or so, then he produced a vial of white powder from his shirt pocket and hauled up the silver coke spoon he wore around his neck. He offered me some. I declined. Giving me a wry smile, he took a hit in both nostrils. Emilio looked on indifferently.

I glanced at my watch, "We're too early," I said. "It's not even six-thirty yet."

Jaime didn't say anything. He was going through this whole routine of sniff-sniff-sniffing and focusing his eyes. At last he said, "You sure you don't want any? It's prima stuff."

"Yeah, I'm sure it is."

"What the fuck is that supposed to mean?"

My heart dropped like a lead sinker. What's his psychopathology, I wondered. *This* was the guy I was going to commit a burglary with?

"I meant just what I said," I told him. "I'm sure it's good stuff or you wouldn't be putting it up your nose."

"You better believe it."

"I believe it."

"*Okay!*" He turned away from me suddenly and began strutting around the big gallery room. "I'm ready! I'm *ready!*"

"I still think it's too early." I said it in a nice, even tone. Sure. Just try to reason with a guy when his feet are four feet off the ground.

Predictable response. He turned on me like I was the enemy. "*No!* You don't tell Jaime when it's time and when it's not time. I got the word. *Tengo el poder. Yo sé! Yo—*"

Just then—and was I ever glad for the interruption— there were three loud bangs on the steel doors. Carlos was back. Jaime turned to Emilio and jerked his head in that direction. Emilio trudged off obediently.

Jaime looked at me and tapped his forehead. "I know." At least he wasn't shouting.

So how do you deal with a megalomaniac? You humor him. "All right," I said, "all right."

He nodded, satisfied.

On the ride up on the elevator he seemed to have calmed down. As a matter of fact, he seemed almost too calm. There was a kind of remote languor to the way he stood

151

leaning against the wall of the elevator car, staring straight ahead, a half smile on his face. I didn't like this any better than the performance he gave in the utility room.

The guard in the lobby had given us a kind of funny look when we came through the rear doors and headed for the bank of elevators, pushing the big trolley-mounted trash barrel with its rack of brooms and mops. But the guard was a long way off, sitting behind the curved desk that faced the revolving doors that led out to Wilshire. Was he one of the guys from Intertel? Not one I recognized, anyway. Did his look say that he made us as imposters? Or just that we were early? I never found out because just when he might have gotten up to take a closer look, somebody came through the revolving doors, walked up to the desk, and signed in.

Then the elevator arrived.

It was pretty crowded in there with the four of us and that big mobile trash barrel. Emilio farted. Carlos laughed. Jaime pushed off the elevator wall, turned rigidly toward the two of them and gave them a fierce look.

The elevator slowed and stopped at the Intertel floor. The doors slid open. And there was the boss, Bill Wallace, standing tall no more than six feet away. I saw him, but he didn't see me. I ducked my head and suddenly got very interested in a bottle of window cleaner in the rack behind the trash barrel. What he saw was just another Mexican with the cleaning crew in work clothes and gloves. I managed to keep the barrel between him and me as we pushed out of the elevator and onto the floor. He wasn't interested in me, anyway. He just wanted to grab that elevator and get out of there.

"*Ándale! Ándale,*" he urged.

Where was he headed? What was he up to? Probably just going out to dinner, but with him you never knew. I wanted to follow him to be sure—or maybe I just wanted to get away from Jaime.

Wallace was on the elevator without so much as a second

look at me. Then he called out, "If any traffic comes in for me, I should be back by mid evening."

I heard the elevator doors shut behind me, and only then did I risk a look at the two big men slouching in the chairs exactly where they had sat a couple of nights ago. Only this time instead of Artie and his buddy from before, it was Artie and the even bigger guy who had been following Alicia around. But they weren't interested in us, either.

"Hey," said Artie to the big guy, "did you hear what he said—'if any traffic comes in'? Why the fuck can't he just say phone calls?"

"Yeah," said the big guy, "jeez."

"And 'mid evening'—when the fuck is that supposed to be?"

The other one laughed.

"A joke, huh?" He raised his voice. "Hey, I got another one for you. Didja ever hear that statistics prove that eighty percent of all accidents are Mexican related?"

A slow smile spread over Jaime's face. It looked like he was about to say something.

"Hey, you understood that, huh, Ho-zay?" Artie started laughing.

"Vamonos," I said to Jaime. *"Vamonos—a la derecha."* I got the wheels of the trolley turning and begun pushing it for all I was worth. Carlos and Emilio fell in step beside me. But Jaime stood where he was for a long moment smiling that bland smile at Artie.

"Come on!" I rasped it out at him in a whisper.

Then, with a shrug, Jaime turned and started after us into the hallway. I could still hear Artie laughing a full minute after we had left him behind.

By time that time we were pretty close to Wallace's office. I eased off on the trolley and pulled it to a halt. Three of us turned to Jaime. Maybe he really was in charge.

"Hey, that guy back there," he said, "he's pretty funny, huh? A real comedian."

"Yeah, sure," I said in a low tone. "Look, I think we're in luck. Nobody's around."

"But that guy at the elevator, he said he was coming back."

"Yeah. In a while."

"You know him? You sure didn't want him to see you."

"He knows me. He saw me when I was here before. All three of them saw me before."

"Who is hc, that guy at the elevator? It seemed like he was the boss."

He had me.

He pressed his case. "Is he the guy who came on to Julio?"

"Not the guy I had in mind," I lied.

"You better be playing straight with me, Mr. Detective. Otherwise . . ." He jerked an imaginary rope above his head.

Terrific. Why should I lie to protect Wallace? After all he'd done, didn't he deserve whatever Jaime had in mind for him?

"Okay, look," I said, trying to sound like I knew just what had to be done, "if we set up Carlos and, what's-his-name, Emilio, here in the hall, they can sort of stand guard if one of those guys should decide to come back here and take a look. Put one of them on this side of the corner office, and the other one on the other side."

Jaime nodded. His mouth dropped into a crooked smile. "That's your plan, eh, 'mano?"

"Well . . . yeah."

"You and me, we go in there, and we look for . . . what?"

"Information. Evidence."

He threw his head back and laughed loudly. "Hey, that's good! Evidence! What the fuck do we care about evidence? I think, Mr. Detective, we're in here for two different reasons. Am I right?"

I started to speak, but—

154

"No, listen. You're trying to make a case for the guy you work for. We could care less, you know? We're here for one thing only—a payback, blood for blood."

"Yeah, but you want to get the right guy, don't you? The guy who set Julio up?"

"That'd be nice, but it's not, you know, a high priority."

"Then come on," I said, just like I knew what I was doing, and I started off down the hall for Wallace's office. You get to a point when you're more annoyed than scared. And that's where I was then. I didn't look back to see if they were following. I just went.

Circling the secretary's desk, I noticed—really for the first time—the computer off to one side of it. I know I'd seen it before, and I knew there was one on Wallace's desk, too. But I hadn't really thought about what that meant. My heart sank right down to my running shoes.

I continued on into Wallace's office. It was just about as I remembered it from my visit there. Except then I hadn't noticed how bare the place was. Oh, there was plenty of furniture, good stuff, too, including a nice big L-shaped desk with that computer on the short leg of the L. What there weren't were file cabinets.

Jesus, Mary and Joseph! I came in here with only one name to go on, and now it looked like there weren't even any files to search. But maybe the desk . . .

I went around and looked it over. It was one of those modern jobs, slim-lined polished wood with a long, shallow center drawer and two on either side not much deeper. It didn't take me long to jimmy them open. The Finns, or whoever they were, made them for looks and not to with-stand an assault with a good piece of steel.

I dug through the drawers in a hurry. There was stuff in them that might turn out to be interesting—but no files, nothing organized at all. I pulled the contents of the drawers out and set them on top of the desk. As for the rest of it, well, the computer sat on one gorgeous slab of wood and beside it a flat device with paper feeding into it

155

that I vaguely recognized as a printer. They took up all the space on the base of the L.

That damned computer. All the files, with everything I wanted, were inside it. I was ready to lift the damned thing up and throw it out the window onto Wilshire below. I hit at the screen in frustration instead, and hurt my knuckles in the process. *"Chinga!"*

There I was, behind the desk, squeezing my hand and then shaking my fingers when I looked up and found Jaime in the doorway, watching me with a crooked smile on his face. I had no idea how long he'd been there.

"What's the matter, Mr. Detective," he said, "you got problems?"

Why hide it? "Yeah, I got problems."

"What kind?"

"Everything I'm after is in there," I said, pointing with my sore hand at the computer.

Jaime shrugged. "Maybe the Compañeros got the answer." He half turned and called back into the hall, "Emilio, *ven acá.*" Then he moved over in the doorway, and a moment later Emilio stuck his head inside. "He knows about that stuff," Jaime said to me. Then to Emilio: "Give him a hand."

The three of us exchanged looks. I must have seemed pretty dubious because I was. Jaime nodded. Maybe he wanted to come across as reassuring, but he only looked sort of pompous, trying to look like the man who could handle any situation. Emilio glanced up at him—he was about six inches shorter—then over at me. I thought he looked like a nerd at first, and he still did. There was a kind of round innocence to his face, an anomaly.

"Have fun," said Jaime. He turned away and went back into the hall. A moment later I heard him kibitzing with Carlos.

Emilio came in sort of diffidently, nodding, a little half smile on his face. "What's the trouble?" he asked. I realized then that it was the first time I had heard him speak. He had a kind of squeaky tenor.

"Well, I'm after files—information on this guy who set Julio up. Him and whoever is paying the bill."

"Yes? So?"

"Well, there's nothing here—no paper files. I haven't gone through these drawers yet, but they don't look too promising. All the stuff I want is probably in the computer."

He nodded again and smiled. "Probably."

"Well, I was thinking maybe they've got these, what do they call them, floppy disks around here with the files on them. Only I don't know where they'd keep them. In one of those rooms along the hall maybe. I could dig around in them, and . . ." I was sort of babbling, and I knew it.

"No," he said, "don't bother. You won't find anything."

"Why not?"

"What you're thinking of is a home computer, see, like an Apple or an IBM PC." He looked at me in a more or less neutral way. "You don't know anything about computers, do you?"

"I guess that's pretty clear, huh?"

"It's okay. See, a PC, something like that, they store information like you said, on floppy disks, hard disks, you know."

I nodded just like I did know.

"But, like, this one, it's not that kind. It's not even a whole computer."

"It isn't?"

"No, see, it's just a terminal hooked up to a mainframe computer someplace else. Maybe a pretty big one."

"So we gotta find that, huh?"

"No, no, no. A terminal, it's like a telephone, see. You call in and you get what you want. The mainframe, it's probably not even here, maybe hundreds of miles away, thousands. Who knows? Doesn't matter."

"So we can just call them up and get what we want?"

"Sure. All you need is the right telephone number—the log-in and the password."

"Like a key to open it up?" I sighed. "Well . . ."

157

"You don't have that, huh?"

"No."

"That makes it hard." He came around the desk and sat down in the chair in front of the computer. "But maybe not impossible."

He punched a button. I leaned over and watched as the black screen lit up in green characters.

WELCOME TO THE INTL COMEX-3 COMPUTER

PLEASE LOG IN NOW

LOG IN:

The pulsating dot hung there right after the colon.

"This works sometimes." He typed in the word GUEST, and the computer responded:

SORRY, TRY AGAIN

"Didn't work, huh?"

"Well, we know GUEST isn't a valid username."

"That's good?"

"It's a start." He hesitated, then turned back to me. "Who uses this, anyway? Whose office is this?"

"A guy named Wallace, Bill Wallace."

"Well, if I'm right, this takes a maximum six characters on log-in. That's a seven-character name, so I'll try some short versions of it."

"Okay," I said, "I'll go through the stuff in these drawers." I stood behind him a moment and watched him work. Jesus, I thought, how did this guy get mixed up with Jaime?

But—back to work. I began shuffling through the papers in one of the two side drawers. Not much there—some blank expense forms, a desk dictionary (I shook the pages, but nothing fluttered out), and that big loose-leaf tome on Intertel Wallace had entertained me with the other night (I gave that a shake, too—nothing). But there, at the bottom, was a file—or at least a file folder. Was this the one Wallace had had on his desk when he talked to me? The one I thought had information about me? If so, it was just a dummy. The folder contained nothing but a sheaf of old

158

business letters, not much of interest. Wait a minute, here was one from the Office of Probation, State of California. Yeah, there might be something here. I decided to take the letter along.

All this time, Emilio was clicking away on the keys of the computer keyboard. As I glanced over, I saw SORRY, TRY AGAIN flash up on the screen in green. It didn't seem to faze him. He started over immediately.

And I started in on the middle drawer. Mostly junk—paper clips, pencils, ballpoints, more office forms. But there, taped to the bottom was something interesting—a card with a series of characters, five of them. You could tell they had been added one at a time because they were in different color ink. The first four groupings of letters—you couldn't call them words—had lines drawn through them. Only the last, *SPNQRD*, had not been crossed out.

"Bingo!" cried Emilio and let out a giggle that told me the kid was really enjoying himself.

"What is it?" I leaned over his shoulder. "What've you got?"

"I got his log-in. WILWAL—how do you like that?"

"Sort of poetic. I didn't think he had it in him." Then I saw ENTER YOUR PASSWORD up there on the screen, and I realized we weren't home free.

He looked up at me. "Any ideas?"

"Me? No."

Well, let's begin at the beginning. He typed in USER.

The response was a quick SORRY, TRY AGAIN.

"Look," said Emilio, "what kind of place is this anyway?"

"What do you mean?"

"I mean, what do they do? Is it, like, some kind of detective agency or something?"

"Yeah, basically." I could have filled him in all night on that.

"So, basically, like security and shit like that, right?"

"Right."

159

"Well, then, they want to keep their information secure, too. And one way to do that is to use computer-generated passwords. They let the computer think up its own passwords—sort of nonsense words. Have you seen anything around here that—"

"Try SPUHNQUHRD!"

"Huh?"

I pushed the middle drawer across the desk to him, so he could see the card taped to the bottom of it.

He smiled. "See, they change these every month or so, and people can't remember them because they're not real words, so they write them down and stick them in places like this. Well, let's try it." He typed it in—SPNQRD. The computer liked it: SIGNED ON.

"Bingo," I said.

He hit a couple of keys and called up a list of coded headings that took up most of a screen. "Okay, these are the guy's active files," he said. "You want to read them all? It's going to take a while. And it's going to take even longer to print them out."

"I've got a name," I said. "Is there any way you can look for it fast?"

"Oh, yeah. I'm sure this has got a search capability. What's the name?"

"Norman Collinson." I spelled it out for him.

He typed it in and hit the execute key. The screen went blank for a moment and then on came one of the files. It was classified highly confidential, and it was headed, "Majestic Pictures." Client contact was identified as Norman Collinson, President. There were various notes on a client interview. I saw the Toller name and then an address in Munich, and that was all I needed.

"Look," I said to Emilio, "is there any way you can get this out of there and on to paper?"

"You mean print it out?"

"I guess so. Yeah."

He hit a couple of keys, and the file went off the screen.

Then, seconds later, the little machine next to the computer terminal began humming and zipping away as paper began to flow through it.

I looked at him—and I hoped my look showed the respect I felt. "Amazing," I said. "What do they call you guys? Hackers?"

"Yeah." He had that innocent look again. "I'm a hacker."

"Tell me something. How do you fit into this . . ." My fingers drew a vague circle in the air; I was looking for a nice, neutral word. "How do you fit into this organization, anyway?"

He grinned. "I'm just the bookkeeper." So Toller had his Herr Klemper, and Jaime had his Emilio. Then, as if answering a question I hadn't asked, he added, "You ought to see the setup I got at home. I can do anything with it, go anyplace, get into anything. A setup like I got costs money."

"But how come you're along on this—"

A voice interrupted. "What the fuck are you doing in here?" That voice didn't belong to Jaime or Carlos. It belonged to Artie. He had a pistol, some kind of automatic, pointed in our direction. How had he gotten past the two in the hall?

"Okay," he said, "come out from behind there." He meant both of us, but he was looking hard at me. Then something in his eyes told me he'd made me from the night before. "Hey!" He fairly shouted it. "I know you. You're the guy who—"

Then something strange happened. He was just taking a step into the office when his eyes widened very suddenly. He took another step, and he stumbled and fell onto the carpet, about five feet from the desk. His body curled, then kicked out in a spasm and went still. He had Jaime's knife in his back. From the pages of *Soldier of Fortune* right into his back.

Jaime stood for a moment in the doorway looking down

161

at Artie, no expression on his face at all. Then he strode in, bent over the body and pulled the knife out. What next? Well, I wish I hadn't seen it, but he pulled Artie's head up by the hair, exposing the throat and cut him across the windpipe. There was blood, but no gush. Artie was already dead. Jaime wiped the knife on Artie's clothes and looked me straight in the eye. Still no expression.

"Jesus," I said, "was that necessary?"

"To make sure," he said.

I glanced over at Emilio. He gave a little shrug and turned away.

"Okay, Mr. Detective, did you get what you came for?"

Funny thing, I hadn't noticed before, but the printer had quit humming and zipping and a good yard of paper hung out of it. Emilio scooped up the paper and tore it off, then handed it over to me.

"Well, we got what we came for, too," said Jaime. "Let's go."

We followed him out into the hall. Carlos was there, just back from the corner, motioning us to get behind him. He had a smile on his face and in his hand a big automatic made bigger by a three-inch silencer.

What was this all about? I understood when I heard Artie's companion, the big guy who followed Alicia around, lumbering noisily down the hall, calling out for Artie, asking where he was and where the fuck all the fucking Mexicans were. Something in me wanted to yell out and warn him to get out of there. But I didn't say anything. For a few seconds I didn't even breathe.

He got louder and louder as he got closer, and finally he turned the corner, all three hundred pounds of him, and looked not at us but right into the silencer at the end of that automatic.

"Do him," said Jaime. I heard him say it just like that.

Carlos fired three times—*phut-phut-phut*—and the guy didn't move. He just stood there, looking surprised. He didn't even have a gun in his hand. But still he stood. Car-

162

los fired again. The shots were grouped in the chest. Then again and again. The big guy stood swaying and finally fell, crashing like a redwood onto the tile floor.

Then Carlos walked over and put a shot—*phut*—into the back of his neck.

I was dripping with sweat, panting for air, and holding tight to that clump of paper under my arm.

I'd learned something. Your enemy's enemy will probably turn out to be your enemy, too. I'd made a deal with these guys, thought I could waltz them in and waltz them out, use them to find out what I needed to know. Now two men were dead. Never mind that they were professional muscle and may have deserved what they got. I felt guilty. And I *was* guilty of thinking I could control these guys in some way, get them to trash the place and leave it at that. Or something. Well, it had gotten out of hand. The whole operation had taken on a life of its own. And Jaime was fully in control.

On the way out he produced a can of spray paint and outlined a crude drawing of a skull on the wall.

14

The apartment was both less and more than I expected. It was a condo north of Sunset, good location, but the building wasn't much. There were million-dollar places around it, but this apartment would have gone for about half that. On the other hand, it was bigger than I would have thought and better furnished, with pictures on the wall—one of them looked like a David Siqueiros—and a couple of pieces of sculpture. It had some class, some taste—and that, I was sure, had been supplied by Jaime's mother.

That's right. Jaime Fernandez, *el gran jefe de los Compañeros de la Muerte* lived with his mother.

She floated around the room like a dark ghost in a silk robe, her black hair pulled back and trailing past her shoulders, her cold brown eyes shifting restlessly around the room. When those eyes settled on me the first time, I sensed recognition and—yeah, unmistakably—contempt. When she crossed over to her son and passed close to me, the smell of her perfume placed her down in the basement of Esperanza the night before. Yeah, she was the one. The *Colombiana,* a blood tie to the coke trade.

She whispered something to Jaime. He looked my way and nodded. Then she settled into a chair in the corner and waited.

"Let's see it," he said.

"See what?" I asked. As if I didn't know.

"Hijo la! Don't fuck around with me. Let's see what you been holding onto so tight ever since we left that place. What you got out of that computer."

Carlos leaned forward in his place on the sofa and adjusted his clothes so I couldn't miss the blunt handle of the automatic sticking out from under his jacket. They had taken my .38 away from me the moment we left the building.

Emilio was there, too, at the other end of the sofa, sitting back, taking it all in. He had removed himself from the action and was now no more than an interested spectator. But it was Emilio who had started it all. It was because of him I was here in Jaime's apartment.

On the way down in the elevator of Intertel's building, while Jaime was still breathing hard from another hit of coke, Emilio had started whispering to him. I wanted to get close enough to listen, but it was clear I was the guy who wasn't supposed to hear. Emilio couldn't really have said much—but it was evidently enough. When we hit the lobby and wheeled out the big dolly-borne trash barrel with the mops and brooms, the guard at the front door gave us another funny look. Again, he seemed like he was ready to get up and check us out. He could get dead that way.

"We go now. Eat!" I called to him, making like Cheech Marin. "Come back later."

He seemed satisfied at that. He nodded and waved and settled back in his chair. I had the feeling I'd saved his life.

Once through the doors to the back, Carlos gave the

cleanup wagon a big push and laughed like a kid as it went careening down the hall and crashed out into the big room beyond.

Jaime stopped me then. "Hey, *'mano,*" he said, giving me a playful punch on the arm, "you were pretty good out there. 'We go now. Eat.'" He punched me again, a little harder this time and laughed like it was funnier than it really was. "Hey, you sounded like a real homeboy from the barrio."

"Yeah, well, I think we better get out of here."

"You're right! What can I say? You're right. Only we got a little change of plans, see."

"What's that?"

"You're coming with us, Mr. Detective."

There was no arguing with him. They had me out of there in less than a minute. Carlos lifted my .38 and tucked it away.

"Just to make me happy," Jaime explained. "You gonna ride with me, and I get nervous when the guy beside me got a gun, you know?"

"You seemed pretty steady earlier today."

"Oh, I was shakin', *'mano.*" He laughed. "Inside I was shakin'."

And so of course we did it his way—Emilio and Carlos up in front of the limo and me beside Jaime in back. A good yard separated us there in the backseat of the Lincoln. Jaime was high, on the coke but mostly on himself. He was in no mood to talk—at least not to me. He called up to Emilio and told him to put on a Carlos Santana tape. Beating out the rhythm on his thighs, he began singing along on the refrain. *"Oye como va!"*

He was off somewhere by himself. Let him stay there. From out of my jacket I pulled the wrinkled roll of printout from the computer and began reading through it.

The whole case was right there in dot matrix. The first item in the file was the longest and the most revealing. It was Wallace's record of his meeting with Norman Collinson, CEO of Majestic Pictures—in effect, his marching orders. Collinson outlined the contractual arrangements with Toller that set it all up. Apart from the usual agreement to distribute *Faust* in the United States and Canada, Majestic had put up forty percent of the financing for the film on very stiff terms: If Toller should fail to deliver the rough cut of *Faust* by the appointed date—it tallied with the four-week deadline that Ursula had given Denison, the director—then ownership of the film at whatever stage of completion would pass to Majestic. But a rough cut? Why? Why? Guys like Toller delivered finished films. He must have needed the money pretty bad to go along with that.

Collinson had told Wallace that a few things had been done in Germany to slow the production down, and the director, Derek Denison, was a notoriously slow worker, anyway, but it looked as if the Tollers had better than an outside chance of making the delivery date. Collinson made it clear that this was not to happen.

Then Wallace had written: "When I started to suggest to Collinson that a hostage situation might prove effective, trading hostage for film, he stopped me and said he didn't want to discuss methods. That, he said, was my department. After giving me his home number, he instructed me not to call him at the studio. I asked how often he wanted me to report, he said he would rather not hear from me at all. If he could read his report in the newspaper that would suit him fine."

The telephone number was down there together with the amount paid in cash—American currency, denominations not less than fifty dollars—$250,000. Wallace had made the notation: "Downpayment, remainder to be paid upon successful closure of the file."

That was quite a retainer. I searched the elongated single sheet of script from the printer for the total amount Intertel would collect—or wouldn't, if I had anything to do with it—but I couldn't find it anywhere.

I did, however, come up with a few interesting tidbits—

that address in Munich, a name, a phone number, and then a report on the Munich operation—marked, "Telex, book code, decode as follows." The size of it was that the hired hands in Germany hadn't expected such resistance from the bodyguard. "Our man inside"—the chauffeur—"became fearful for his own safety when bullets hit the Toller car, and he drove away, taking with him the designated target." Ursula, of course.

A little farther down was Julio's name, with a notation Club Dos Mundos, the address on Sunset—"(Bernie's recommendation)"—then my name, PI license number, auto license and make, address and phone number—notes on me and on Alicia. I could read all that stuff later.

I looked up. Jaime was watching me. How long? He wore a tight little smile. "Pretty interesting, huh?"

"Yeah, well, sure." I shrugged. Be casual.

"It better be. You took a chance getting it."

What was I supposed to say to that? That the real chance I took was going in there with him? Jesus, what a mess this was—two bodies and a finger pointing straight at me.

All I said to Jaime was, "Right." I rolled up the printout and tucked it back inside my jacket.

He didn't say anything more and neither did I.

The trip was shorter than I expected. When we turned off Sunset and started up the hill, I guessed we were headed for Jaime's place. I don't know why, but I thought I'd be a little safer there.

So here was Jaime in his living room, hand outstretched, demanding what I'd risked my neck to get. Well, I'd be risking it even more if I held back now. And besides, I'd decided I wanted him to have it. I hauled the rolled yard of paper out once again, and not bothering to flatten it out, simply tossed it over to him.

He nodded. "Smart." Then he began to read.

I glanced around the room at the others. Now that there

168

was no need to make a threat, Carlos pulled back his jacket and covered up the butt of the automatic. Suddenly he was out of it. He didn't fall asleep or anything, but the lights behind his eyes went down to dim. I've seen animals, dogs, go into that half-awake state—and I knew how fast they (and he) could rouse out of it.

Emilio, on the other hand, was alert but lost in his own thoughts, maybe designing software in his head, maybe figuring how he could stick up the Bank of America with his computer.

Only Jaime's mother took much interest in what he was reading. She leaned over his shoulder and scanned the long sheet with him. Suddenly, he laughed.

"Hey, Mr. Detective," he said, "the guy who wrote this, he don' think much of you."

"Yeah?"

"Listen to this. He calls you 'a man of limited capabilities.' Pretty bad."

"I didn't read that part."

"Well, it's right here. You wanna hear some more?"

"No."

Señora Fernandez gave me a sharp look and a crooked smile. Then both of them returned to the printout. They read to the end, then the two of them held a quick, quiet conversation. She took the printout and retired to her chair in the corner to study it. Jaime leaned forward, clapped his hands, and rubbed his palms together. Across from me, Carlos roused.

"I think we're gonna be partners, 'mano," said Jaime.

"Oh? How's that?" I said very innocently. Let him tell me what I already knew.

"For my money, you're no man of limited capabilities. You went in there, and you got what you wanted. You couldn't do it without us, but you did it. So we're already partners, see?"

He had this way of making speeches.

"Emilio helped you a lot, right?" He was stating the obvious.

"Sure, right.'

"Well, Emilio happened to notice some pretty big names on that stuff you got, and he passed the word to me. He thought I might be interested. Emilio's a pretty smart guy. I *am* interested."

"Two big names," I prompted.

"That's right. Collinson and Majestic Pictures. Now, reading through this I get part of the picture, and remembering some of what you said last night I get some more. But I don't know, maybe I wasn't listening so good before." He laughed. "But hey! You weren't talking so good then, either, you know?"

"So?"

"So I'd like you to take me through it all again."

And that's what I did. This time I tied what I knew last night to what the printout now proved. Naturally I called attention to Julio's name in the file. That was when Jaime asked me if I knew who this guy Bernie was. I told him I didn't. I didn't tell him I had sort of an idea who Bernie was, though. Anyway, I laid it all out before him. Yet I did a little acting, too. I wanted to seem reluctant. I wanted to create the impression that he was pulling the story out of me. At a couple of crucial points I hesitated and got him to ask more questions. I knew where we were headed, and I liked where we were headed, but I didn't want him to know that.

When at last I finished, Jaime was silent for a long moment. He glanced over at his mother, as if he was looking for confirmation. She gave a nod, the kind of nod you might miss if you weren't looking for it. Then he clapped his hands again.

"Okay," he said, "like I said, partners. You supplied the raw material. Now we supply the *huevos*."

"What does that mean?"

"You don't see it, Mr. Detective? I think we got the stuff here to put the squeeze on Mr. Norman Collinson."

"You mean blackmail?"

He gave an indifferent shrug. "I don't know that word. It's too big for a barrio boy like me. All I know, you got information on somebody he doesn't want to get out, then somebody's gonna pay. That's the way it works. The bigger that somebody is, the more he'll pay."

"I don't like it," I said. That was a lie. I liked it just fine.

"Oh, you don't like it, huh? *Hijo la!* You got no sense at all? This guy paid a quarter mill to get this caper started. He's gonna pay at least that to end it. That's what you want, isn't it?"

"Yeah, but not like this."

"What you gonna do? Go to the cops with what you got? They say, 'This is very interesting, my friend, but how'd you get it?' Then you tell them there was this little matter of a burglary and a couple of bodies your friends left behind. Then they say, 'Fuck this movie stuff. Tell us about your friends who leave dead bodies behind.'" Jaime shook his head slowly but very emphatically. "No, my frien'. Believe me, my way is better."

"Well . . ."

"What's the matter? You think I won' cut you in? Maybe no fifty-fifty, but you get a piece of the action. Say ten percent. It's—what do they call it?—a finder's fee."

"But don't you think—" I began.

But Jaime cut me off with a quick chop of his hand. "*Bastante, maricón!* You got no say in this. *Hijo la!* I try to treat you like *un hombre,* but you got no *huevos.* My mother got more *huevos* than you!"

Señora Fernandez smiled at me coldly. Both Carlos and Emilio were paying attention now.

"Carlos!" Jaime yelled it out like he was in the next room. "Bring me a telephone."

Carlos was on his feet instantly. He went off at a quick march and returned with one of those cordless jobs. He pulled up the aerial and handed it over to Jaime. Then he looked at me, snickered, and gave me the finger.

"*Jesus, Maria y Jose!*" I exploded, grabbing my head

171

with both hands. "You're not going to call Collinson right now?"

"*Callate!* We got his private number here."

His mother called it out to him, numeral by numeral in Spanish, and he dialed it. There was a pause then as he waited for an answer. When it came, he held up a finger, winked, and opened with the most outrageous pitch any blackmailer had ever used.

"Norman Collinson, have I got a deal for you!"

I was still laughing about it after Carlos dropped me off and I was driving home. Jaime let him know right away what he had and what he knew. He didn't want Collinson hanging up on him. But once he had the hook in, he played him just right. No threats, no tough talk. He just sort of kidded him along, telling him he was sure they could work things out, because after all they were both businessmen, weren't they? Then there was a lot of "Of course" and "Naturally" and "I couldn't agree more." This was Jaime's class act, and he was playing it for all he was worth. He ended it with a suggestion—well, it sounded like a suggestion, but it was really an order—that they meet tomorrow morning at nine in the Griffith Park Observatory parking lot. And then he said: "Oh, I'm sure your chauffeur can find it. And just one more thing. Keep this confidential. Don't ask for help from anyone. My people will be there. You won't see them, but they'll be there."

Then Jaime pressed the button on the cordless that ended the conversation. "*Hijo la!*" he crowed, jumping out of his chair, "I'll own the fucking studio before I'm through!"

I doubted it. But I tried to look concerned, shocked and apprehensive during all this. On the way out I even went so far as to tell him I thought he was going too far. Actually, I thought he'd gone just far enough. I couldn't have done it better myself, and in a way I felt I *had* done it myself.

I was feeling proud and confident when I turned into the

building garage. Things were working out. I might really be able to pull this off. I glanced at my watch. It was late, nearly ten. I hoped Pilar had stuck around. I wanted to get both of them out of there, but I wanted Alicia to have the little protection—and the good sense—the older woman might provide. I swerved into my parking space, jumped out, and hurried to the garage elevator.

But I was still riding high as the elevator took me up to the second floor. This was going to work out. I knew it would.

Down the hall then, key in the door, and just as I swung it open, Alicia let out a cry—a warning, I guess. She lay there on the sofa, Pilar bending over her. And there behind them both Bill Wallace stood.

I reached into my jacket for the .38, but I was too late. I saw the automatic in his two hands pointed straight at me. And from the wild look in his eye, I knew he was ready to pull the trigger.

173

15

It turned out he had been there only about five minutes. I had thought that damage control at Intertel would keep him occupied half the night. But no. He must have made a couple of phone calls, not one of them to the cops, and come right over here. He got into the building some way—it really wasn't that hard—and had gotten into the apartment by beating on the door and shouting loudly that I had been hurt in an accident, probably the oldest dodge there is for getting inside anyplace. But it worked. Pilar had thrown open the door, and there stood Bill Wallace, gun in hand, with the same crazy look in his eyes that was there when I stepped inside.

Just guess what he was after.

"You . . . you . . . you . . ." The guy was so excited he could hardly speak. Where was that smooth operator who sat across the desk from me the other night? I noticed sweat on his forehead and his upper lip. He seemed to be having a pretty hard time controlling his breathing. "You . . . have something of mine that—shut that door! Shut it! Shut it!"

I closed it behind me, careful not to bang it. I didn't want to upset him.

"Now that gun you reached for. Take it . . . take it out very slowly with two fingers and put it down over here." He indicated a place on the floor about midway between us.

I did it just the way he told me to do it, bending down very slowly and laying it softly on the carpet. Then I stepped back.

"Back," he said, "farther."

I took one last step back, and my back came in contact with the wall right near the door.

Just then Alicia let out an awful bellow, and I jumped. All that kept me from running over to her was the gun that Wallace waved in my direction.

"Can't you shut her up?" Wallace demanded. "If she keeps on like this, I'll—I'll have to shoot her to put her out of her misery."

"What's the matter?" I called over to Pilar. Alicia seemed at that moment beyond any sort of communication.

"It's her time, *Señor*," said Pilar.

"*Sí*," wailed Alicia, "it's my *time!*" And then she lapsed into a series of low, racking moans.

Wallace advanced carefully, bent down and picked up my old .38 Police Special. Maybe it was then that I noticed that the automatic he was holding so tightly in his right hand was a Walther PPK. Was that how he saw himself—as some kind of James Bond?

He retreated just as slowly and seemed to be getting hold of himself—until Alicia let out another bellow. He whirled suddenly in her direction, and I tensed, ready to leap across the ten feet or so that separated us because it looked for just a split second as if he might shoot to keep her quiet. Then just as suddenly he whirled back toward me. Maybe he sensed that I was ready. Or maybe he was just jumpy. I wanted him to settle down.

"A loose cannon," he said.

"What?" He wasn't making sense.

"You—a loose cannon. Just slamming around the deck, wrecking things, a lot of careful work, all destroyed."

"Well, I—"

"Never mind. Give it to me."

I knew I was taking a chance, but I asked anyway. "Give what to you?"

But he held steady, enunciating very precisely. "Give me the goddamned printout."

"Look," I said, opening my jacket very slowly. "I haven't got it. You want to look for yourself?"

I could tell he was tempted for a moment to do just that. But caution won. "Where is it?"

"I wasn't alone there, you know."

He let out the kind of *ha-ha* that was more a sneer than a laugh. "You think I don't know that? You think I'd suppose for a minute that you could wreak that kind of havoc alone? No, it was you and that—that cleaning crew. And I let you past, didn't I? Well, it won't happen again, I promise you."

This time it was a scream that erupted from Alicia. She dug her heels into the cushions of the couch and arched her back in agony.

Pilar fluttered around her, unable to do much to help except stroke her forehead. But then she stiffened, turned to Wallace and shook her finger at him. "You don' understan'," she shouted. "This woman is going to have a baby. Soon! You better let her go to the hospital."

He looked from me to her and back to me again. "That's up to you, Cervantes. You tell me who's got the printout and where they are, and I'll let these two go."

Pilar made a big show of sniffing the air. I smelled something, too—food cooking. *"Ay de mi,"* she wailed. "The soup! The soup will burn on the stove!" She hustled fearlessly past Wallace before he could stop her. With a gun in each hand, all he could do was shoot, and he wasn't ready for that—yet. She made it to the kitchen.

He yelled at her, "Come back in here."

But Alicia all but drowned him out with two great whoops of pain that ended in a long, gurgling groan.

I took a step toward him, and he retreated just as far, raising both pistols and pointing them straight at me. He couldn't miss.

"Listen," I said. "You let them go. Then I'll tell you."

"And lose my leverage?" Then he half turned toward the kitchen and called out to Pilar, "You come out of there right now!"

She was banging pots and pans around. "Oh, I'm afraid the soup is ruined," she answered mournfully, "all burned." There was the sound of running water then. It continued as she emerged behind him from the kitchen, moving silently onto the carpet, supporting the biggest pot I owned between her two hands with just a dishtowel to protect them. Steam rose from the pot.

I took another step, laterally this time in the direction of the couch—and Alicia. He trailed with me. His back was to the kitchen. And as I moved, I made my speech. "Okay," I said, "I guess I don't have much choice. It's a gang—the Compañeros de la Muerte. That skull they sprayed on the wall is their sign. They've got this bar on Sunset in Silverlake—Esperanza. Uh, Hope."

"I know what it means," he said.

But that was the last intelligible thing he said for a long while. Just as Pilar came up behind him, he turned his head in her direction. He couldn't have heard her. He must have sensed her there.

She pitched the steaming contents of the pot into his face. He screamed. I dove for the floor. The two pistols were still pointed in my direction. They went off just about simultaneously. Two bullets slammed into the wall, one of them where I had stood.

But he never got off another shot because Pilar was suddenly all over him with the empty pot, banging him as hard as she could on the head, in the face, on the shoulders. He dropped my .38, trying to protect himself with both hands.

177

I was up from the floor covering the distance between us n a diving tackle. But somehow somebody got there before me. It was Alicia. She was grabbing at the hand holding the automatic. When I hit Wallace at the knees, all four of us went down in a tumble, with him on the bottom.

He was doing the moaning now. Pilar pulled away and, kneeling, she went right on hitting down at him with the pot. Alicia kept a tight hold on his wrist, fighting the pistol away from him. Now she was biting his hand. He let the PPK drop.

And I? What did I do? I was sitting on his back. I had his left arm behind, holding it at the wrist, then I pulled in the right. I could have cuffed him then and there—but no handcuffs. Also no need. He was inert, completely unconscious, or maybe even dead.

Pilar knelt over him, panting, the pot raised high above her head, ready to bring it down on him again if he should show any sign of movement.

"That's enough, Pilar," I said. "Go in the kitchen and see if you can find something to tie him up with. I think there's some rope under the sink."

She nodded and pushed herself heavily up to her feet and, still breathing heavily, made her way back to the kitchen without a word.

I looked at Alicia. She was grinning triumphantly. She started to laugh. "Ui did itt, Chico!" she said. In Berlitz English, no less.

"Yeah," I said, "we did it. Or maybe it was mostly Pilar."

"Ies, shi uoes uoenderful!"

"Wait a minute. Weren't you in the throes of childbirth or something?"

In Spanish: "Oh, I just did that to fool him, *como se dice,* distract."

"Well, you fooled me, too."

Pilar returned with a handful of rope, good, strong stuff I used a couple of years before when I moved into the apartment. I took it and began untangling. Then I happened to look up and noticed the awful look on Pilar's face as she stood staring at Wallace's body.

"What's the matter?" I asked.

"Is he dead?"

"No, I don't think so." I bent down and took his pulse at his neck. It wasn't strong, but it was slow and steady.

"Will he die?"

As I started to say no, Alicia cut me off with a sharp *"Naturalmente!"*

Did she mean what I thought she meant?

Yes.

She handed Wallace's PPK to me. "Here, Chico," she said, "You shoot him with his own gun. It's better that way."

I took it and looked from her to Pilar. The expression on her face was not exactly alarm but a look of, well, call it consternation. It was like she was saying, "I hope this terrible thing won't be necessary." But she didn't say it. She just looked.

I jammed the automatic into the pocket of my jacket and began tying Wallace's wrists. Not a word.

Alicia gave me a punch on the shoulder. *"Hombre,* don't tie him up. It's not necessary. Shoot him! Do it in the back of the head, the way they do. That way it's sure."

Do it in the back of the head? Where had she heard about that? Or had she seen it done down in Culiacán?

"You don't want the noise? I'll get a towel from the bathroom. We wrap the towel around the gun and nobody hears nothing."

I finished with his wrists, satisfied he couldn't work loose, even if he was conscious. Then I turned to Pilar. "Get me a knife," I said.

She hesitated a moment, then went off again to the kitchen.

Alicia gave me a pat where she'd punched me. "Ah, Chico, you're smart. A knife is much more quiet. No noise at all, and then it's done." She drew her finger across her throat.

I stared at her for a long moment, then shook my head. Pilar came back with a long saw-toothed knife. I cut the rope. I had just about enough left to wrap his ankles a couple of times and tie them.

Alicia struggled up to her feet and stalked away. Angry, disgusted, and making a show of it. She plopped down heavily on the sofa, let out an *"Ay, de mi!"* and then glowered at me.

I finished with Wallace's ankles and turned him over. Pilar caught her breath and clamped a hand over her mouth. I could understand her reaction. He was a mess. His gray hair was matted with blood from Pilar's blows. There was blood on his forehead, too. It looked like his nose was broken. But worst of all were the burns from the soup she had thrown in his face. She had caught him across the right cheek with most of it. It was swollen and raw. His right eye was swollen, too. You wouldn't recognize him as the same man. I almost felt sorry for him.

Alicia came over and took a look. "He would have killed us," she said. "You know that. All three of us, as soon as he got what he wanted. Isn't that true, Pilar?"

"I believe so, yes."

Alicia bent down and spoke quietly and slowly, the way you'd talk to a child. "Don't you understand, Chico? You kill him, and it's done. You let him live, and you got an enemy for life."

All I said was, "I'm going to need a blanket to wrap him in."

He was heavy. Lean and above my height, he couldn't have weighed as much as I do, but he was dead weight on my shoulder. I staggered with him up the stairs of the loading dock behind Intertel's building on Wilshire. When I reached the service door I went down on my knees and

180

eased him onto the cement, taking particular care with his head. Then, taking the same sort of caution, I eased the blanket out from under him. I stood and looked down at him. On the drive over, he had let out a couple of moans and once shifted in the backseat. He was still breathing. I knew that. But looking at him there in the dim moonlight, he seemed more dead than alive. I didn't want him dead. He had a message to deliver.

I listened at the door. Nothing. But I gave it three solid bangs, rang the bell long and hard, and then ran back down the stairs to my car. Without waiting to see if anybody opened up, I started the Alfa and was out of there within seconds.

I felt bad about leaving like that. Somebody was sure to find him—a guard or somebody—but how long would it take? I had to make sure they got him. With a sigh, I turned onto Wilshire and began looking for a pay telephone.

There was one at a Mobil station near the San Vicente turnoff. I pulled in and parked close to it, then went through Wallace's wallet and pulled out one of his business cards. I went over to the phone and dialed the Intertel number on the card. I waited. There had to be somebody there. Finally, on the fourth ring, there was an answer.

"Yes, hello. Who is it?" Out of breath, abrupt, but he didn't sound like one of Wallace's muscle brigade. Maybe this guy was in the management training program.

I decided to go fishing. "Who is it?" I blustered, "just who do you think it is?" It worked.

"Mr. Collinson? Look, I'm sure you want to talk to Mr. Wallace, but he's not back yet. We expect him just any time, but I'm sure he'll tell you what he told you before."

"Tell me again."

"Make the meeting. String them along. Tell them you couldn't get . . ." He stopped, aware at last of how he'd been babbling away. "Wait a minute. Just who is this?"

"Not Collinson," I said. "Just the delivery man. There's

181

a package out on the loading dock for Intertel. A package of meat. Better get it before it turns rotten." And then I hung up.

Well, he'd flunked the course, but he gave me a little information I didn't have before. Or maybe just confirmation of what I might have expected anyway. As soon as Collinson got the call from Jaime, he got on the horn to Wallace screaming bloody murder that he was being blackmailed—and it was all Wallace's fault! And I also knew what Wallace had advised him—probably told him he'd have it all under control in twenty-four hours or something like that.

Twenty-four hours. Maybe it really would be all over by then. God, how I hoped it would!

As I settled in for the long drive to Cousin Pancho's place in Silverlake, I began thinking about that whole scene back there at my apartment. Alicia really wanted me to kill the guy, didn't she? And Pilar would have gone along with it, too. Jesus, I still had a lot to learn about women. They'll do what has to be done. They're tougher than we are, the good ones are. Anyway, I knew for sure that for all of Alicia's histrionics and childishness, there was something deep in her that was cold and hard, something I didn't have and didn't want.

Was this some kind of middle-class squeamishness of mine? Or was it the fact of the "hyphen": Mexican-American, instead of just plain Mexican? I wasn't sure about that, but I was certain about a number of other things.

I had a reason for keeping Wallace alive—but that, finally, didn't matter. I couldn't have killed him as he lay there on the floor—either with his pistol, or his pistol wrapped in a towel, or with a knife. I couldn't do it. That's one thing I was sure about.

I was also sure that everything Alicia had said was true. Certainly Wallace would have killed all three of us—me because I'd seen what was in that printout and because I'd messed things up for him. And because the two women were around to see him do it, he would have killed them, too.

She was right, too, about having an enemy for life. It was that kind of cold logic Alicia was capable of. Well, I'd just have to deal with Bill Wallace in my own way. For the time being, I just hoped he hadn't gone into a coma or something.

When I had called Pancho up and told him we were in trouble, he told us to come right over. I didn't even have to ask. I had sent Alicia on ahead with Pilar. She packed a few things. I made sure she took the pills the doctor had given her. And I had them out of there in five minutes. Then I struggled getting Wallace down to the garage. I always kept a change of clothes and a pair of running shoes in a gym bag with the car tools, so I was set for a while at least. I had the PPK and my .38, and some extra rounds for mine. And I had emptied Wallace's pockets and had the contents on the front seat beside me. I'd give them a closer inspection when I had the time.

Pancho lives on a winding uphill street just off Silverlake Boulevard. It's a nice block, and he's got the nicest house on the block—a big Spanish colonial with a tile roof in good shape and a six-and-a-half-foot wall running all around. He likes the old neighborhood. That's why he stayed there. But Pancho, being a realist, has a very pretty wrought-iron gate that would take a good charge of C-4 to open without a key, another gate on the front door and another on the back, and iron bars on all the windows. If you looked closely, even in the moonlight, you could see shards of broken glass evenly embedded along the top of the wall. I looked. I felt reassured. We would be safer here than anyplace I knew.

I rang the bell. The intercom above it crackled. "It's me. Chico."

I heard the front door open, then the barred gate attached to it swung out, and a moment later Pancho appeared at the wall gate. He was in his robe and slippers.

His right hand was in the pocket of his robe, which seemed to contain something heavy. But when he saw it was really me and not some imposter, he smiled broadly, undid the lock with both hands, and threw open the gate.

He grabbed me with both arms in an *abrazo.* "Ay, Chico, *primo,* you're in trouble, uh? You come to the family. Well, that's the way it should be. Come, come."

He banged the gate shut and threw the lock, then led the way inside the house, pausing twice more to secure his fortress.

"I'm really grateful to you, Pancho," I said. "Things were just a little too hot to stay where we were."

"I know! I know! Pilar told me all about it." He led me into the living room and pointed to a big, soft easy chair.

"Yeah," I said, collapsing into the chair, "I'm really sorry she got involved. I remember I promised you there wouldn't be any . . . danger to her."

"You make a joke, uh? Listen, Chico, you should hear her tell it. She had the time of her life. She'll be telling her friends about it for years to come. Did she really do all she said? The soup in the face? Beating him up with the pot?"

"Absolutely."

"Que cosa! Asombroso!" He shook his head and chuckled, like he was particularly proud of her. Then he glanced over at me. "You want something to drink? Some Cuervo Gold maybe?"

I sighed. "No. I'm going to bed if it's okay with you. I'm exhausted."

"Sure, Chico, sure. Your girl's up there now. First door at the top of the stairs. Christina's old room."

"How is Christina?"

"Oh, good, good. Two babies already. Her husband's a nice guy but you know how it is, they're living way out in Simi Valley, so we don't see them as much as we'd like to."

"I guess that's the way it always is."

He shrugged and nodded. "It's true. They got their own lives now." Then Pancho looked at me slyly. "Hey, *hombre,* when you gonna marry that girl upstairs?"

"She hasn't asked me yet." It sounded funny to say it, but that's how it was. The subject hadn't come up.

"Well, you two better hurry up if you want to beat that baby."

I nodded. "About a week."

"That's a good-looking woman, Chico."

"Yeah, well . . ."

"You're not talking, uh? She didn't have much to say either."

"She didn't?" That was a first.

"No, she said she was tired and went right to bed."

"I'm not surprised. She was down on the floor wrestling with the guy, too. She got the gun away from him. Bit his hand."

He laughed. "These women. They surprise you, uh?"

"It's true. They surprise you." I hauled myself out of the easy chair. "I'm going to bed. But I'll need an alarm clock. I have to go someplace, seven o'clock at the latest."

"It's okay. I'm up at six. I'll knock on the door. Go to bed."

"Thanks, Pancho." I gave him a wave and headed up the stairs. There was no light under the door and the only sounds were those Pancho made, making the rounds, switching off the lights. I entered the bedroom as quietly as I could and undressed in the dark. I could hear Alicia breathing lightly as I slipped into the bed beside her.

She sat up. She'd been playing possum. "Who's this coming into my bed?" she asked dramatically. "*Dios mio!* It's a saint! *San Antonio el Bueno!* I know I have nothing to fear from a saint—and *neither does anyone else.*"

I looked at her. I couldn't see her, really, just her shape beside me. "*Mira,*" I said, "I'll make a deal with you. If you don't tell me how to run my business, I won't tell you how to have your baby."

She hovered there for a long moment without a word. Then she threw herself down on her pillow and shifted heavily so that her back was to me.

I pulled up the covers and turned away from her. Already I was sorry I'd said it.

W hen they built the observatory in Griffith Park, Los
Angeles was a lot different. There wasn't much but
farms and a few oil wells out beyond Hollywood. But anticipating growth, the county fathers had set aside a huge tract
of land for a park on either side of the thickly wooded hills
above Hollywood and Burbank. Then they decided to build
the observatory. Since the air was so clear and the view
from the hills so open, it would have been a terrific place to
scan the dark night skies and contemplate the mysteries of
the universe. So they put it up there on a hill—not the
highest hill, because they wanted it to be easy to get to, but
a hill. Now, many decades and many millions of tons of
smog later, you can't see the night sky so well, not even
with the big telescope they've got there in the observatory.
And if that wasn't enough, all those lights down in the
basin that made Los Angeles so beautiful at night keep it at
a kind of dim dusk all night long, the light curtaining off
the deep dark beyond. I guess you could say that astron-
omy is definitely not a growth industry in Los Angeles.

What this meant was that there were seldom a lot of people up there at the observatory and almost none on a weekday at nine o'clock. Jaime had chosen well. The parking lot was a good place for a meet. A little while later the tourists would come for the view. And after that the school buses would arrive with loads of kids there for the lectures they give at the observatory.

Now it was about eight-thirty, and here I was waiting for the arrival of the opposing teams, just hoping the game would start on time. I'd been there for about an hour. Driving into the parking lot, I saw that the only cars parked there were in spaces reserved for the observatory staff. The spaces were not only reserved but roped off with cable and padlock. Well, I had a bolt cutter to take care of that, and nobody was around to see me do it. I pulled the Alfa in between a Nissan and a Buick and hoped it wouldn't stand out. Then I dug out my Zeiss binoculars and my camera bag from the trunk and began looking around for a good point to watch from. There wasn't much in the way of high ground. The only spot elevated above the parking lot was the observatory and the two stairways leading up on either side. But they were completely exposed. But at the far end of the lot there was a wooded area that would hide me pretty well and give me a good view as long as the parking lot stayed empty. That's where I settled in.

It was cold. The sun was up, and the predicted high was in the low eighties, but that didn't help how I felt then, stretched out on the ground behind a tree, taking a test scan with the binoculars. The way I was dressed didn't help much. I buttoned the top button of my shirt, pulled the collar up and zipped up the windbreaker. That was all I could do. I got the Nikon ready with the longest lens I had, and then I waited.

Too much of my time was spent just this way. Waiting. You called it stakeout, and most people thought you were either playing peeping tom, or anticipating the commission of a crime so you could rush in and nab the perpetrator.

No. What you were doing mostly was just waiting for something to happen so you could see it happen, or better yet, take a picture of it happening.

Just to pass the time I pulled out Wallace's wallet and began going through it methodically. He had the usual credit cards, quite an assortment, and the usual official ID. His California DMV driver's license told me where he lived—not too far from me and even closer to Jaime—up above Sunset in that part of West Hollywood that was almost Beverly Hills. He'd be as easy to watch as I was, if it should come to that. And then the business cards—his own, of course, and a variety of others. Some of them, I assumed, were clients, or had been clients. But Norman Collinson's Majestic Pictures card was notably absent. There was a surprise in that collection of cards, though. I turned over one for Joseph Jarasek, Business Writer, *Los Angeles Tribune*. My boy Joe—sometime drinking companion, willing supplier of information, friend to those who needed a friend. Interesting. Naturally I wondered what business the two of them had together, and I decided to check it out, adding Joe Jarasek to what was shaping up to be a pretty full schedule.

Jaime's limo rolled in about eight-forty. Carlos and another guy, not Emilio, got out of the front yard and eyeballed the situation in a casual way. Then, with a little encouragement from inside the limo, the two walked the perimeter of the lot, checking around corners, in the public lavatories, and inside the few cars parked in the observatory staff spaces, including mine. Carlos might have thought the Alfa looked familiar, but it was the other guy who checked it out. Carlos came up my way. When I saw him coming, I retreated a little deeper into the woods on my belly and found a good-sized bush to hide behind. He walked right on by and then circled back to the limo.

Then, and only then, did Jaime emerge. He looked around, satisfied, then placed his two Compañeros where he wanted them—Carlos at the door to the men's room,

188

within pistol range, and the other up on the side of the observatory stairs to serve as lookout. All this took about ten minutes, but it gave Jaime the opportunity to strike a casual pose as he waited for Collinson's arrival.

I was back in place behind the tree when, about five minutes later, the lookout man gave a wave and a Cadillac limo even longer than Jaime's Lincoln pushed up the hill and into the parking lot. It pulled up not exactly next to it but close. Jaime beckoned Collinson out. During a pause of nearly half a minute I saw the man on the stairs come down and take a position near the Cadillac, out in the open. He opened his jacket and put his hand on the handle of a big automatic he had slung in a shoulder holster.

Jaime beckoned again. At last the rear door of the Cadillac swung open. I'd been watching all this through the binoculars, but the moment Collinson emerged, I picked up the Nikon and started shooting. I wanted the two of them together in the same frame, and that didn't prove hard at all.

Jaime advanced upon him, a smile fixed on his face. He even offered his hand. And Collinson, looking slightly bewildered and not knowing what else to do, shook it. This was the first look I'd had at him. He was younger than I had expected, about forty, six feet tall, tanned, and even in his business suit and tie, he was athletic looking—one of those baby moguls I used to read so much about. His face was interesting—not because it was strong or had a lot of character, but because of the contradiction in it at this moment. You could see the petulance of the spoiled child there, and the downward turn of the mouth that said he was used to voicing automatic disapproval. But this same face was now struggling with itself to appear pleasant, in control, and tough all at the same time. It wasn't working.

Jaime started talking, and Collinson was nodding, looking cooperative. I got a picture, but this wasn't what I wanted. Then Collinson began talking. Naturally I was too far away to hear, and I'd never learned to read lips, but I could tell what was being said. With an earnest look on his face and using those same forthright gestures Richard Nixon used to, he was explaining to Jaime that he couldn't possibly raise that kind of cash on such short notice. He had to have time. I got all this on film.

In response, Jaime stepped back—out of the frame, dammit!—and simply looked at Collinson for a long moment. Then that knife of his was suddenly in his hand. He moved fast, but I found out where he kept it—up his left sleeve, probably in some kind of spring scabbard on his forearm. But he just stood there with it, staring blankly at Collinson. It made a good picture—but move in, Jaime, move in! Glancing up from the camera, I saw that the guy who had been posted on the observatory stairs had edged closer to the Cadillac, just so the chauffeur wouldn't get any brave ideas about protecting his boss.

Back to Jaime. Look at him! He was cleaning his nails! The weighted throwing knife in his hand had become a nail file, and he was using it to dig along the cuticle of his fingers with the sharp point. That looked dangerous to me. You could lose a joint off your finger that way. He was talking, too, very calmly, but the smile was gone from his face.

Then in two quick steps, he practically leaped across the space between them—he was nose to nose with Collinson. My God, I could even hear him, sounds not words. He was yelling into his face, tapping him hard on the chest with the knife, maybe digging little holes in his suit. Great, Jaime! Great! Keep it up! This was just the stuff I was hoping for. I clicked away without much regard for how many frames I was shooting, then I checked the count and eased off. I was glad I did because the next thing I knew Jaime had the knife up to Collinson's face, next to his cheek. Click! Then he jerked out Collinson's tie, held it taut, and cut it off at the middle with one quick sweep of his knife. Click! Click! Click! I got it all on film, including the look of consternation on Collinson's face as he watched the big piece

190

of the tie flutter down to the ground. And all the time Jaime kept right on talking—no more yelling; his lips barely moved. Speak softly and carry a sharp knife.

Then, just as suddenly as the attack had begun, it ended. Jaime took a step back, turned stiffly and walked back to his car. He got inside and slammed the door. Carlos and the lookout ran over and jumped into the front seat of the long limo. And then they were gone, leaving Norman Collinson staring after them, looking like he was about to cry. I got a picture of that, too.

Once the Cadillac had left, I waited a minute or two, taking the time to pop out the roll of film and pocket it, and then pack away the camera and the lens. Still I waited, listening, and satisfied that nobody had decided to return, I made for my car and got out of there fast.

Calling from the photo lab on Highland, I got hold of Joe Jarasek at the *Trib* and asked kind of bluntly just what he had to do with Bill Wallace.

There was a long silence at the other end of the line. Finally: "Where did you hear about that?"

"Never mind that now. I need to know."

He lowered his voice. "It's kind of secret," he said.

"You can't talk about it?"

"I can't talk about it *here*."

He said he'd meet me in half an hour at Vickman's, the old cafeteria downtown on Eighth Street. It was right around the corner from the Tribune building, and at mid morning it was a good place to talk.

Then I put in a call to Billy Jay, my old buddy at Rampart narco division, and told him—that's right, *told* him—to meet me for lunch. When he started to give me an argument, telling me how busy he was, I said it was police business and in his own best interest to see me. He shut up then and agreed to go just as far away from the station as I could get him.

As I hung up and turned to go, the counter man called after me, "Hey, are you sure about this?"

"Sure about what?"

"This order. I mean, you want *three* eight-by-ten glossies of *everything* on the roll?"

"That's what I said."

"You don't want to see a contact sheet? The way you shoot, Chico, some of that stuff won't be worth printing."

"Hey, come on," I said indignantly, "I hit on about one out of three. That's a pretty good average."

"In baseball maybe. Look, it's going to take time to do all this."

"Mid afternoon, like I said."

"And it's going to cost you."

"I can handle it."

He shrugged. "Okay."

Here's my take on Joe Jarasek. He's a good reporter, the best they've got on the business section of the *Trib*—and a pretty good writer, also the best on that section. But like every other journalist of his age (over forty) and qualifications, he's looking to get out. He talks about it a lot. After he's had a couple of good belts, he'll start in on how newspapering is a young man's game, and how he's got this theory that a reporter only has so many deadlines in him. What happens then? I would ask him. "Well," Joe would say, "one of three things. Either he keels over at his terminal, or they put him on the rim, or he goes into public relations." Since those three options were obviously unattractive to him, I wasn't surprised to learn that morning at Vickman's that he had a secret fourth; he was working on a book. That's what he called it: *The* book.

He had only done a little writing on it and was researching as he went, but the way he saw it, he had hold of something that would sell. The book was his ticket out of the *Trib*.

All this had taken about half a cup of coffee to tell. That was okay with me. I didn't have to be anyplace until I met Billy Jay for lunch. But when Joe came to a sort of full stop at that point, I got a little impatient.

"So?" I prompted. "What's it about? What's the subject?"

He looked around him like somebody might be listening. The only soul in sight was a *mamacita* sitting three tables away. He leaned forward anyway and dropped his voice to a whisper. "It's about the business intelligence community," he said.

All I did was nod.

"Well," he started, "ever since Pinkerton's in the eighteen hundreds the big agencies have been spying on labor for business, right? You know about the Molly McGuires and all that? Okay. But in the last decade or so business intelligence has gotten to be *very* big. A lot of new players in the game, a very sophisticated high-tech operation, massive files on computers and all that."

"Yeah," I said, "I'm . . . aware of that."

"Okay. But with some of them today it goes beyond gathering intelligence in the usual ways. I mean, there's a lot of industrial spying going on, and even though you don't hear much about it, some industrial sabotage, too. That's with a few agencies, not all. But with a couple, maybe two or even just one, it goes way beyond that—dirty tricks and even what they like to call wet work."

"And this is where Intertel comes in?"

"Exactly. I'd heard rumors for a while, and they centered on this guy Wallace—Bill Wallace. So I called him up and asked for an interview, told him it was for a book I was working on, everything on the up and up. He gave me plenty of time, well over an hour, and it was pretty interesting in a weird sort of way. Mostly I just let him talk. I've got him on tape if you want to hear it. But he began by giving me this big pitch on Intertel—worldwide network, offices in foreign capitals and so on, which is mostly bullshit, I found out. Anyway, I'm not dumb enough to confront him with some of the rumors I've heard—some of them are pretty hairy—but I asked him very innocently, 'Just what is Intertel equipped to do?' And he gets this funny look on his face and says, 'Anything.'"

"Anything? He said that?"

"Anything. I asked him what that meant, and he got kind of cagey. I began throwing hypothetical situations at him, and he kind of laughed them off and said he certainly wasn't going to cite case histories because that stuff was confidential. Actually, I think he said, 'top secret.'"

"But then came the weird part. He starts telling me about himself, how he was in Vietnam and all. He had to have been in the Green Berets or the CIA. He was kind of unspecific about that. But anyway, he begins telling me war stories, 'deep country operations,' and so on. Piles of Vietcong heads up to here. That stuff. Frankly, I wasn't too entertained because I was a big peace marcher back then. But I was fascinated because I realized that what he was telling me was, 'I'm not going to tell you what we do, or don't do, but I just want you to know who you're dealing with, kid. There's nothing I haven't done, or can't do.' That was the message."

Again, I just nodded—shocked but not surprised. Maybe Wallace's conceit had led him to run off at the mouth. Or maybe he figured that in a perverse way this was good public relations—and maybe he was right.

Joe seemed kind of disappointed at my reaction or lack of it, because he came back at me kind of aggressively. "Okay. Now. You tell me how you plug into all this. What do you know about Wallace?"

"I can't tell you now."

"Oh, shit." He shook his head in disgust. "I give you my best stuff, practically bare my soul to you, and you can't tell me now."

"Listen," I said, "that doesn't mean I won't tell you. That means I can't tell you *now*. I will just as soon as I can."

He slouched back in his chair, took a swig of cold coffee, and drummed on the table with his fingers for a moment. Then I asked him, "What do you know about Norman Collinson?"

"You're a real vampire, aren't you?" Then the light went on: "You mean Collinson's involved with Wallace?"

"I can't—"

"I know, I know," he interrupted. "You can't tell me now, but you sure as hell better tell me later." He hesitated, collecting data. "Well, all right. Norman Collinson, president of Majestic Pictures. He's had the job for five years now. Which these days in that industry is practically unheard of. He's a real iron ass for work, the way all those guys are, and he's got a reputation for being a pretty mean bastard." He paused. "Are you sure you want to hear this? It's really pretty boring, an unbroken string of successes, except . . ."

"Except what?"

"Except he broke into the business with old man Toller—Heinrich Toller. You know about that?"

I tried to play it cool. "Uh, no. Tell me."

"Well, this was about a dozen years ago or more, when Toller was really on top. Collinson ran his West Coast operation, and the two of them were turning out one big prestige hit after another. And then suddenly he got fired by Toller. Nobody knew why. Nobody ever found out. Collinson was out of work for about a year, then finally he got in at Majestic as a lower-echelon production executive. Essentially, he had to start all over again from the bottom."

"Well," I said, "that's interesting, isn't it?"

Joe gave me a look that was about equal parts annoyance, frustration, and restrained affection. "You really aren't going to tell me a fucking thing, are you?"

I thought about that a moment. "Maybe just one thing."

"What's that?"

"You know all those wild rumors you heard about Intertel?"

"Yeah?"

"They're all true."

The Columbia Grill is there in Hollywood at the corner of Sunset and Gower. It's not exactly a landmark, but it's named after a landmark that isn't there anymore. Columbia Pictures used to be right down Gower a block or two before it moved out to Burbank to share studio space with Warner Brothers. Then, about fifteen years later, this posh restaurant opened up and what did they call it? Naturally— the Columbia Grill. Hollywood is like that. They're always erecting memorials or naming streets (and restaurants) at least a decade after the fact.

I picked this place out for lunch with Billy Jay for two reasons. First of all, I wanted it to be someplace where we weren't likely to run into any other cops. And chances were just about zero here. Second, well, I'll admit it, I wanted to dazzle him just a little.

He was impressed, all right. When the maitre d' ushered him over to the table, I saw he'd even buttoned the top button of his shirt and pulled his tie up for the occasion.

He sat down and looked around. "I suppose you tellin' me you eat here all the time."

"All the time."

His gaze had fastened upon a face from television at a nearby table. She was another one of those Barbie Dolls, but she played the mother on a sitcom that had run a couple of seasons. It was shot right down the street.

"Then you must be pretty well acquainted," he said. "Why don't you take me over and introduce me to that good-lookin' lady over there?"

I made a big show of turning around to take a look. "She must be new here. I don't know her yet."

He laughed his big laugh at that. "My, my, my, you sure have come up in the world. But Chico, you the same old bullshitter I know and love."

196

The waiter made a quick stop at our table and took our order for drinks. Billy Jay didn't hesitate—double Chivas on the rocks with a twist of lemon. I made it two.

He kept on looking around the place really shamelessly. Not gawking but just taking it in, amused, enjoying himself. He made a few choice comments, too—calling into question the masculinity of our waiter, noting the absence of steak on the menu, and giving me his wisdom on all the table hopping going on around us ("dogs smellin' each others asses"). It was like the ruler of some distant country had been dropped in this foreign land and was engaged in a little amateur anthropology, just studying the social environment.

But when our drinks came and we ordered lunch, he dropped all that and suddenly got serious. "Now just what is so goddamn all-fire important you had to pull me way up here when I told you I was busy?"

I told Billy Jay that I thought he had a leak in his operation. He wanted to know who, and I told him Ray Jorgensen. There was no reaction. He was good at that. He just looked at me, took a solid gulp of his scotch, and looked at me again. That second look meant, "Put up or shut up."

So I told him what happened to me the night after I saw him at Rampart. I had seen Jorgensen at the Dos Mundos in the company of the Compañeros just before I got taken out. Then I described the mock hanging in the basement and how, right after that, Jorgensen showed up to rescue me. "A little too neat," was how I put it.

"That ain't much," said Billy Jay. "I'd say you got reason to be grateful to Ray. Might've happened just like he said."

"It might've," I admitted. "But why did they keep that hood on me all the time I was in there?"

"Maybe just didn't want to look at your ugly face."

"Come on, Billy Jay. There was somebody there they didn't want me to see. I thought at first that was Jaime's mother, but they let me see her later on."

"Tell me about that."

"Later." Maybe never. "I think they had Jorgensen there to tell them if the story I told them matched with the little bit I told you. Or maybe just because he's in that tight with them. And another thing . . ."

"Yeah?"

"Did he tell you any of this? About seeing me at the Dos Mundos? About letting me loose?"

"No." The great stone face had spoken.

"You say he makes a lot of arrests. Has he ever pulled in any of the Compañeros?"

"No, that's his long-term deal. That's why he was up there every night talking to that guy Julio. Said he thought he could turn him, get a man on the inside."

I sat back and studied Billy Jay. He was just sitting there like a black Buddha. "Well," I said at last, "what do you think?"

"I think what you just told me is enough for me to keep an eye on him. That's all."

"Okay, listen. I want Jorgensen to deliver a message to the Compañeros for me. I think he will. Only they can't know it's from me. Just drop it as information in front of him. If they get the message, then we'll know about it and where it came from. If they don't, then we'll know Jorgensen didn't deliver it, and I'll shut up about him."

"What's the message?"

"There's going to be a big shoot-'em-up, a raid, tonight at Esperanza, the Compañeros place."

"Who's doing this raid? Colombians?"

"I don't know exactly." Well, that wasn't really a lie. I didn't know their names. "But they'll be pros, and they'll probably have automatic weapons."

"Now, how does this tie in with Jorgensen?"

"Okay. The Compañeros are going to get hit whether you pass the word on to Jorgensen or not, so what's the difference? Well, the difference is that if he delivers the message, instead of the three or four Compañeros who might be hanging around the place, you'll have the whole gang there. When the shooting is over, you can rush in and get them all, whoever's left."

Billy Jay gave me a long, funny look. "Uh-huh. Uh-huh. Yeah. But tell me something, Chico. Why is it I get this funny feeling when I hear you say, '*you* rush in?' Something tells me you trying to get us to do your work for you. Could that be?"

What could I say? "Sure! Right! Of course I am! You don't think I'm giving you this out of the goodness of my heart, do you? Listen, Billy Jay, this is going to happen, and it's going to happen tonight. I guarantee it. If you want to take advantage of it, okay. If not, then we're both out of luck." I hesitated. Then I said, "Only one thing."

"Yeah, okay, let's hear it."

"Jorgensen can't know the tip came from me. Tell him it came down from intelligence or maybe from a Sergeant Gulbransen in homicide over in the valley. He's got a piece of this case."

"I had dealings with him once. Maybe I better talk to him about it."

I sighed. "Go ahead."

Just about then the waiter came back with a plate in each hand, and not a moment too soon.

Well, I'd guaranteed it, hadn't it? My credibility was on the line—not to mention an old friendship. I wouldn't be able to show my face again at Rampart or any other cop house in town unless Esperanza got hit that night. And now I had to see that it happened.

That was why I had come here, to the combination office, garage and clubhouse of Angel Flight: the Macho Messenger Service. These guys weren't kidding. This wasn't the kind of macho they sold in the butch gay bars on Santa Monica Boulevard. The Angel Flight riders all were or had been Hell's Angels. Or wait a minute. I take that "had been" back. Beefy told me once that the Angels were like the Mafia. "Once you're in," he said, "you're in for life. Unless you get kicked out, then you better get your ass out of town fast."

I remembered that as I made my way across the greasy, gritty, oil-soaked concrete that led to the little shack that served as an office. Over to the right of it was the open garage. There were three bikes and a pickup truck parked off to one side, and inside it a BMW in pieces on the floor. It was the first time I'd ever been here, though I'd heard about it often enough from Beefy. We used to drink together a lot at Barney's Beanery before the place got kind of yuppie and he quit coming. He told good stories, had an interesting view of the world, and no matter what you'd heard about the Hell's Angels, he was a pretty good guy.

When I got to the door of the shack I was half inclined to knock, but in crudely painted red letters above the door it said OFFICE, so I walked right in. There were four of them sitting around a folding card table in the corner. They were playing gin rummy. Three of them looked up as I closed the door behind me. The fourth, the one with his back to me, turned around and gave me a cold, hard stare.

"Yeah?" He didn't sound glad to see me.

"Got a delivery I want made."

"Why the fuck didn't you call? We do pickups, you know."

"Yeah, well, I was in the neighborhood."

He continued to stare at me. He had greasy black wavy hair and a Vandyke beard. I saw some pictures of Freewheelin' Frank once. This guy looked like him, probably by intention. He sighed a disgusted, "shit," laid his cards down on the table, and stood up.

"This is for Beefy," I said, holding up the thick envelope in my hand. "I want him to deliver it."

"He's on a run now. We got other riders here."

"No," I said, "it's got to be Beefy."

"You queer for him or something?" He waited for me to

200

respond. I didn't. "All right, fuck, I don't care." He sat back down at the table.

"I'll wait outside," I said.

"You bet your ass you will."

It didn't take long. I spent about ten minutes running through a checklist of things I had to take care of in preparation for tonight. Details, it was all details. Then I heard a deep chug-chug-chug, turned around, and there was Beefy coming through the gate in the chain-link fence on his big Harley. You could hardly tell one from the other. They were both about the same size.

When he spotted me, he steered over and came to a halt close by. He gave me a big grin and stuck out his hand. We did an elaborate handshake that he had drilled me on once at Barney's. And as he took me through it, he crooned out in singsong, "Hey, Chico! Rico Chico! The man who buys me drinks. How you doin'?"

"Doing fine, Beefy. But I can use some help."

"Then I'm your man. Whatcha got in mind?"

"I need something delivered. But it's got to be you who does it."

He giggled. He had a silly laugh for a guy his size. "You tell them that inside? I'll bet that went over big. Why me?"

"Number one, I know you, and I don't know those other guys. Number two, it's gotta be somebody big enough to hold onto this package until you can put it right into the hands of the man it's addressed to—Bill Wallace of Intertel on Wilshire."

"Don't worry. I ain't gonna let no one-hundred-pound receptionist get the better of me. I'm tough. Yeah, but how'm I gonna know it's him? Should I say I hafta see his driver's license?"

"No. I have that."

"Why, you sneaky little bean eater. You into pickpocketing now?"

"Not me. He just left his wallet lying around, and I picked it up."

Beefy giggled and snorted and giggled again.

"The thing is," I continued, "this guy, Wallace, he probably won't be at that office. He'll either be at home, which is at this location"—I slipped him a card on which I'd written Wallace's address—"or, well, he might even be in the hospital."

"Hoooo!" he howled. "You put him there?"

"I had some help."

"Okay. I guess he won't be so hard to pick out from the crowd."

"He'll have bandages on his face and head."

Beefy nodded. "Anybody says he's Wallace, and he's not dressed like that, I don't give it to him."

"Right. No matter how nice he asks."

Beefy walked back over to his bike and pulled a clipboard out of the saddlebag on the near side. "Gotta make this legal," he said. He pulled a ballpoint pen out of his cap and started making out the order form.

"Put me down as John Doe," I said.

"Not even Juan Doe?"

"Nope. You never saw me."

"What if they ask where I picked it up? Some of these receptionists can get pretty mean, y'know. Do I just tough it out?"

A sudden inspiration. "No. If anybody asks, and they probably will, tell them you got this package at the Majestic Pictures gate."

He kind of smiled and nodded, then handed the clipboard over to me. I signed the form "John Doe" and handed it back to him with a hundred dollar bill I'd picked up for the occasion. "That should cover it," I said.

"And then some." He gave me the yellow copy underneath the top.

"Keep the change. Buy yourself a beer." It was Toller's money, so I might as well spread it around. "But I'll want to talk to you about it afterward," I added. "I'll call around six." I handed him the package, a full set of glossies from the roll I'd taken that morning in Griffith Park.

*   *   *

The light was fading to dusk as I pulled up in front of the Toller mansion. No trouble at the gate. My name had been left there—probably by Urbanski—and the guard let me right in. That was a switch.

So here I was, and I had what I figured to be a difficult job ahead of me. It was up to me to convince Ursula to leave this place and come along to Pancho's house—humbler surroundings, but the way I figured it, a lot safer. There was just a possibility that if Wallace had enough men he might divide his force and try to pull off here what had been bungled in Bavaria. If he could do that and take out Collinson's blackmailer all in one night, then he just might be able to win back his client. Ursula was probably safe enough here with Urbanski, but she'd be safer at Pancho's.

I banged on the door with the big brass knocker. I was surprised when it was Hans-Dieter who opened it up and not the maid. He had a stapled sheaf of papers in his hand. He barely looked up from it to note my arrival. "Oh," he said, "it's you."

He stepped aside to let me in, then without another word, started down the hall, still studying the document. He seemed different somehow—distracted, certainly, and if I wasn't mistaken, in need of a shave—but it was something more. There was some subtler change. Could it be that he seemed smaller? No longer the quick-stepping young executive, he was slumped and he shuffled slightly as he walked away. It was like someone had let the air out of him.

"Hey," I called after him, "I need to see Casimir. You know, the cop?"

"They're in there, I think," he said, pointing to the library door as he shuffled past it. He disappeared down the hall, turning off into some room I hadn't seen. Did he live here, too? I wasn't sure.

I started into the library, even had my hand on the handle of the door, when I heard somebody laugh. Somebody

203

female. I was pretty sure it wasn't the maid, so I knocked on the door very politely. There were whispers behind the door. I knocked again.

"Yeah . . . uh, yeah?" It was Casimir Urbanski, who seemed to have subcontracted his way to glory. "Who is it?"

"It's me, Chico," I called through the door. "Come on out. We need to talk."

"Just a minute, like two minutes, yeah?"

"Yeah."

There was the sound of shuffling, moving about, and more whispers. I took a couple of steps back from the door and waited. Now I understood why Hans-Dieter seemed so completely deflated. From the moment I first met him I understood he had ambitions to marry the boss's daughter. But now it looked like this Polish policeman was here to stay. That romantic interlude the other night wasn't just Ursula's passing fancy and Casimir's reward for a job well done. There was something going on here that neither Hans-Dieter nor, for that matter, Antonio Cervantes could hope to control. Next thing I knew I found myself humming that song from *Casablanca* as I waited. Amazing.

The library door opened. Urbanski emerged, tucking his shirt in his jeans. He turned and said something to Ursula in a quiet tone, and as he shut the door I got a flash of her adjusting her clothes.

"She's something," he said with a big grin, "really a sweet kid." That was the second time he'd said that. It made you wonder.

"Where's the maid?" I asked.

"She gave her the day off."

"The cook?"

"Her, too."

"But Hans-Dieter's still here."

"If he wants to hang around, that's his problem, you know?" Casimir had taken charge.

"Well, come on," I said. "Let's go outside and talk. I've got some things I want to tell you."

204

He followed me out front. We leaned up against his car, and I told him everything.

I must have trusted the guy. I mean, off duty or not, he was LAPD, wasn't he? After all he heard from me, he could have arrested me on the spot for breaking and entering, theft, accessory to murder, and aggravated assault. But all he did was nod sympathetically and ask a question or two. He didn't even object when I lit up a cigarette there in the dark.

But when I started explaining what I was trying to put together that night, I lit up a second, and he said, "You're making a bad insult on your body." I wanted to keep him on my side, so I put it out.

Anyway, I told him about the message I was sending through Ray Jorgensen, and then I said, "I guess a lot depends on whether I was right about him."

"And whether that guy—what's his name? Wallace— ain't too sick to get out of bed."

"Yeah, and on whether or not he remembers what I told him before he got the pot of hot soup in the face."

Urbanski nodded sympathetically. "That's a lot of depending."

"Yeah—hey, that reminds me." I looked at my watch. It was five to six. "I've got to make a call in a couple of minutes. But look, before I do, let me tell you I think we ought to get her out of here tonight. I want to keep her safe until this is over."

"Oh yeah. That's okay by me."

"I've got a place. Can you talk her into it?"

He looked at me oddly, like I'd seriously misjudged her or something. "Oh, sure," he said. "No problem."

As he went off to take care of that, I made for the telephone in the hall to call Beefy. I pulled out the yellow copy of the delivery order he'd given me, found the number, and dialed it.

I got the guy with the greasy hair and the Vandyke beard. "Closed." That's how he answered the phone. "No more runs tonight. You want a delivery for tomorrow, I'll take the order."

"Let me talk to Beefy."

"Oh," he said, "you. I'll call him."

It took a couple of minutes to get him on the line, but when he was on, he was really on. "Hey, rico Chico! My man! My man!"

"How'd it go, Beefy?"

"Just like you said it would. It's like you got eyes in the back of your future. You know what I mean?"

"Sort of."

"Sure you do. Anyway, I did a real number with this young guy. First he said he was Wallace, then he said he'd sign for him, and then after I explained to him how I felt about that, he finally decided that an interesting solution might be if he drove over to Wallace's house and kind of showed me the way. Terrific idea, huh?"

"Oh, yeah. Terrific. So you got to see Wallace, huh?"

"I literally put the package in his literal hands. Made him sign for it, too."

"How did he look?"

"Well, let's put it like this, Chico. I think he can see pretty well out of one eye, and one hand seems to work, but besides that—"

"Can he walk?"

"Oh, yeah, he can walk. He answered the door. You did a real job on him, though, Chico."

"That's all I need to know, Beefy. That's all I need to know."

17

If Jorgensen had done his job, then there was no way the Compañeros could be surprised there inside Esperanza. Wallace couldn't go in through the front door—Sunset was too wide open, too well patrolled—only through the back, right at this alley entrance I was looking at now. He couldn't hit it too early, and he couldn't hit it too late. It would have to be about closing time, probably just after 2 A.M.

So here I was on top of a garage across the alley from the place. I had all my tools laid out in front of me—the Walther PPK I had taken off Wallace, my .38, which I had extra loads for, and the MAC-11 machine pistol Urbanski had handed over to me before I left the Tollers'. It was almost one-thirty. If I had figured right, then it wouldn't be too long before things started happening.

Here was the game plan I worked out with Billy Jay: As soon as the shooting started, a black-and-white would pull up, with lights flashing, at either end of the alley, blocking it off. Once the shooting died down, Billy Jay and the boys from narcotics would come in and grab the survivors. I remember he had objected he wouldn't have warrants. "I promise you, you'll have probable cause," I told him.

And me? Why was I up here? To make sure Wallace didn't get away. This was personal. I had taken the silencer off the MAC-11. If I shot at anybody with it, I wanted to make noise. I wanted them to know they were being shot at.

I heard somebody coming down the alley moving quietly and slowly. Whoever he was, I couldn't see him, because he was moving down my side from the right. I didn't want to risk exposing myself over the little parapet by taking a look, so I just hung on where I was, kept my head down, and waited. He was getting pretty close. Maybe it was only some guy coming home late and taking the back way in. Then why was he being so quiet about it? Or maybe it was Wallace's point man, scouting the territory by foot. The sounds had stopped almost directly below me. I wrapped my hand around the butt of my .38.

A whisper. *"Chico."*

What in the hell? Was it Billy Jay come to call it all off?

"Chico!" whispered again. "You by here somewheres?"

That could only be one man. "Casimir?" I whispered back. "Up here." Only then did I risk a look down. I gave him a wave.

"How do I get up there?"

"The fence along the side." I pointed. "I'll give you a hand."

I left my post and scrambled along the top of the flat garage roof.

He was already at the fence, ready to climb. "Heads up, here, catch."

Both hands came up in a toss. Not knowing what was coming my way, I almost bobbled the object and let it drop back down to the walkway beside the garage. But managing to hold on, found I had an Uzi machine pistol up there with me.

"And these ones, too," he called in a whisper. "You can just let them drop." He lobbed twice with his right hand, and two extra clips for the Uzi dropped on the roof. "Here I come."

He hauled himself up the fence, then balancing there for a moment, made a grab at the rooftop. I put out a hand to him, but he didn't need it. He was up beside me before I knew it. Muscles did make a difference.

"You shouldn't have come, you know that." Not exactly hospitable but true.

"Oh, Uschi's okay. All those bars and stuff. When I left her, she was having a real good time talking to your girl friend. Hey, she's very pregnant, huh?"

"That's not what I meant."

"So? What?"

"You're a cop. I'm here on my own. They find you up here with me, and you'll get busted off the force. At least."

"Well," he said, "maybe that's okay by me. I'm planning about going in the movie business, anyways."

"Oh? Yeah?" I wonder who put that idea in his head.

"Yeah," he said, daring me to sneer.

Who could sneer? Sam Goldwyn never made it through grade school. He talked funny, too. "Well," I said, "it's also not a good idea for you to be here because you might get killed."

"No, I won't. You'll protec' me."

"Come on." I handed him the Uzi and the two clips and led the way to the observation post I'd set up.

We stretched out there, and I pointed out where I thought Bill Wallace and his guys would have to park—the only wide spot in the alley anywhere near the rear door of Esperanza. Then I told him about the cop cars blocking off the alley and Billy Jay coming in the front.

"What do we do up here?"

"Keep the Wallace guys inside."

"Neat. Hey, I brought some peanuts with. You want some peanuts?"

I laughed. "Sure."

He hauled a big one-pound bag of roasted and salted out of his jacket and opened it up, and we began munching away.

"Hey," he said, "you know what this reminds me?"

"What?"

"Up here like this on a roof, eating peanuts, just waiting around, it reminds me of Detroit on the TAC Squad. That was fun."

"A lot of bang-bang?"

"Oh, yeah. Fun."

We waited. "You found the Uzi," I said, stating the obvious.

"Yeah. You remember you said the chauffeur had it? We looked in the Mercedes. We looked in the garage. Right?"

"Right."

"Well, after you left and Uschi was packing, I started thinking around to myself, and I said, 'I'll bet that prick Hans-Dieter knows where it is.' He knew, but I had to do a persuasion on him."

"He won't like you."

"He never did. Also him I don't like, either."

Urbanski rolled over and stared up at the stars. He was a big, happy kid. I liked him. I was hoping hard he wouldn't get hurt. I took a look up and down the alley. Nothing. There were only a couple of lights on in the windows around us. There'd be more when the shooting started. If the shooting started. I looked at my watch. It was 1:43. Maybe it wasn't going to happen, and I'd wind up with egg on my face and a lot of enemies for life. That reminded me of Alicia, of course.

I turned to Casimir. "You said Ursula and Alicia were talking up a storm when you left them."

"Her and your girl friend, yeah."

"In what language?"

"English, sort of. They were acting a lot, like, you know."

"I know."

"Women, they—"

"Shhhh." I heard something. Casimir rolled over and put his hand on the Uzi.

A car had entered the alley from off on our left. We kept our heads down. It moved along very slowly, but it didn't stop. It kept right on going the length of the block and out the other end of the alley. At last, Casimir and I exhaled simultaneously.

"False alarm," he said.

"I don't think so. They'll be back."

"Last call for peanuts," he whispered. He grabbed a handful and started crunching, then offered the bag to me.

"No thanks." My mouth had suddenly gone dry.

He nodded and tossed them aside. They shook as they landed a few feet away.

"Shhh," I whispered. "Don't do that again."

"I can't do that again," he whispered back. "I already t'rew 'em away." Now he was using logic on me.

"Okay. Shhh."

We waited there silently on the garage roof, listening in the dark. It was a full five minutes before the car came back, running without lights this time, hunching over into that wide spot just down the way I had picked out for it. Casimir and I kept down flat. All we did was listen.

There wasn't much to hear for another five minutes. Somebody in an apartment house behind and above us had the radio on at a rock station. Sounds of Poncho Sanchez drifted down. I sensed, rather than heard, voices inside the car. Only, was it a car? Something about the way it had moved before, and the way that voices were now muffled inside told me that it might have been some kind of truck or van.

At last a clear sound—doors opening, first one and then another. Then the scraping of feet on the pavement of the alley, the faint crunching of gravel and bits of glass. There were a couple of clanks, and something suddenly hissed, the closest thing to a word spoken yet.

Looking at each other, Casimir and I counted the separate treads as the party made its way down the alley to a point just across from us—the back door of the Esperanza. Casimir looked at me questioningly and held up four fingers—his guess. I shook my head no, and held up five.

They were in no hurry. They moved slowly and cautiously about their business, whatever it was. A good three minutes had elapsed since they had reached the back door. Not an audible word had been spoken, but they were busy at something.

I raised my wrist just high enough to read the face of my watch. It was two o'clock precisely.

The sounds of weapons cocked.

A voice counting down in a soft whisper: ". . . seven, six, five, four, three, two, one."

The explosion that came surprised me. They didn't just blow the door open. They blew it off its hinges, and it slammed against the pavement of the alley. It was still skittering along when I popped up to take a look. I expected to see them disappearing inside. But no. They were flat against the wall, waiting. Then one of them stepped forward and sailed an object underhand through the door. He drew fire from inside, but he slammed up against the wall, apparently unhurt. About a second later there was another explosion, this one inside—a fragmentation grenade! The Compañeros couldn't have expected that. Then all five of them swarmed inside, the lead man firing as he went on full automatic.

"Jeez," I said to Casimir, who was up beside me now, "it's the A-Team."

But wait a minute. Not one of those guys had bandages on his face or head. Wallace wasn't among them.

Lights were on in windows all around. I got a good look at the van that had carried them in. I could see somebody behind the wheel. Was it Wallace? Could he see me?

Then, down at the entrance to the alley, the black-and-white pulled into position, his dome lights sending weird shards of red, yellow and blue all the way down the alley. The driver of the van began honking.

But what about the other one at the alley exit? Nothing. Nobody there. As of that moment the van had a clear path out of there.

All this time there was fierce firing inside the club, most of it long bursts of full automatic with a few single shots in response. This lasted about a minute, then tapered off to short bursts of automatic.

The van moved forward and pulled up just ahead of the gaping hole that had been the door to Esperanza. Its back doors were standing wide open. I looked down the alley to my right. Where was that other cop car?

"Get ready," I said to Casimir.

He pulled the slide on the Uzi, cocking it. I did the same with the MAC-11. We blessed ourselves like the good Catholic boys we were, and he kissed a medal. We were as ready as we'd ever be.

Firing had stopped.

Then there was the sound of a voice from the club. Although I couldn't make out the words, I could swear it belonged to Billy Jay. In answer, a burst of full-automatic. Then—*ka-boom, ka-boom, ka-boom*—police shotguns, and a muffled, funny pop that had to be a tear-gas grenade going off.

Casimir caught the first of them coming out of the back door—a short burst of three or four, and the guy was down on the ground, crawling back for the shelter of the door. I'd been glancing down the alley looking for that other damned black-and-white.

Another guy stuck his head out to help the one who was hit. We shot on either side of the door, knocking up chunks and chinks of brick and mortar, and he pulled his head back in again.

What could I do to stop that van? By now I was sure that

213

Wallace was inside. I couldn't hit the tires. The angle was all wrong. And the van was squared off in the front, the engine tucked underneath somewhere. There was nothing to shoot at except the top of it, so I tried that, emptying what was left of the clip down there just below me. That did no good at all. There were dents all over it—but no holes. They had all ricocheted off, left, right, backward and forward. I threw down the machine pistol and picked up my .38.

There was automatic weapons fire, but mostly the great roaring booms of the shotguns from inside the club. But in between all this we could hear them coughing at the doorway. Casimir used up his clip keeping them there. I took over and began potting away as Casimir started changing clips.

A hand, head, and half a body appeared in the doorway. I shot twice, expecting him to duck, but he stayed out just long enough to toss something up in our direction.

"Grenade!" I yelled.

That's what it was, and it landed on the roof, just to our left within arm's reach of Casimir. In a single motion, he scooped it up with his left hand and dropped it over the side.

It exploded. That could have been us. We would have been in pieces. I wanted to say something to Casimir, but he had just slapped the clip into the Uzi and cocked it and was now angrily looking for someone to shoot at. No more Mr. Nice Guy.

The shooting inside had stopped. Completely. Silence. Then, surveying the scene, I happened to look down and saw that the grenade had put the van out of commission. It sat at a crazy angle on its right rear axle. I also saw that the door on the driver's side was standing open and a figure was disappearing around the front of the van. I caught a glimpse of head bandages as I fired down—three, four times—emptying the .38.

"He's getting away," I wailed. I could already hear him

running along the walkway that ran alongside the garage, *our* garage.

"Who's getting away?"

I grabbed up the PPK and scrambled for the edge of the roof. I dropped off the far end, hung suspended for a moment, then kicked off and landed soft in backyard grass.

As I got back to my feet, I could hear footsteps—running footsteps—almost to the street beyond. I took off after him. I used to be pretty fast, fast enough to be a middle-distance runner in high school, but time and too much beer had taken their toll, and I was soon panting hard in pursuit.

I could see him, all right, and it was Wallace, about forty yards ahead. But he was pulling away from me.

He was a full fifty yards ahead when he reached the corner and came to a high fence running the length of a big lot.

"Stop! Police!" I yelled. It was a lie, but what the hell.

He didn't stop. He turned and fired. The bullet hit a car off to my left. I kept on coming, but just as I was getting close enough to shoot back, he reached up, grabbed hold of the top of the fence and practically vaulted over.

I reached the fence and stood there for a moment, trying to catch my breath and figure out what to do next. The guy was really in shape. He had to have at least five years on me, and he was running around with a concussion—at least a concussion—and half his face burned. And he'd made *me* look sick.

But here I was—and what was I going to *do*? If I tried to go over the fence the way he did, I'd make a terrific target. He must have been on the other side just waiting for me to come.

What was this fence? What was behind it? It looked like a construction site. And a construction site meant kids. They were always getting in, playing around in piles of dirt, stealing things. I trotted the length of the lot, turned the fence corner, and found what I was looking for. There were two loose boards together. This was where the kids got in. Maybe I could, too. I pried the boards back. It was a tight squeeze, very tight—but I was inside.

He was in here. I knew it. I crawled along for a short distance and stopped to get my bearings. He was around here somewhere, probably pretty close to where he had come over the fence and where he expected me to appear. It wouldn't be long until he would get tired of waiting. He'd feel trapped and begin to look for a way out. That's when I'd get him.

Had he seen me come in? Had he heard me? I didn't think so.

This was a construction site, all right. Having run out of lots in West LA and Sherman Oaks, they'd started in on Silverlake. From the size of the hole they were digging, I'd say it was going to be a condominium. There was a big pile of dirt off to one side. Trucks would come in the morning and cart it away, and then there would be another pile the following morning.

I listened and waited. I heard something stirring back where I'd been. It was him. It had to be. I crawled forward, ten yards, fifteen, and then I waited again. I crawled another ten. Maybe he'd try to go out the way he came in. If he did, then I had him—the way he would have had me.

Forward a little, maybe five yards along the side of the hole. My wind was back, and I was using it sparingly. The ground was soft, turned over in crumbling chunks. Just right for moving quietly on my belly.

I had my head pretty close to the ground, right where it was supposed to be. I raised it slowly for a look around, and there was Wallace maybe fifteen yards away. He was half turned away from me. I held my breath, brought the pistol up very slowly and trained it on him.

Then: "Gotcha. Throw the gun away."

But before I quite got it out, he turned and fired twice at the sound of my voice.

He turned too fast, and he was standing too close, and he

216

toppled backwards into the hole. All he said was, "Ahhhh," as he went down.

I ran ape style on four points to the edge of the hole and looked over. He was only about seven feet down, on his back on soft earth. He wasn't hurt, couldn't have been. At the most, he'd had the wind knocked out of him.

With just the top half of my head exposed and the PPK pointed down at him, I knew I was a very small target, and he was a very big one. "Okay," I said to him, "get up very slowly."

He pushed up on his elbows. "Who is that?"

He got up to his feet. Standing, he was really pretty close. He still had the pistol in his hand, both hands above his head.

"Throw that gun away."

And then an awful look of frustration and rage came onto his face, and he screamed, *"It's you!"*

He brought the gun down and fired as I fired at him. He got one shot off. I put three into his face.

I lay panting there for I don't know how long, maybe seconds and maybe minutes, staring down at that destroyed face half bound in dirty bandages. And then I began to cry. I don't know why, but I began to cry.

"Come on, Chico. Let's go. Let's get out of here."

It was Casimir, putting a soft hand on my shoulder.

"How'd you get in?" he asked. "I don't think you can make the fence the way you are now. Let's *go!*"

He got me to my feet, and I pointed the way. "Two loose boards," I gasped, "over there."

He moved me along firmly, quickly, and we were out of there in no time at all. The only problem was, Casimir was too big to get through the kid's hole in the fence. He had to go over.

I was still quivering a little on the drive to Pancho's. At one point, I tried to explain to Casimir—and to myself—why I reacted the way I did. But I began panting again. He

217

reached over and gave me a pat on the knee. "It's okay, Chico. It's okay by me," he said. "I understand."

He got us there in his car. I couldn't even remember where mine was, much less drive it. He took over. It was all right with me.

There was a parking space across the street and just down from Pancho's. We got out of the car and walked slowly over to the gate without a word between us. I had a key and let us through. Just as we were trudging up to the front door, it flew open and Ursula emerged, half supporting Alicia, who was walking kind of funny.

"What—?" I never got a chance to ask that question because as soon as she was close enough, Ursula hauled back and gave me a slap on the face. It hurt.

"Where were you? This woman is going to have a baby," she said angrily.

"I know," I said stupidly. "She's pregnant."

"She's going to have a baby *now,* you dumbhead! Take us to the hospital."

Alicia nodded. "It's real this time, Chico."

18

I was asleep in the obstetrics waiting room when the nurse shook me awake and said, "You have a nice baby daughter."

That flustered me—or maybe I was just groggy, still half asleep, but I found myself denying it. "Oh, no, you don't understand. I—"

"Aren't you the father?"

But by then I'd recovered. "Yes, sure."

"Would you like to see her?"

"Alicia? Certainly."

"No, I mean the baby."

"Oh, well, yeah, right, of course."

I stood up and rubbed my face, trying to get it together. Casimir was still asleep, snoring, three chairs down from mine. There was no need to wake him. Where Ursula was I had no idea.

The nurse led me down the hall. At one point she said, "The mother's still in the recovery room. She'll be out soon. You'll probably be able to look in on her after you see the baby."

"Yeah, I'd like to do that."

We turned a corner, and I caught sight of Ursula. She was staring like she was hypnotized through a big window. And the look she wore was pretty hard to describe. It wasn't just the big grin she wore, it was the fascination in her eyes—or no, call it awe. I'd never seen that before on anyone, and I never expected to see it on her.

She was looking at babies. There was a whole roomful of them there behind the glass. Not a big roomful—but it was impressive the way they kicked and squirmed and cried and slept, just like real people, almost. It was kind of frightening to think we all started out this way.

The nurse left me there. I took a place beside Ursula and stood watching. A nurse wearing a surgical mask was moving among them, looking efficient and at the same time pleased to be doing what she was doing. She came over toward the window and looked at me inquiringly.

Ursula turned to me. The expression on her face didn't change, so I knew that all was forgotten, if not forgiven. "They just brought her in. She's right over there." She pointed. "See her? Third from the right. She's so cute, so . . . *süss.*"

The nurse behind the window nodded and went over to the crib Ursula was pointing at. As she bent down and picked up the bundle in a blanket, I noticed that the name on the crib was not Ramirez but Cervantes. So that was the way it was.

She brought her over and held her up for me to see. It's hard to describe them, the way they look fresh from the womb. This one was nice and healthy looking with big, round cheeks and a pouty lower lip. Her eyes were shut tight, but the way she squirmed she didn't seem to be sleeping. She had a lot of black hair, plastered on her head with wet stuff, and her face was kind of wet, too. On the one hand, she didn't look like much, but on the other she was very, very impressive.

Ursula was overwhelmed. "*Ach!* Look at her! Look!"

She ducked down and spoke through the glass to the baby. *"Du bist so lieblich, du! So schön!"* She wiggled a finger at her. The baby moved her head like she was responding to that, but the eyes stayed shut tight.

The other nurse, the one who had brought me over, came back and told me I could see my wife now. (*But she moved back to Seattle a year ago!* No, I didn't say it.) I followed her again back the way we had come, down the long corridor, almost to the nurses' station. She stopped at the last room and nodded at the door.

"She's still kind of out of it," she said. "Just stay a little while. Then you'd better go. She needs to rest now."

I nodded and stepped inside. There was a woman sitting up with a magazine in the bed nearest the window. She was reading by a bed lamp. Dawn was just breaking over Hollywood. The middle bed was empty, and there were screens on rollers around the one close by. That had to be Alicia.

I slipped in between them and took a look at her before I said a word. She looked like she'd been through the war, not me. Her face was pale and sweat stood out on her forehead and upper lip. She was breathing steadily—but a little fast, not sleeping. I came close, and she stirred a little and half turned in my direction.

"Chico?" She spoke drowsily, not nearly out from under the anesthetic.

"Estoy aquí." I took her hand.

She shook her head slowly and said just as slowly in Spanish, "No. Speak English to me. I have to learn."

"All right," I agreed. "How do you feel?"

"Funny," she said. "They gave me something. It makes me feel funny." She stopped, and I began to try to think of something to say. But then she started up again. "But they were very sympathetic. They helped me."

"Good."

"You see? You do your business, and I do my business."

"Yeah, well, I'm sorry I said that."

"No, it was right. You were right." Another pause. "Chico?"

"Yeah, babe, what is it?"

"Give me a kiss and tell me things are all right between us."

I bent to kiss her on the cheek and she moved her mouth to mine.

Her eyes half opened for the first time, and I touched her damp cheek. "They're better than all right," I said. "I love you."

"I love you, Chico." She said it in English.

I cleared my throat. It was kind of hard to talk just then, but I managed to say kind of brightly, "I saw the baby."

"Is she beautiful?"

"She's as beautiful as any baby in the world has ever been." I tried to be honest but sound very enthusiastic.

It satisfied her. "That's nice," she said.

"What are you going to name her?" It was funny. We'd never talked about that. It said a lot, didn't it?

She was quiet for a while. Her eyes had closed again, and I thought she might have drifted off to sleep. But no. "I'm going to call her Marilyn."

"Marilyn?" I said. "That's kind of gringo, isn't it?"

She smiled. "She's a *gringa* now. Besides . . ."

"Yes?"

"I call her after Marilyn Monroe. My baby's going to be a big movie star, just like her mama."

The nurse came in then and told me it was time to go.

I probably would have slept the clock around if the telephone hadn't awakened me in the middle of the afternoon. I should have pulled the plug and set the alarm, but I was too tired to do even that when I collapsed in my own bed at about seven o'clock in the morning. It took me three rings to bring me up on one elbow and another one for me to find the phone on the bedside stand. Just as I was saying

222

hello, the machine kicked in from the living room, and I gasped out assurances over my own voice that I was on the line, and if whoever it was would just hang on we could talk after the beep.

At last it beeped.

"You know who this is?" The voice was familiar but threatening.

I thought about it. "Billy Jay?"

"That's right, and I want you down here in an hour."

He hung up then, and I held the receiver, looking at it for a long moment before I finally reached over and returned it to its cradle.

Although I was moving like a zombie, I managed to get ready and get over to Rampart in time to make Billy Jay's deadline. I had time enough to take a detour along Sunset for a last look at Esperanza—but I didn't go by there.

Casimir and I had driven by a little after six in the morning to look it over. The alley was sealed off, but I got a glimpse of the van, broken down, still there. The front of the place was cordoned off with a couple of cops out in front. The windows were broken down to the frames and the door hung open in a way that looked like it would never close again.

My car was on the next block. Casimir pulled over close to it, and we both got out. He walked around to my side and looked me up and down. "Big night," he said at last.

"Yeah, well, I want to thank you."

"Bullshit."

"Bullshit, maybe, but thanks, anyway."

Then, without warning he threw his arms around me and gave me the *abrazo* to end all *abrazos,* almost crushing me between his eighteen-inch biceps.

"We made it, you little beaner. We made it!"

"Yeah," I gasped, "we did."

Then he released me.

"And you had a baby—all the same night." Not quite the way I would have put it, but . . .

He started back around the car and opened the door. Then, with a grin, he said, "You get her christened, and my mother gonna say a novena for her. She says novenas all the time!"

With a wave, he jumped into his car and drove away.

When I walked through the door marked NARCOTICS, conversation stopped. There were three of them sitting at desks in the outer office. Ray Jorgensen wasn't among them. All three stared at me. They knew who I was. I wasn't sure whether that was good or bad. The one nearest me, heavyset and a little older than the others, stood up and pointed to Billy Jay's office in back. I nodded and went right on past them. When I reached his door, I walked right in.

Billy Jay looked up sharply. "Sit down," he ordered.

I closed the door and sat down.

"Pretty careless of you," he said.

"What do you mean?"

"Not reporting that burglary six months ago."

"What? I don't—"

"Shut up. That's your story, and you stick to it."

"Okay, okay, but—"

He raised his hand and shut me up. "Among the items you neglected to report stolen was this." He opened up the top drawer of the desk, took out my .38 in an evidence bag, and laid it on top of the desk between us. "You'll never guess where they picked it up. It was the crime-scene team, not us. They found it up on the roof with a little machine gun and about a million empties. I wonder how it got up there. Anyway, they took it, ran it through records, and found out it was your service revolver. They brought it to me, and I told them I'd talk to you about it. We just talked, and you told me how you got burglarized and didn't report it. That was pretty dumb."

"Yeah," I said, "it sure was."

"Take it. You'll have to sign for it out front, but take it."

I picked up the .38, still in the evidence bag, and set it down on my lap. "What was the body count?" I asked him.

"Well, there were a dozen of those Compañeros. Seven of them killed in that big shoot-out, four of them wounded pretty bad."

"That leaves one."

Billy Jay sighed. "Yeah, well, that was kind of a special case. When we went in there and started looking around, all of a sudden one of our guys lets go with his shotgun. *Bam-bam*—you know. It was Jorgensen. The way he told it, this guy was lying there just pretending, you know? When Jorgensen got up close to take a look, the guy went at him with a knife, so he let him have it. Blew out the guy's insides pretty good. It was this Hymie Fernandez."

"Pretty convenient for Jorgensen. That way, Jaime couldn't tell on him."

"Yeah, pretty convenient. Of course Fernandez did have a knife in one hand, or right near him, and a gun in the other. There'll be a hearing, of course, but Jorgensen'll probably beat that. Even so, Ray and I had a talk about an hour ago, and we decided between us that it might be best if he did a transfer. I got a feeling that Wilshire division's loss will be our gain."

"You're booking the four wounded?"

"Oh, sure, on narcotics and weapons charges. The crime-scene guys found about fifty kilos of coke hidden in the basement." He paused. "Also something else. They found a guy hiding in this little room, kind of a storage room with a bed in it, a cell. He claims he was just a customer who was in there when the shooting started. He ran down to get out of the line of fire. You know anything about that?"

"A little guy named Emilio?"

"That's him."

I thought about that a moment. "He was just a customer."

Billy Jay gave me a funny look. "Okay. If you say so. I'll

225

pass that on." He leaned back in his chair then, clasped his hands behind his head and grinned. "My, my, my, Chico. You delivered."

"Yeah, well, thanks, but what about those other guys, the ones who shot up the place—who were they?"

"Somethin' else, huh? There were just five of them—but man, the way they went through that club!"

"Yeah, but who? Where were they from?"

"They were a bunch of Vietnam veterans, consider themselves some kinda vigilantes or something. Kinda old for playing games like that, if you ask me. Anyway, they got called up in a hurry by this guy they call the Major, some kinda blood oath. We got all of them. One got shot in the leg trying to get out. Nobody got out. Seems like they were detained by heavy fire from that garage roof where that burglar left your service revolver. Now, they claim the Major told them they were just cleaning out a bunch of drug dealers, which was true enough but maybe not the whole truth, if you know what I mean."

"I know what you mean." I kept waiting. He was taking a long time leading up to it.

"'Course the Major isn't around to tell what he said."

"Oh?"

"No, they found this body in a lot about a block away. I guess he was the Major, all right. His name was . . ." Billy Jay glanced down at a sheet on his desk. "Wallace, William Wallace. Does that ring any bells?"

"Can't say that it does."

"He didn't have any ID on him, but one of the commandos took a look at him and said that's who it was. Now, the way he must've died, he got so embarrassed at how bad the operation went that he ran away, jumped down in this foundation hole they were digging in the lot. Then he committed suicide by shooting himself three times in the face. That's just a theory, y'understand, Chico. We're still working on that one."

With that, he raised his hands in an expressive shrug, as

if he was saying, "We can only do so much." But he didn't say that. Instead, he just looked at me with that no-expression expression of his and asked, "You got any questions?"

I guessed that meant I could go. I stood up, shook my head no, and took a step toward the door. Then something occurred to me. "Yeah," I said, "just one more thing. There was supposed to be a black-and-white at each end of the alley, but the one that was supposed to block the exit never showed up. What happened?"

"Oh, that. Well, you might say it was a typical police fuckup. Those two guys claim they got the cross street wrong. They were two blocks down from where they were supposed to be. You want my guess, they sized up they'd draw the heat and decided to fuck up. Anyway, they're going over to Wilshire with Jorgensen."

"That's all, Chico. Don't forget to sign for that .38."

Because it took the cops a while to release Wallace's name and even longer for anybody to put him together with Intertel, I didn't hear from Joe Jarasek until the next day. He wanted to know all I knew. I couldn't very well deny him now, it seemed, and so I invited him over. He agreed to take me as a nameless source. He didn't like it much, but he agreed. When he switched on the tape recorder, I asked him to turn it off. He didn't like that, either, but he took notes just like reporters used to. We talked for most of the morning, and although I was kind of selective in what I told him, he seemed pretty pleased with what he got. That, together with the other research he'd done, gave him a series on the business intelligence community. The Wallace-Intertel hook was enough for the *Trib* to give it a big play. They started it on the front page the following Sunday and ran it inside the news section through Wednesday. I read it all. It was pretty good.

It seemed like most of my time that couple of days was taken up going back and forth to the hospital. Alicia made a good comeback, and the baby—Marilyn? wow!—seemed just fine. My next visit I brought roses. I remember when I walked in, the two of them were there together in the bed, and I just stood and looked. Alicia had this big smile on her face, playing with the kid like a little doll. She didn't even know I was there for a while. It looked—well, it looked wonderful. She liked the roses, too.

I hadn't made any effort to communicate with the Tollers. I just waited them out, half expecting Hans-Dieter or Herr Klemper to call and terminate my services. When at last the call came, it was from neither of them but from Henrich Toller himself. The old man was in a great mood, calling me De Quincey, of course, joking on the line about jet lag, telling me he'd heard I'd just become a father and promising me he could give me a little advice on that subject. He schmoozed like that for nearly five minutes, and then he got around at last to inviting me over. I asked him when, and he said, "Oh, well, whenever you can make it." Then he added very directly, so there couldn't be any argument, "Now."

And it was Toller himself who opened the door. Oh, the maid was around. She waved and twittered a *"Guten Tag!"* from down the hall. Suddenly it was an altogether cheerier place. The old man had worked the change. He greeted me with a broad smile and a strong handshake, looking ten years younger. With a hand on my shoulder, he herded me into the library and shut the door. The room had been straightened up since my last visit there.

"Can I offer you something?" he asked. "A snifter of brandy, perhaps?"

"Yeah, why not?"

"Good." He poured one for me and another for himself. He held up the bottle. "Napoleon—one hundred years old."

He offered a *"Pros't,"* and we both took a sip. It didn't taste a hundred years old. It tasted as good as new.

228

"Sit down, De Quincey, sit down." He nodded at the sofa, and I took a place there. Toller sat down behind the desk, giving me a look at last at the commanding executive who had run an independent operation for nearly fifty years. He took another sip of cognac, then, with a serious frown, leaned forward and began.

"I called you here because I wanted you to hear about this from me and not simply read about it in the papers tomorrow. You may have wondered that I left town during this . . . this recent crisis."

"Well, I figured it was business."

He nodded curtly. "Yes, business, exactly. There is a man in Germany I know named Friedrich Neubauer. We started out in Berlin together before the Hitler time. We were friends then. Hitler came. I left Germany. Neubauer stayed. He rose in the German film world. The war ended. He reemerged in television manufacturing, then bought into publishing, computers, many different areas. The name of the conglomerate he put together is Kommunikat. You've heard of it?"

Who hadn't. "Sure, I have."

"Neubauer and I, if no longer friends, have remained in contact since the war. To make a long story short, I have persuaded him to buy Majestic Pictures."

I think my mouth popped open about that time.

"I used two arguments. First, it would be wrong to let the Japanese take over Hollywood completely. Second . . . well—I trust you, and this is in strictest confidence—I have something on him from the Hitler time. Anyway, the transaction has been completed, a straight money deal between two conglomerates—you knew Majestic was owned by Compucom? The amount may or may not be announced. I don't even know it myself. Kommunikat simply made an offer they couldn't refuse."

"And Norman Collinson?"

"Ah, you found out about him, didn't you? Of course you did. Ursula told me. Norman Collinson is—how do you say it?—out on his ass. I am to be chief executive officer and Ursula will be production head of the studio."

At that I burst out laughing. Collinson was out of his league entirely! He'd been slapped down twice in a lifetime by the old man. Toller smiled and let me laugh. Finally, I calmed down enough to ask, "He used to work for you, didn't he? This was personal."

Again, that curt nod. "Yes, very personal. He worked for me and I gave him considerable independence. I trusted him. And you know? I caught him skimming!" He brought his fist down on the desk with more force than I thought he had in him. "And in my organization, nobody skims but me!"

I wanted to laugh at that, too, but I didn't.

"So he became powerful. He wanted revenge—to put me out of business, and he went to very unscrupulous people to do it. So! Now I have revenge for his revenge."

He sat back and gave me that same big smile he'd greeted me with at the door. He raised his glass and took a big gulp of brandy, very pleased with himself—and why shouldn't he be? But then he got serious again.

"Another matter," he said. "This man"—he pronounced the name carefully—"Casimir Urbanski."

"Yes? What about him?"

"Ursula wants to marry him. She asked him."

It had come to that, had it? "Well, that's . . . interesting."

He waved his hand, brushing that aside as an unsuitable comment. "This man seems uncultured."

"Yeah," I said, "that's a fair estimate."

"Even stupid."

"He's not stupid."

"Hans-Dieter would be a more suitable match."

That did it. "Listen," I said, "Hans-Dieter is a pain in the ass, he brings out her worst qualities."

He thought about that and nodded. "True," he said.

"Let me ask you something, when you came to Hollywood, were you cultured?"

He pulled a face. "Well, I was young. I was ambitious. I had a *Gymnasium* education in Germany. Compared to the rest of them out here, yes, I was cultured."

"Exactly! 'Compared to the rest of them.' The people who ran things then were a bunch of grade-school dropouts. They made good movies, though, because they had some of the same qualities Casimir's got."

"Name one."

"He's brave."

He looked at me and blinked. "Brave?" He thought about that. "Well, that's certainly a very unusual quality in the movie business today."

"Yeah, and it might help him handling Ursula, too."

He pinched his lower lip thoughtfully. "You might be right."

We didn't say another word about it. I finished off the Napoleon, and just as I stood up to go, he pushed something across the desk toward me. "Here," he said, "I want you to have this."

It was the edition of Thomas De Quincey I'd been reading when we met. I smiled and opened it up. The inscription said, "For my friend, Antonio Cervantes, with honor and respect, Heinrich Toller" and then the date. I thanked him, and we shook hands.

He went with me to the front door and we said good-bye. As I was walking to my car, he called after me, "Oh, De Quincey, the check is in the mail. You won't be disappointed."

I wasn't disappointed. It was double the biggest I'd ever gotten. It helped a lot when Alicia came home from the hospital, and we began to put our lives back together. I hired Pilar to come in a few hours a day and take care of the baby. She and Alicia get along just fine now that the baby's here. But now that the baby's here, I'm thinking about opening an office, maybe down on Hollywood Boulevard where rents are cheap. There's this building at Hollywood and Ivar that's got some history to it.